ALL THAT GLITTERS

ALL THAT GLITTERS

A Sgt. Windflower Mystery

by
Mike Martin

OTTAWA PRESS AND PUBLISHING

MYSTERY

Ottawa Press and Publishing
Copyright © Mike Martin 2023

ISBN BOOK: 978-1-990896-09-5
ISBN E-BOOK: 978-1-990896-10-1

Cover design and interior layout: Patti Moran / Patti Moran Graphic Design

Printed and bound in Canada

Library and Archives Canada Cataloguing in Publication

Title: All that Glitters: a Sgt. Windflower mystery / Mike Martin.
Names: Martin, Mike, 1954- author.
Identifiers: Canadiana (print) 20230221300 | Canadiana (ebook) 20230221351
| ISBN 9781990896095 (softcover) | ISBN 9781990896101 (EPUB)
Classification: LCC PS8626.A77255 A75 2023 | DDC C813/.6—dc23

*To Joan. The Windflower adventure continues
thanks to your enduring love and support.
Thank you for being my muse and inspiration.*

1

Winston Windflower looked out his window at the dogberry tree next door. It was so full of berries that the branches almost touched the ground. According to local folklore, many berries meant a miserable and hard winter ahead. Windflower wasn't that sure. Late August in Grand Bank, Newfoundland, on the eastern tip of Canada was nearly perfect. All the summer heat and humidity had burned itself out, and the forecast called for sunny, mild days all week.

That was good. For two reasons. First, he hoped to go blueberry picking a few more times this season when the B&B finally started slowing down after a very busy summer. But even more importantly, next week he would start a new job as Community Safety Officer for the combined communities of Grand Bank, Fortune, Garnish and Frenchman's Cove. He sipped his coffee and wondered how that happened.

Not that long ago, he'd been an RCMP officer, something he once thought he'd be forever. But a series of events propelled him towards his current situation, not the least being that the powers that be had decided to close the Royal Canadian Mounted Police station in Grand Bank. But he'd been thinking about this eventuality and leaving the Mounties for some time now.

He didn't figure on being a Community Safety Officer for the same region. But that was what was going to happen next week. Not only that, but the last request Mayor Jacqui Wilson had made as they concluded their negotiations was if he would mind still using the title "sergeant" in his new position. She said it would make people more comfortable.

He agreed, but he wasn't sure he was completely comfortable with all this. One thing that suited him perfectly was the fact that the councils had agreed with his request to hire Betsy Molloy as his assistant. Betsy had been his admin assistant for years in the RCMP detachment, and she knew everything and everybody in Grand Bank and the surrounding communities. And they would be able to still work out of the old detachment building. The RCMP had leased it to the communities for a dollar a year.

How it would all work was a big question. But that was next week, thought Windflower as he drained his coffee and put his cup in the sink. Today he had to go to the B&B and get going on tonight's dinner menu. He was just leaving his house when his wife, Sheila Hillier, pulled into the driveway. His two daughters, Stella, almost six, and Amelia Louise, three and a half, ran up to meet him first.

He struggled to get away from them but ended up on the grass on his front lawn when Lady, the family Collie, lovingly attacked him from behind. He pulled himself away from the dog and children and went to help Sheila bring in the groceries. He was walking back to the house with both girls chattering in his ears and noticed the final member of his family, Molly the cat, observing the goings on from her perch in the window. She was clearly not amused and slunk from sight before Windflower had opened the front door and the two girls ran in.

"It was a moose, Daddy," said Stella.

"A big moose," added Amelia Louise.

"Just past Garnish," said Sheila, who had come in behind him and was already putting groceries away in the kitchen.

Windflower listened patiently while his daughters told him several variations of the same story and only got away when Sheila offered the girls a cookie.

"I've got to get supper ready at the B&B," he said as he snatched his own cookie from the package. When he looked down, he saw Lady waiting hopefully for her own treat. He grabbed a Milk Bone and handed it to a grateful Collie. But she now had a companion. Molly was sitting beside her, looking expectantly at Windflower.

"How does she do that?" asked Windflower.

"What?" replied Sheila.

"How does the cat know when there's treats? She's invisible until she hears Lady getting one," said Windflower.

"Female intuition?" offered Sheila.

"Yeah, right," said Windflower as he handed over the cat treat. "I'll be back in an hour or so."

"Great," said Sheila. "I have a couple of potential buyers on a Zoom call later on."

After hugs and kisses and pats on the head all around, Windflower managed to get out of the house and walked to the B&B. He had just opened the front door of the beautifully restored inn when Levi Parsons, the manager, came running towards him.

"We think he's dead," said Levi.

"Who's dead?" asked Windflower.

"The man in Room 12," said Levi. "Beulah tried to get in to make up his room, but the door is locked and bolted from the inside. And there's not a sound."

Beulah, the cleaner and part-time server, came around the corner from the kitchen when she heard Windflower arrive.

"I don't know for sure, but there's something funny going on," she said. "We haven't really seen him all week, and now there's no answer when I knocks on his door."

"Maybe he's sleeping," said Windflower.

"His breakfast tray is still outside his door. I knows we don't see much of him, but he always takes his meals in and leaves the empty one outside. Then he often goes out in the morning, and that's when I cleans up," said Beulah.

"Sneaks out," said Levi. "I only seen him once. When he checked in. I haven't seen him since."

"Let's not jump to conclusions," said Windflower. "What's his name?"

"Robert Smart," said Levi. "From Burlington, Ontario. That's his Cadillac parked on the side. He wanted a safe and secure place for his car."

Windflower climbed the stairs to the second floor and walked down the corridor to Room 12. He knocked on the door and called out the man's name. No answer. He took the keys from Levi and tried the lock. But they were right. The deadbolt was locked from the inside.

He looked at Levi and then at Beulah. "Do you have a couple of hair pins I can borrow?" he asked Beulah.

The woman looked at him funny but reached into her hair and pulled out one bobby pin and then another. She handed them to him.

"Don't look," he said to Levi as he inserted the closed side of one bobby pin into the bottom portion of the lock. Then he broke the other pin in half and pushed it into the top of the lock and jiggled it back and forth. After a little while he could feel the deadbolt moving and finally unlocking. He swung the door open.

2

Windflower carefully entered the room. His long career as a police officer made him both cautious and careful not to disturb any situation before it was completely inspected. You never know when you might find a crime scene.

Levi and Beulah crept behind him, with Beulah peeking around the men, half afraid to see what was in the room but more afraid of missing out on something.

Windflower noticed the lump on the bed first. He turned around and motioned Levi and Beulah to leave. Neither moved initially, so he indicated more forcefully for them to go. Reluctantly, the pair retreated to just outside the door.

Windflower walked to the bed and gingerly lifted the covers. "Mister Smart, are you all right?" No answer, so he moved a little closer and touched the man's hand. It was cold to his touch. Not a good sign. Neither was the fact that he couldn't feel a pulse.

"Call the paramedics," he shouted. "I think he's dead."

Minutes later, everybody in Grand Bank could hear the sirens, and soon a small crowd congregated across the street to watch the arrival of the ambulance. Two paramedics ran inside and were directed upstairs by Levi. He'd been assigned front door duties that included letting the professionals in and keeping any gawkers out.

Windflower stood outside the door of Room 12 and nodded to both paramedics as they went in to see the man in the bed.

"Dead," one of them said. The other did not disagree.

"Can you keep the area safe for a little while?" the first paramedic asked Windflower. "We have to call Doctor Sanjay."

"Sure," said Windflower.

The paramedic picked up his cell phone and made the call. The other one hesitated for a second and then asked Windflower another question. "Do you know who we're supposed to report this to now?"

"I guess you have to call the RCMP in Marystown," he replied after thinking about it for a second or so.

"Okay, great," said the paramedic, happy to have somewhere to start dealing with an unexpectedly dead person. Soon he was on his phone too.

"Doc Sanjay will be right over," said the first paramedic.

"Corporal Tizzard is on his way from Marystown," said the other a few moments later.

Windflower nodded at both of them and went downstairs to call Sheila with the less than good news about the late Mister Smart. He paused for a second when he saw the familiar black car of Doctor Sanjay pull up in front of the B&B. The diminutive doctor got out and pulled his black bag out of the trunk. Was that a wave his old friend gave to the growing number of onlookers across the street?

He finished his call with Sheila, who was certainly concerned but not very upset. That didn't surprise Windflower in the least. Sheila was the rock of the family, and everyone, including him, leaned on her for emotional support. She only had two questions: were he and the staff okay? And how long did he think this would delay him from getting home? She didn't want to miss her sales call.

Then he went upstairs to see Doctor Sanjay, who was still huddled with the paramedics inside the room. His eyes brightened when he saw Windflower.

"You'll have to wait around until the RCMP gets here," he said and went to greet Windflower.

"Winston, my friend, how's she going b'y?"

"It's going good," said Windflower. "Considering the circumstances."

"Indeed," said the doctor. "I hear young Corporal Tizzard is on the way over. This will be like old times."

Windflower smiled. "Everything's a little different right now," he said. "Eddie landed a great job as assistant to the new inspector, whomever he or she may be."

"And Carrie is over in Marystown as well," said Sanjay. "Are you as happy with your new assignment?"

"I'm okay for now," said Windflower. "Nobody really knows how this will work."

"Do you have time for a cup of coffee at the café?" asked Sanjay.

"I seem to have nothing but time," said Windflower. "Let's go. I'll even buy."

"Ah, time, that precious quantity," said the doctor. "As you grow older, like me, it feels like it is slipping away far too quickly."

"You're still quite young," said Windflower, although Doctor Sanjay was now into his eighties, and except for some autopsies and suspicious deaths, he was mostly retired. "Didn't you tell me once that 'the butterfly counts not months but moments and has time enough'?"

"Touché, my friend," said Sanjay. "But I am honoured that you think of me and the great Bengali poet, Tagore, in the same breath."

The two men left the B&B and went over to the nearby café. The crowd parted to let them through, and soon they were safely inside the now deserted coffee shop. The Mug-Up was the best and only café in Grand Bank, known for its great coffee and even better cheesecake. It was owned and operated by Moira and Herb Stoodley, long-time friends of Sheila and Windflower.

Herb and Windflower had grown especially close over the years that he'd been in Grand Bank. They'd bonded over many pieces of chocolate peanut butter cheesecake that Windflower had consumed and Herb's love of classical music, which he was passing on to his friend. Herb was also an avid fisherman and had introduced Windflower to the joys of trout fishing in the many ponds and rivers in the area. It didn't hurt either that Herb was a retired Crown attorney, and Windflower had often used him as a sounding board on difficult cases or how to navigate the justice system.

Herb was standing in the doorway of the Mug-Up when Sanjay and Windflower came over from the B&B. He got them both a cup of coffee and took one for himself as they sat in the window and now became the observers of the scene outside.

"Lots going on this morning," said Herb Stoodley as a lure to see if either the doctor or Windflower would bite. But neither man rose to take his bait. Windflower just smiled and thanked Herb for his coffee.

Doc Sanjay offered a cryptic quote: "'Gray hairs are signs of wisdom if you hold your tongue.'"

"'Speak and they are but hairs, as in the young,'" added Windflower.

"I guess that means you're not going to tell me what's going on over at the B&B," said Stoodley with a laugh.

Windflower and Sanjay laughed as well.

"We actually don't know much," said Windflower. "We have to wait for the RCMP to find out for ourselves."

"Ah, I guess that means someone is coming over from Marystown," said Stoodley. "Tizzard?"

"One and the same," said Sanjay.

"It'll be very interesting to see how all this works out," said Herb. "Can I offer you gentlemen a snack, a piece of cheesecake perchance?"

"I'd like that," said Windflower. "But Sheila says I have to watch my girlish figure."

"Well, you will need to stay in shape if you are going to be running around the region all the time," said Sanjay. "Here comes the cavalry." He pointed outside where an RCMP Jeep had parted the wave of people and stopped next to the ambulance at the inn.

"Thank you for the coffee," said Windflower and went to the cash to pay.

"On the house," said Stoodley. "We have to look after our new law enforcement personnel."

Sanjay and Windflower waved goodbye to Herb and walked across the street, where Corporal Eddie Tizzard was talking to one of the paramedics.

"Hey Sarge," Tizzard called out when he saw Windflower. "And Doc Sanjay too. Just like old times, eh?"

"That's what we were just saying," said Doctor Sanjay.

"Nice to see you, Eddie," said Windflower. And he wasn't just saying that. He and Eddie Tizzard had not only been associates in the RCMP— they were more like brothers. Tizzard was almost a local. His family had lived in Ramea, a little fishing community down the coast from Grand Bank. They left when the inshore fishery collapsed and Eddie's father moved with Eddie and his two sisters to Grand Bank. Eddie had joined the RCMP and somehow landed a position in his adopted hometown. He'd been around about as long as Windflower, with some time away when he ran afoul of a belligerent supervisor.

But all that seemed like ancient history, and now Tizzard was in Marystown with his wife Carrie Evanchuk and their young child, Hughie.

"How's that kid of yours?" asked Sanjay.

"Hughie is almost a year old," replied Tizzard. "Can you believe it?"

"Happens fast," said Windflower.

"I hear there's a dead body inside. Can we take a look?" asked Tizzard.

"Sure," said Windflower as they walked inside the B&B. "We found him this morning. Don't know much about him. Robert Smart from Burlington, Ontario. Quiet, stayed to himself. I never actually met him. Until this morning. The door was locked from the inside, but I jimmied it open. This is how we found him." He walked into the room, followed by Tizzard and the doctor.

"He was pronounced dead a little while ago, but I suspect he's been dead for a while. He's cold but not completely frozen up," said Sanjay. "I would estimate time of death to be twelve or fourteen hours ago."

"Cause of death?" asked Tizzard, moving closer to get a better look.

"Unknown," said Sanjay. "I assume you want me to take a look."

"That would be great," said Tizzard. He motioned to the two paramedics who were standing in the doorway of the room that it was okay to take the body. They quietly entered, put the deceased on their gurney, and carried him out.

3

"I think we'll need you to keep this room free until we can do a full examination," said Tizzard. "I'll call for someone to come over and do a full sweep."

"No problem," said Windflower. "We're slowing down now anyway. Let me know if there's anything else you want me to do."

"Will do," said Tizzard.

"I guess I'll go back to check out your late hotel guest," said Sanjay. "I am hoping that you will be able to come visit soon. Repa and I would love to see you and Sheila and your wonderful girls. And, of course, I have a new Scotch for you to try."

"That would be very nice," said Windflower. "I'll talk to Sheila." His mouth watered at the idea not just of trying the good doctor's new whiskey, but also at the prospect of some of his wife's excellent Bengali cooking.

Doctor Sanjay gave a short wave and took his leave. The two other men watched as he drove off with the ambulance in a solemn procession. "So, how is it over at Marystown?" asked Windflower.

"It's okay," said Tizzard. "We're really lucky to have been both placed in the same detachment. It would have been horrible to be separated."

"How's the new boss? What's his name?" asked Windflower.

"It's a she, Diane Forsythe," said Tizzard. "And she's great. Her last assignment was in Halifax working as 2IC to Majesky."

Windflower knew Superintendent Wally Majesky very well; they had worked through some difficult situations together. "If Majesky likes her, she's probably pretty good."

"She's been good to us," said Tizzard. "Although not everybody is as happy to have a female boss."

"Issues?" asked Windflower.

"More grumbling than anything else at this point," said Tizzard. "Locker room stuff. They don't say too much around me, but you can feel the chilly vibe."

"How's she taking it?" asked Windflower.

"She's a pretty cool lady," said Tizzard. "I've yet to see her upset, and you know how rare that is in our line of business."

"You talking about me?" asked Windflower, feigning outrage.

"If the shoe fits…" said Tizzard, walking away. "I've got to call in."

Windflower could hear shuffling noises as Tizzard went downstairs. When he went out into the hallway, Levi and Beulah were standing there, looking a little sheepish.

"We were just…" started Levi.

"Snooping," said Windflower, finishing the sentence. "Okay, you know that we need to block off this room. And I would strongly suggest that you avoid talking about what happened here with anybody else. First of all, we don't know what happened, and secondly, we don't need any more negative publicity. Having someone die in here is bad enough."

Beulah's cheeks reddened a little at his last remark, but she nodded, along with Levi.

"Let's get dinner organized," he added. "Maybe all this excitement will generate a few more diners. Even if they are only curious about what's going on."

An hour later, he and Beulah had the salads made, vegetables peeled and chopped, the fish thawing and the beef filets wrapped in bacon and ready for the broiler. He left Beulah to clean up and walked home. He had a couple of hours before dinner, and he knew that Sheila needed a break.

As he was walking away from the B&B, he saw a white van pull up. He recognized it as the forensics van from Marystown. Not as fancy or well-equipped as the one from St. John's, but enough to look after this crime scene. If it *was* a crime. Eddie Tizzard's Jeep was parked in front of the café. A part of Windflower wanted to go and follow Tizzard around as he supervised the inspection of Room 12. But a bigger part just wanted to go home to Sheila.

That was interesting, he thought as he strolled along the narrow streets to their house along the water's edge. Very interesting.

Eddie Tizzard saw the van pull up as well. He paid his bill and said goodbye to Herb Stoodley. He waved to the two RCMP officers who were unloading their equipment and walked across to join them as they went into the B&B and upstairs to Room 12.

He watched as they stripped the bed and went through the dead man's belongings. He followed behind and did his own mini-search. Not much, really. Clothes, a nice-looking camera and one book on his bedside table. There was also a briefcase with some papers and a laptop. All of which would go back with the forensics guys for further review.

Not much so far, thought Tizzard. The bathroom proved more interesting, though.

"Pills," he heard one of the RCMP forensic guys say. "Lots of pills."

Tizzard walked into the bathroom. There must have been twenty bottles of pills, all of them in prescription bottles. All made out to Robert Smart, from the same pharmacy in Burlington.

"Put them all in an evidence bag," said Tizzard. "Record them and drop them off to Doctor Sanjay at the clinic."

When he came out of the bathroom, the other officer was starting to put away his fingerprint kit. "Prints?" asked Tizzard.

"Just one set," said the officer. "Likely our vic."

"Okay, run them through when you get back," said Tizzard. The two other officers put all of Smart's belongings into clear plastic bags and brought them to their van for the return trip.

Tizzard was starting to think about heading back to Marystown too when his phone rang. He checked the number. It was his boss, Inspector Forsythe.

"Inspector, how can I help you?" he answered.

"Are you still in Grand Bank? What's going on over there?" asked Forsythe.

"Just wrapping up," said Tizzard. "Suspicious death at the B&B. Not much to report yet. We found a lot of prescription meds in the room. Our guys are bringing them over to Doctor Sanjay, who's taking a look at the body."

"I'm on my way to Fortune," said Forsythe. "I have to see the Customs people about the transfer over next week. If you hang around, we could have dinner. There's a few things I want to talk to you about."

"Okay," said Tizzard, wondering what the new inspector wanted to talk to him about. "We could have supper here at the B&B. They make really good food."

"That's Windflower's place, isn't it?" asked Forsythe. "And I forgot you call it supper over here," she said, laughing.

"Yes, ma'am," said Tizzard. "This is Windflower and his wife Sheila's place. And dinner is what we get at lunchtime around here. But as long as we get fed, I don't really care."

The inspector laughed again. "Okay, I'll meet you there at around six."

Tizzard smiled as he made his way to the desk and booked a table with Levi Parsons for six o'clock. That left him about an hour and a half to kill. Perfect, he thought as he jumped in his Jeep and drove to his dad's house for a visit.

4

Windflower didn't have the luxury of time off for visiting. But he was just as happy. He and his girls and Lady were strolling along the beach, looking for the perfect rock. Well, the girls were. Lady was hoping to find something dead to sniff or maybe one of those delicious sea cucumbers she'd developed a recent taste for. Windflower had to spend his time inspecting the latest finds from the girls and making sure that Lady was unsuccessful in her quest for something dreadful or awful-smelling.

He managed to pull off both feats and everybody, except Lady perhaps, was quite happy on the walk back home. She cheered up considerably when the girls decided to have a race home. The girls were more than a little competitive, but the Collie was just happy to be part of their game, whatever it was.

The girls burst yelling into the house before Windflower could catch up. It was okay because Sheila had finished her call and was writing up her notes.

"How'd it go?" he asked.

"Great," said Sheila as she fended off both girls and hit *Send* on her laptop. "We've got another supplier for New Brunswick and our first for Ontario. He's in Ottawa, but he's got a supply network all over the province. We should be able to get tons of sales through that connection."

"Excellent," said Windflower. "Your little co-op will soon be sending Newfoundland crafts all over the world."

"Baby steps," said Sheila. "But it's coming. Do you need me tonight? I can get Debbie to come over."

"No, we should be good," said Windflower. "Beulah is there, and I think we've only got six people coming for dinner. It's our last dinner night for the season."

"Okay," said Sheila. "It always feels a little sad to come to the end of summer, don't you find?"

"New beginnings," said Windflower. "New business opportunities for you. New job for me. Life would be 'as tedious as a twice-told tale' if it wasn't for changes."

"'The web of our life is of a mingled yarn, good and ill together,'" replied Sheila.

"What are you guys talking about?" asked Stella.

"Your mother was giving me a lesson in how much she's been studying the Bard," said Windflower.

"Who's the Pard?" asked Amelia Louise.

Windflower laughed and went to have his shower. He stayed in the hot water as long as he could stand it, then got dressed in a clean white shirt and jacket and went back downstairs.

"You clean up pretty good," said Sheila, who was in the kitchen chopping vegetables for supper with the girls.

"You smell funny," said Amelia Louise. "Like Mommy's perfume."

"Aftershave lotion," said Windflower. "It's what men use."

Both girls pretended that he stank and turned up their noses. He kissed them both, and Sheila, too, before leaving for the B&B.

Beulah had all the meat and fish out when he arrived. All he had to do was apply the spices and get the sauces started. He made the fish sauce first. It was the easiest. He mixed the butter, cream, garlic, mustard, and lemon, along with some sea salt and three hefty shakes of black pepper. He poured it over the platter of fish and placed it back in the fridge. Once the first guests arrived it could be put into individual baking dishes that could be put in the oven.

Next, he made the sauce for his beef. He melted butter and stirred in onions and garlic until they were soft and then added a tablespoon of Worcestershire sauce and little bit of dry mustard and two tablespoons of whiskey. He liked bourbon, Jim Beam for this, and he added a dash of Tabasco sauce to give it an extra bite. Once it was ready, he tasted it, pronounced it perfect and put it aside as well.

He heard people talking outside and went to greet his guests. Levi had ushered the first couple in from the front desk, and Beulah was already on the way with their water and menus. It was Melvina and Jack Fitzgerald, two neighbours of the B&B who came every couple of weeks to check out Windflower's cooking. Windflower said hello and took their drink orders, a glass of Chardonnay for Mel and a Merlot for Jack.

The other guests arrived soon after, and Windflower was very pleased to see Doctor Sanjay and his wife Repa among them. He didn't have too much time to talk now but promised to come back for a chat after dinner. Then he was very surprised to see Eddie Tizzard and his new boss walk into the dining room.

"Winston Windflower, this is my new boss, Inspector Diane Forsythe," said Tizzard.

"Very nice to meet you, Inspector," said Windflower.

"It's my pleasure," said Forsythe. "I've heard many things about you. You are a bit of a legend in these parts."

"I hope you haven't been listening to Corporal Tizzard," said Windflower. "He's been known to spin a few tall tales."

Tizzard pretended to be insulted. "My dad told me that it's better to tell the truth because 'if you tell the truth you don't have to remember anything,'"

"I think that might have been Mark Twain," said Forsythe.

"Maybe my dad told him, too," said Tizzard.

"Enjoy your meal," said Windflower. "Maybe we can have a coffee later if you have time."

"That would be nice," said Forsythe.

Windflower had to hurry back to the kitchen to get the food going. Beulah had the orders from everyone except Tizzard and Forsythe, so she went to do that while Windflower got the salads ready. The salads were quick and easy, and by the time Beulah came back with the final order Windflower had them laid out and ready to go. He put the fish orders in one oven to bake and put the steaks under the broiler in the other oven.

Everything ran smoothly, and the food was plated and served right on schedule. Windflower made some fresh coffee and brought out the wine to see if anyone wanted a refill with their dinner. The diners seemed happy, and so was Windflower as he helped Beulah clear tables and get the coffee ready. Dessert was courtesy of Beulah, who was known as the best baker in town. Tonight's offerings were lemon meringue and a dark chocolate mousse that Windflower topped off with fresh berries.

Beulah served desserts and Windflower the coffee. Once that was done, the pair went back to the kitchen to start the clean-up. When the majority was done, Windflower went back out to say goodnight to his guests. He spent a few moments with Repa and her doctor husband with plans to come visit soon. Then he brought the coffee pot and an extra cup for himself and sat with Tizzard and Forsythe while Levi took payment from the other guests on the way out.

"That was a fabulous dinner," said Inspector Forsythe. "The fish was perfect."

"I loved the beef," said Tizzard. "But dessert is my favourite."

Windflower smiled and poured them all some coffee. "Glad you enjoyed it. It's our last supper for the season."

"Will you close down completely?" asked Forsythe.

"No, we'll keep a few rooms open through the fall. But only serving breakfast for our guests from here on," said Windflower.

"I guess you'll be busy with your new job," said Forsythe.

Windflower nodded and sipped his coffee. "Anything on our late friend?" he asked, looking at Tizzard.

Tizzard paused for a moment and checked with Forsythe, who smiled at him. He took that as a sign to continue. "I just got a text from Forensics. Apparently Smart is a very interesting man," he said. "Turns out he's wanted or was wanted by Interpol and at least three other police forces in Europe."

"For what?" asked Windflower.

Tizzard looked at his boss again, and seeing no red lights there, he continued. "Diamond smuggling."

5

"**D**id you find any diamonds?" asked Windflower.

"No," said Tizzard. "Not yet, anyway."

"It's very strange to have a diamond smuggler in this part of the world," said Forsythe. "What's he doing, or what was he doing here?"

"Probably going across the water to Saint Pierre," said Tizzard. "Our guys found a plane ticket and his passport."

Forsythe looked puzzled. "I know that there's a rum and cigarette smuggling trade going on. But diamonds?"

"They have an international airport with direct flights to Paris," said Tizzard.

"We've had some dealings before with international guests," said Windflower. "I guess the airport is slightly underpoliced. That makes it very attractive to criminal types. Even European ones."

"Anyway, the higher-ups will sort this one out," said Forsythe. "But I'm glad to have a chance to say hello before next week. How do you see the new process working?"

"That's the million-dollar question," said Windflower. "I guess I see my job as more prevention and information gathering. I'm not sure anybody has thought through the enforcement part."

"Well, we're only a call away if you need us," said Forsythe.

"Thanks, I appreciate that," said Windflower. "Anyway, I have a pile of dirty dishes waiting for me. Nice to meet you. See ya, Eddie."

The RCMP officers finished their coffee and left while Windflower went back to join Beulah in the cleaning up. An hour later, he said goodnight to Levi, who was holding the fort at the B&B overnight, and walked home.

The night was clear, and Windflower looked up as he walked along. He could clearly see the moon, and if he remembered right, this was called a

Waxing Moon. He knew that because there was a New Moon a little while ago; now, they were moving towards a Full Moon. It meant that you could only see a thin fraction of the moon's illuminated side while most of the moon was submerged in its own shadow. But Windflower knew that the whole of the moon, Grandmother Moon, was still up there.

He had learned about Grandmother Moon and the role she played in Cree culture back in his home community of Pink Lake in Northern Alberta. His Auntie Marie had taught him the most, including the fact that there were thirteen moons, each reflecting different aspects of the seasons in the sky and on the earth. They were now moving out of the Flying Up Moon in August, when the young fowl are ready to fly, and into the Rutting Moon of September, when the bull moose scrapes the velvet from antlers as a sign of mating to begin.

He thought now about Auntie Marie, who had passed over a couple of years ago and how much he missed her guidance and support. He said a silent prayer to Grandmother Moon to watch over his special aunt and to look after the other women in his life, starting with Sheila and his daughters. His daughters were both in bed when he arrived home, but Sheila was waiting with a smile and a fresh pot of tea. Windflower was happy to be at the end of what seemed like a very long day.

Tizzard's day was not nearly over. Inspector Forsythe had invited him to come to her car to chat before they went back to Marystown.

He slid into the front seat beside her.

"Thanks for doing this," she said. "I didn't want to talk in there, and I sure wouldn't want anybody to overhear this back in the shop."

"Sure," said Tizzard.

"You know I've been facing some challenges," she started. Tizzard nodded. "I thought I could weather the storm. Still think that. But the super said I should seek out some allies."

"I'm honoured that Superintendent Majesky thinks kindly about me, but I'm not sure what I can do to help," said Tizzard.

"I just need some eyes and ears to back me up," said Forsythe. "That's what Majesky suggested, anyway."

"I support you, for sure," said Tizzard. "I know how hard it is for a woman officer in our outfit. I'm married to one. But maybe you should ask her."

"Not the same," said Forsythe. "Listen, I understand if you don't want to…"

"I didn't say no," said Tizzard quickly. "Let me think about it, okay?"

"Okay, that's great," said Forsythe. "Thanks for talking with me."

"No worries," said Tizzard. "Watch out for the moose on the way home." He walked back to his Jeep and drove out of town. He waited until Forsythe's car moved. Then he waited a few more minutes. He needed some time to think.

Windflower didn't want to think one second more. He and Sheila shared a cup of tea and the story of their days. Sheila's sounded like the most fun, but Windflower's dinner guests might have been the most interesting.

"I'll call Repa on the weekend and see if we can find a good time to get together," said Sheila. "I love seeing them, and they are so nice to the girls."

"That would be great," said Windflower.

"You're just trying to get some of Doc Sanjay's Scotch," said Sheila.

"Maybe a wee dram," said Windflower.

"Tell me about the new Inspector," said Sheila. "A woman. That's a surprise. How's she doing with that old-boy outfit of yours?"

"I am no longer in that outfit, I'll have you know," said Windflower. "I think she might be struggling a little. Tizzard said that some of the guys were being jerks. But she seems very nice. We're going to talk more about how our new arrangement will work."

"We're all waiting to see how that will unfold," said Sheila. "If you'll look after the pets, I'm going upstairs."

Windflower carried the tea tray out to the kitchen and let Lady out back for her nightly routine. Molly opened one eye to check on him and see if there were any treats on offer. Seeing none, she closed her eyes and went back to sleep. Windflower filled their bowls, let Lady in and turned off the lights. Twenty minutes later, he was fast asleep. Five minutes after that he was awake again, in a dream. He didn't know it was a dream right away. He saw a light outside his bedroom door and assumed one of the girls had gotten up to go to the bathroom. He got up and walked towards the light. That's when he knew it must be a dream.

He was in a stadium. All the lights were on, but there was no one on the field. No one in the stands. When he looked up, he saw his name, "Winston Windflower," flashing on the giant scoreboard. He stood there for more than a few moments. Transfixed.

"Pretty good, isn't it?" said a voice behind him. He turned around, and standing there was a man that he thought looked familiar but couldn't quite place. He was short and stout. Kind of like a fire hydrant.

"It's me. Harvey Brenton," the man said. "Remember me now?"

Windflower knew exactly who he was. Brenton was the perpetrator in one of the very first cases that he had dealt with when he came to Grand Bank. "B–but…" he stammered.

"I know, I know. I'm dead," said Harvey Brenton. "They don't normally let me out of that other place. But they made an exception. I'm here to warn you about something. If you get out of it, I might get a reprieve of sorts. Fifty years off eternity, I hear."

Windflower had been in strange dreams before. His whole family, led by his grandfather, were dream weavers. They had taught him to understand and interpret dreams, although he had the most problem with his own. His main teachers had been his late Auntie Marie and his Uncle Frank. One of the tricks Windflower had learned was always to look for his hands in a dream. That would let him know that he was having a dream, but it also allowed him to be more alive and alert during the dream itself. So, tonight he did just that. He looked down at his hands and realized he was indeed in a dream. This one was stranger than usual.

But the only choice he had was to play along. So, he did. "Harvey, can't say it's nice to see you. You were a very bad man. But I'm ready to hear your message."

"Still as righteous as ever, I see," said Brenton. "Someone you know is in danger. More than he knows."

"Who?" asked Windflower. But Harvey Brenton and the scoreboard and the stadium went black. Windflower heard a voice calling his name.

Was that another dream? No, turned out it was Sheila standing in front of him in the hallway.

"Are you okay, Winston? You look like you've seen a ghost."

"Just a dream, Sheila," he replied groggily. "Just a dream."

But he knew as he lay next to Sheila, listening to her gentle breathing, that dreams always meant something. Sometimes they meant a lot. He started rolling over the dream in his mind but couldn't make any more sense out of it. He was starting to grow frustrated when he remembered that he could always ask for help. Uncle Frank might be just the person for it. He'd call him in the morning. Now he could relax. He snuggled into Sheila and was soon off to sleep again.

6

Eddie Tizzard was still driving as Windflower was falling asleep. He'd started to come into the Marystown area and could feel his body relaxing as he looked forward to getting home to see Carrie. Then he saw red taillights on the road ahead. Probably Forsythe, he thought. He saw the lights flash and the car slow and spin out of control. He thought he saw something, an animal, by the side of the road. He knew what that was, and it wasn't good.

He ran to the car, which was crumpled at the front. Inspector Forsythe was inside, and it didn't look like she was moving. The horn on her car was blaring, likely from the exploding airbag that had pushed up against Forsythe. He tried to open the driver's door, but it was jammed. He smashed the window with his flashlight and felt for Forsythe's pulse. She was alive.

He let out one long breath. Hadn't realized he'd been holding it. He called back to the office in Marystown. Easier to get them to dispatch an ambulance and the fire department than go through 911. He set up flares around the scene and turned on her flashing lights. Then he went to the large female moose that was lying by the side of the road, bleeding. He knew what he had to do. He walked over to the moose, which was moaning on the ground. He took out his service weapon. "Sorry," he said. Seconds later the moose was still.

He went back to Forsythe's car and looked in again at her through the broken window. He couldn't see much, but there were cuts on her face that were likely caused when the windshield collapsed. It was hard to see any other damage. That would have to wait for the paramedics. Eddie wasn't a very religious person, but tonight he said a prayer for his inspector. He also prayed that the paramedics would get there quickly. He could hear that last prayer being answered.

The paramedics arrived first, and they confirmed that Forsythe was still alive.

"How bad is it?" asked Tizzard.

"Hard to tell until we get her out," said one of them.

"And we have to wait for the fire department," said the other. "But it sounds like they're coming."

Two fire trucks from the Marystown Fire Department, along with an escort of three RCMP cruisers, came into view shortly after. The firefighters quickly surveyed the situation and soon had the door chopped open. The paramedics bundled Forsythe onto a gurney and wheeled her into the ambulance to take her to the hospital in Burin.

Tizzard gave them a thumbs-up as he barked orders to the other RCMP officers. He had them secure the scene and assigned one of them to write up the accident report. He dictated what he had seen and then assigned another one of them to talk to Wildlife and arrange disposal of the moose. Two others were told to direct and divert traffic from both ends of the highway. Once everything was in hand, he drove as fast as he dared to the hospital to get an update on Forsythe.

She was already in the examination area when he arrived. He tried to peek in through the doors, but a nurse shooed him away. He would just have to wait like everybody else. While he was sitting in the emergency room waiting area he called Carrie, who'd texted him three times.

"I'm okay, but Inspector Forsythe is in bad shape. Hit a moose. I'm in Burin now waiting to see what they say," he said.

"Oh my God," said Carrie. "That's awful. How long do you think you'll be?"

Tizzard's phone buzzed. "Sorry, I've got another call. I'll call you back."

"Tizzard, it's Superintendent Majesky. Are you at the hospital? What's going on?"

"Yes, sir. I'm at the hospital. Don't know much yet," said Tizzard. "She was beat up pretty good. She's being examined now."

"Call me as soon as you know more," said Majesky. Tizzard's phone went dark. He put his phone into his jacket pocket.

"Okay, I'll do that, Superintendent," he said to himself.

"Talking to yourself is a bad habit," said a voice behind him. "People will think you have money or have gone crazy."

Tizzard turned around. It was Doctor Derek Savage, another refugee from Ramea who'd found his way back to the area.

"Hey, Doc, good to see you," said Tizzard. "I guess I better stop talking to myself. I sure haven't got the cash."

"You're here about your colleague, I assume," said Savage. "She's under right now. Lots of swelling. The usual cuts and bruises and multiple broken bones. But you know that the danger is with internal injuries. We won't know that until at least the morning. We'll keep her sedated. You have the next of kin info?"

"No, but I can get it," said Tizzard. "Do you need it right away?"

"We may need permissions," said the doctor. "All possibilities are on the table at this point."

That sank in for Tizzard, who'd been running on adrenalin for the last hour. He gave Doctor Savage his cell phone number and walked back to his Jeep. Time for another prayer, he thought.

Windflower was trying to fall back to sleep when he heard the telltale patter of little feet running down the stairs. He could also hear Sheila trying to hush them, with limited success. But he appreciated the effort. Saturday was his morning to sleep in, and he planned to take advantage of it. But thinking got in the way. He tried to go back to sleep, but no luck.

He accepted his fate and took a long, hot shower instead. Feeling much better, he walked downstairs and gratefully accepted his first cup of coffee from Sheila. The girls were watching Saturday morning cartoons, so he grabbed his smudging kit and went out on the back deck. Lady followed close behind.

Smudging was one of the ways that Windflower tried to maintain connection with his Indigenous spirituality. In fact, it was one of the few ways that he still practiced, and while he didn't do it every day, when he did he found some peace and comfort. Today, he felt a little disturbed, partly because of the dead person found at the B&B, but more about the changes that were happening around him. Having a dream like the one last night didn't help either.

To smudge was to use some special herbs, sacred medicines his people called them, and to use the act of burning them to slow down and become mindful and centred in the moment. He really needed that today, he thought, as he put small portions of cedar, sage, sweetgrass, and tobacco into his bowl and lit them with a wooden match. As the smoke rose, he took his eagle feather and wafted it all over his body. He passed it over his head to help clear his mind and over his heart to help purify his spirit. He even allowed it to pass under his feet because that was a reminder to try to walk a straight and honest path.

When he was finished, he laid the ashes on bare ground so that all negative thoughts and feelings were absorbed by Mother Earth. Then, as in every morning that he smudged, he also prayed. He started by offering prayers of gratitude for the life he had and all the gifts he'd been given. For his family and his ancestors and for the many people who had touched his life in a positive way.

Smiling, he led Lady back in and gave Sheila a big hug.

"What's that for?" she asked in mock surprise. "But I can take some more anytime."

Windflower laughed and hugged her again. "Just grateful," he said. "What's for breakfast?"

"Cereal, fruit and toast," said Sheila. "I got those little boxes of cereal that the kids like."

"I love those boxes," said Windflower as he scoured the counter. "Great, still have Frosted Flakes. All sugar but that's okay." He poured his cereal in a bowl, added milk, and went to join the girls in the living room. His cell phone rang as soon as he finished his breakfast. He checked the number. It was Uncle Frank.

"Uncle Frank, how are you?" said Windflower. "I was going to call you today."

"I know," said Uncle Frank with a chuckle. "You forget sometimes that I can access the dream world, too."

"Indeed," said Windflower. "Is that why you called?"

"Partly," said his uncle. "But also to wonder if it was okay if I came for a visit. I miss the girls and my friends. You and Sheila, too," he added.

"That would be great. The girls would love to see you. So would we. Is your heart better?" asked Windflower. Uncle Frank was supposed to come to Grand Bank for the summer but had a heart problem and couldn't fly.

"Much better, thank you. My doctor gave me the green light," said Frank.

"Do you want us to get your ticket?" asked Windflower, meaning Sheila.

"No, don't bother. I'll get my buddy Jarge to book my ticket. He gets the best deals," said his uncle.

Windflower walked back to the kitchen, put his bowl in the sink and mouthed "Frank" to Sheila as he went back outside.

"So, you know about my dream. What does it mean?" asked Windflower. "Is someone really in danger?"

"I don't know about that," said his uncle. "You know that dreams are sometimes cryptic, even backwards messages. Only you know what's in your heart. But I heard somewhere that dreams about being in a stadium or arena could mean there is something inside that you want to share with the world. Is there anything you want to tell me?"

"Not that I can think of," said Windflower.

"The other thing I noticed was that your name was up on the scoreboard. Not very shy, are you?" asked his uncle.

Windflower didn't know how to respond to that question, so he remained silent.

Uncle Frank continued, "If you are the centre of attention in a dream, it also means that you want to be there for some reason. Can you think why?"

"No," was all Windflower could reply.

"Sometimes the lessons are simple ones," said Uncle Frank. "Our teachings say that humility is not only important. It is essential. And if we fail to practice humility, we will surely fail at life."

"But..." started Windflower.

"I know you're going to say that you try to be humble. And you're probably not bad at it either," said his uncle. "But we have to practice to get better. If we were perfect, we'd stop growing. Ever see a dead tree?" Uncle Frank didn't wait for Windflower's reply this time. "Keep working at it."

"I will, Uncle," said Windflower. "When do you think you'll be here?"

"Early next week, I hope," said Frank. "I'll let you know when I have my arrangements. I hope you'll pick me up in St. John's."

"Absolutely," said Windflower. "I love you, Uncle."

"I love you, too, my boy," said Uncle Frank.

Windflower walked back into the kitchen looking a little more subdued.

"Everything okay with Frank?" asked Sheila.

"He's coming next week," said Windflower. "He sounds good."

"That's great news. And you. Are you okay?" asked Sheila.

"I will be once you give me another cup of coffee," said Windflower.

7

Eddie Tizzard had barely gotten any sleep and was back at the hospital in Burin, hoping to get some news, almost any news at this point, so he could call Superintendent Majesky and then go to bed.

He was nursing a cup of coffee from the vending machine when he saw Doctor Savage come out of the intensive care unit.

"You been here all night?" asked the doctor.

"Just feels like that," said Tizzard. "Can you tell me anything?"

"If I were a betting man, I'd get her next of kin here as soon as possible," said Doctor Savage. "Her vital signs have been dropping, and there's little brain function. Some of that is to be expected from the trauma and sedation, but it's an indicator that things are more serious than we first thought."

"Okay, thanks," said Tizzard. "It doesn't sound good."

"Sorry I couldn't bear better news," said the doctor.

Tizzard nodded and walked back to his Jeep. He called Marystown first to get them to relay the message to Forsythe's family, and then he called Majesky.

"Majesky here."

"Superintendent, it's not good news," said Tizzard. He gave Majesky the information the doctor had provided.

"That's not good at all," said Majesky. "I have a favour to ask, Tizzard. I want you to take over Forsythe's job until we see how things develop."

"But I'm only a corporal, sir," said Tizzard. "What about the two sergeants that are on staff? How can I supervise them?"

"Leave those guys to me," said Majesky. "I can also arrange to have Evanchuk transferred to a special project so there's no conflict there. The two sergeants will stay in place and continue to supervise their divisions.

Nothing changes for them. Unless there's a problem. That's why I want you."

"Can I think about it?" asked Tizzard.

"Give me your answer first thing tomorrow morning," said Majesky.

Tizzard was left holding his cell phone and trying to make sense out of what just happened. He felt like he'd been hit by a truck as the tiredness came over him again and his head hurt. He needed food, a shower and some sleep. He would take whatever came his way first.

Windflower had all of those wishes come true and more by the time he led Sheila and the girls into the Mug-Up at noon for the Grand Bank Saturday tradition of pea soup and por' cakes: creamy split pea soup with lots of carrots and turnip and flecks of salt meat and two por' cakes with either homemade jam or molasses.

Sheila made the rounds of tables to visit. As a local Grand Banker and a former mayor, she knew everybody. Several of the women wanted to talk about the new business and how excited they were to be part of making and selling Newfoundland mitts and souvenirs for the new co-op. Amelia Louise and Stella were left reluctantly behind with Windflower, who was supervising their crayon drawings.

A few minutes later their order arrived and all four of them ate their por' cakes first, dipping them into little bowls of molasses while they waited for their soup to cool.

"You're as popular as ever," said Windflower. "You could run for mayor again."

"I could, but I would not," said Sheila. "I feel like I've done my share in that arena. Besides, I'd be your boss if that happened."

"Then you shouldn't run, definitely," said Windflower, laughing.

"Daddy, why do they call these por' cakes?" asked Amelia Louise.

"That's a good question," said Windflower. "But your mother is the expert in that regard."

"They're called por' cakes as a short way to say pork cakes," said Sheila. "That's because there are little bits of pork in them, along with baking powder and flour. I used to make them with my mom every Saturday morning when I was little."

"That was a long time ago, wasn't it, Mommy?" asked Stella. "Why didn't you go to the restaurant?"

"There was no restaurant then," said Sheila. "All we had to eat was what we cooked at home."

The two little girls looked shocked. No restaurant. What next, no TV or movies? They looked afraid to ask. That surprise didn't last long because Repa and Vijay Sanjay walked into the café, and both girls ran to greet them.

Windflower had tried to slow them down but obviously had little success.

"I'm sorry," said Windflower as the Sanjays came closer to their table.

"No worries," said the doctor and shook Windflower's hand. Repa went directly to Sheila and embraced her.

"It's been too long," said Repa.

"I agree," said Sheila.

"That's settled then," said Doctor Sanjay. "Come for supper on Sunday evening. And you come early so that we can play a game of chess."

"Drink whiskey is more like it," said Sheila.

"Yes, please come," said Repa Sanjay.

"We will," said Sheila. "Now girls, come along and let Repa and Vijay enjoy their lunch."

Sanjay walked with them to the door. Sheila and the girls stopped to talk to Moira Stoodley on the way out. The girls loved her and thought of her as their grandmother. Sanjay pulled Windflower aside.

"I know you are no longer in the business, but I have some news and tried to reach young Tizzard," said the doctor. "But he is not returning my calls. I found something very interesting. Can I tell you?"

"Sure," said Windflower.

"Mister Smart died of internal bleeding caused by punctures in the lining of his stomach and intestines. Do you know what caused those punctures?"

"No," said Windflower.

"Diamonds," said Doctor Sanjay. "Maybe a hundred small diamonds were contained in a small plastic pouch. But somehow the plastic tore and some of the diamonds spilled out. They are the hardest substance in the world, and as they passed through the stomach and down into his intestines, they caused small tears."

"That doesn't sound like enough to kill someone," sad Windflower.

"It might if you had aggravated stomach ulcers," said Sanjay. "I expect that our late friend had terrible pain. Which of course he tried to treat with morphine pills that he somehow had a supply of. That would be enough to knock him out, and he bled to death in his sleep."

"Wow," said Windflower. "You tried to call Tizzard? Did you try his new boss, Inspector Forsythe?"

"Yes," said the doctor. "But no response from her office either. It sounds very strange to me. Anyway, I know it's not your problem and you want to get back to your family, but what do you think I should do with the diamonds?"

"Hold them in a safe place for now," said Windflower. "If you still have them on Monday, you can bring them over to Betsy at our office. She'll put them in the old evidence area. I'll try Eddie and get him to get back to you. Okay?"

"Thank you, my friend," said Doctor Sanjay. "See you tomorrow." He went back into the café to join his wife as Sheila was coming out.

The girls skipped out of the café and ran ahead of Sheila and Windflower on the way home.

"We're pretty lucky," said Sheila.

"Absolutely," said Windflower. "I keep wondering how I got so lucky to have you and the girls."

"Great," said Sheila. "You can have them for the afternoon. I am going to make some house calls on my suppliers to see how they're doing. There's a roast in the fridge if you want to do something with it."

Windflower thought for a moment. "I think I'll dry rub it and then cook it slow on the barbeque."

"Sounds delicious," said Sheila as they arrived at their house. She jumped in her car and drove off waving to the girls, who waved back and then looked at Windflower.

"What?" he asked.

"What are we going to do, Daddy?" asked Stella.

"And how long will Mommy be?" asked Amelia Louise.

"O ye of little faith," said Windflower. "Maybe you can help me cook?"

It seemed to him that the two girls looked at each other and rolled their eyes. "Or maybe you guys can watch a movie while I get the meat ready for supper?"

That brightened their mood considerably when he downloaded *Despicable Me 3* and turned it on for them.

"Thank you, Daddy," said Stella.

"Thank you, Daddy," said Amelia Louise. "But Mommy always makes us popcorn," she added.

8

Windflower went to make the popcorn. Once that was done, he gave them each a bowl and went back to his meat preparation. He rummaged around in the cupboard and found what he was looking for, a slender silver canister. Inside was a plastic bag that when opened filled the room with scents of several kinds of pepper, garlic and a special hot Hungarian paprika. He took the roast out of the fridge and applied a layer of the rub all over it. Then he laid it on a glass plate and put it back in the fridge to chill and allow the spices to penetrate the meat.

The girls were laughing and enjoying themselves, so he took advantage of the time to make some scalloped potatoes to go along with their roast beef. He checked the potatoes and was happy to find that the ones in the bottom cupboard were Yukon Gold. Perfect for scalloped potatoes. The other ingredients were easy to find.

When the sauce was ready, he added a handful of shredded aged cheddar cheese. Then he coated the bottom of the baking dish and laid a layer of potatoes. He seasoned the layer with sea salt, pepper and a dash of garlic power and covered the layer with half of the sauce. He repeated the process, added a sprinkle of thyme and rosemary and then covered the dish with tin foil and put it into the fridge alongside the roast beef.

"Not bad at all, if I do say so myself," said Windflower. He went back into the living room and enjoyed the rest of the movie with the girls. When the movie was over, he suggested a walk to the store to get a treat. No objections from his daughters.

Eddie Tizzard was getting his own treat. Little Hughie was climbing all over him in his bed. Carrie was standing on the side, filming the event on her phone. Eddie pretended that Hughie was holding him down. He tickled his son every time he got close enough, and the squeals of laughter were contagious. Soon all three of them collapsed and were laughing on the bed.

"You were a bit of a zombie when you got home," said Carrie once things had settled down a little.

"Oh my goodness, what a day," said Eddie. "First there was the dead guy at the B&B in Grand Bank, then the accident."

"How is our inspector?" asked Carrie.

"Not good," said Tizzard. "They told me at the hospital that we should get the next of kin here as soon as possible. I don't even know where's she's from."

"She's originally from Winnipeg but has travelled around for years with the Force," said Carrie.

"Family?" asked Eddie as he threw Hughie up in the air and caught him, much to the delight of his son.

"Divorced," said Carrie. "No boyfriend in Marystown as far as I can see."

"She asked me to help her out," said Eddie. "Before the accident. We had dinner at the B&B and then talked after. I guess she's getting a hard time from some of the guys."

"Typical male…buffoonery," said Carrie. "What did she want you to do?"

"Just back her up," said Eddie. "I said sure."

"I've got some news, too," said Carrie. "But why don't you have a shower, and I'll make you some bacon and eggs? You must be starving."

"I'm famished," said Eddie as he handed Hughie over and went to the bathroom. "And an extra order of toast and hash browns if you got 'em."

"Yes, sir," said Carrie. "Coming right up."

Eddie hummed to himself as he showered and was still humming when he came out to the kitchen.

"This smells so good," he said as Carrie filled his plate with scrambled eggs, bacon, toast and two hash brown patties. "Perfect," he added as he started to eat. "Tell me your secret and I'll tell you mine."

"Well, Superintendent Majesky called me and offered me a special assignment," said Carrie. "They want me to serve as liaison with the new Community Safety Officer. Not full-time, but for the next couple of months."

"That's very interesting," said Tizzard. "Here's a funny thing. Majesky called me, too."

"What did he want?" asked Carrie.

"At first, he wanted updates on Forsythe," said Eddie. "Then, when she started to go downhill, he offered me her job."

"Inspector? That's crazy!" exclaimed Carrie. "What about all the other guys? And you're only a corporal."

"That's what I said," said Eddie. "None of that seemed to matter to Majesky. He even mentioned that you were going to be reassigned so we wouldn't have a conflict."

"What did you tell him?" asked Carrie.

"I said I have to think about it."

"And?"

"I don't know," said Eddie. "I really don't. What do you think?"

Windflower and his daughters and Lady were walking back from the corner store when Sheila pulled up alongside them. The girls each had a small bag of candy that they were munching from. They couldn't wait to tell their mother about the movie and the popcorn and, of course, the candy.

"Sounds like all the children had fun this afternoon," said Sheila.

"I do have a spicy roast and scalloped potatoes all ready to go," said Windflower.

Sheila laughed, and despite the girls' pleas, she drove off and let them walk the rest of the way home.

"It'll be good for you," said Windflower.

"It would be good to sit in the car," said Stella. Her sister agreed. But it didn't take long before they quickly forgot about the ride and went back to their candy bags.

I want to be like that, thought Windflower. Let go of disappointments quickly and learn to fully enjoy what is in front of me. His Uncle Frank had always said that children were some of our greatest teachers. Today, that was true for Windflower.

When they got home, Windflower got a brief reprieve from childcare duties and went upstairs to read his book before dinner. It was another Donna Leon mystery. This one was called *Transient Desires*, and once again it was set in Venice, a place that Windflower had long dreamed of visiting. The book opened with the discovery of two young American girls injured on a dock near one of the city's famous canals. He was just getting into the story when his cell phone rang.

"Sorry for disturbing you," said Levi Parsons. "But there were two men here looking for the guy who just died."

"What did they want?" asked Windflower.

"I dunno," said Levi. "But they wanted to see his room. I told them they couldn't, but they just pushed past me."

"Are you okay?" asked Windflower.

"I'm fine," said Levi. "I'm used to bullies. You do what you can and then get out of their way. They're gone now."

"Where'd they go?" asked Windflower.

"I think they were going to the clinic. I told them that's where Mister Smart's body was taken."

"Okay," said Windflower. "Call me if they turn up again. Right away."

"Will do," said Levi.

Windflower phoned Eddie Tizzard, who was finishing up his meal.

"What's up?" asked Tizzard.

Windflower told him about the visitors to the B&B. "They're gone to the clinic. You might to send some backup over there. And Doctor Sanjay was trying to reach you. He found diamonds in Smart's stomach. Thinks that's what killed him."

"What? How did diamonds kill him?" asked Tizzard.

"My question exactly," said Windflower. "But you need to talk to him. Why aren't you answering your phone? He said he called you."

"It's been a little hectic," said Tizzard. "Diane Forsythe is in the ICU and may not make it. She had an accident on the way back from Grand Bank."

Now it was Windflower's turn to be surprised. "Wow. How bad is she? Moose?" Every year there were about a dozen moose-car accidents in the area with the animals that when upright stood about six feet tall and often weighed over a thousand pounds.

"Yup, a big female," said Tizzard. "We're looking for Forsythe's family right now."

"That's too bad," said Windflower. "She seemed very nice."

Tizzard hesitated for a moment. Windflower picked that up. "Anything else going on, Eddie? Carrie and Hughie okay?"

"Oh yeah, everybody's great over here. We should get together for a visit soon."

"That would be nice. The girls miss you," said Windflower.

"There was something else," said Tizzard. "Majesky asked me to take over on an interim basis."

"As inspector? You'd be great," said Windflower.

"It's not that simple," said Tizzard.

"Is there an issue with Carrie?" asked Windflower.

"No, in fact she's being reassigned. You'll be happy to hear that she's your new liaison," said Tizzard.

"That is good news," said Windflower. "So, what's holding you back?"

Tizzard paused again. "I'm not sure people will follow me. Lots of the guys have more experience, and there's two sergeants. I don't want to be fighting off a rebellion."

"Fair enough," said Windflower. "But most people don't look at stuff like you do. They want to do their job and go home safe. The less complications and fewer responsibilities they have, the better."

Now Tizzard was silent.

Windflower went on. "Be not afraid of greatness: 'Some are born great, some achieve greatness, and some have greatness thrust upon them.' Sounds like you are being offered an opportunity. Take it or not, there's no bad decision here. Just don't have any regrets."

"That's helpful," said Tizzard. "I think I'll sit on it for the rest of the day and then make a decision after I talk to Carrie again."

"Good plan," said Windflower. "And call Sanjay."

"Will do," said Tizzard.

9

Windflower hung up and started to go back to his book. But he could hear that things were not going great downstairs. He went to investigate. He helped Sheila separate the warring parties, who were then sent to their rooms for a cooling-off period.

"First peace and quiet we've had all day," said Sheila.

"It's nice," said Windflower. "So, lots going on in Tizzard's world." He told Sheila about the accident.

"Oh my God," said Sheila. "She just got here."

"And they want Tizzard to take over, at least in the short term," said Windflower. "The only really good news out of Marystown is that Carrie Evanchuk is being assigned as my liaison."

"Eddie would be great," said Sheila. "That is good news about Carrie, too. Maybe we'll get to see a bit more of them and their little guy."

Windflower nodded. "I'll put the roast on the barbeque. It'll take a while anyway." He walked outside and lit the barbeque, removing the grill on the left side. That side would heat up quickly, but he planned to put the roast on the other side. A few minutes later, he placed the roast on the cool side and closed the cover.

The girls promised good behaviour and had been let out of detention. Sheila tested this promise by getting them to help her make cookies. True to their word, they emerged into the living room, where Windflower had escaped with his book, and offered him a plate of chocolate chip cookies. He selected one, and they each took one to try them out.

"Perfect," said Windflower. "My compliments to the chefs."

The girls beamed and went out to tell their mother the good news.

Windflower reluctantly put his book away and went out to the barbeque. The aroma emanating from inside was glorious, and when he opened the lid, he was enveloped in what he imagined meat heaven might smell like. Sheila was making a salad when he went back in to turn on the scalloped potatoes.

Half an hour later, the table was set, and Windflower brought in the perfectly browned roast and carved it up on a wooden board on the counter. It was crisp and brown on the outside and well done on the outer ring, growing gradually pinker as he reached the core. He sliced an outside piece for himself and Sheila and a couple of pieces of the more done ones for the girls. He added a few thin slices of the rare, barbequed beef to his and Sheila's plates.

"This is fabulous," she said after her first bite of the crispy outside piece of meat. "And those potatoes."

The girls looked pretty happy with their supper, too, and all of them especially enjoyed their homemade cookies with ice cream for dessert.

Back in Marystown, Eddie Tizzard had finally reached Doctor Sanjay.

"How many diamonds are there, do you think?" asked Tizzard.

"Dozens," said Sanjay. "And some of them are bigger than the others. I have no idea what they are worth, but it's certainly in the thousands."

"Do you have a safe place to store them?" asked Tizzard. "Until I can send somebody over tomorrow?"

"I have them hidden in the clinic," said Sanjay. "I think they can be secure overnight."

"Thanks, Doc," said Tizzard. "Either myself or somebody else will be over to relieve you."

The two men hung up, feeling good about their short-term plan for the precious loot that the doctor had discovered. They didn't know that two others were thinking about those diamonds and how to get them back. And that they were sitting outside of Sanjay's house right now.

Windflower didn't know anything about diamonds or Sanjay or Tizzard or anybody lurking in the shadows. He was happily walking Lady on her last stroll of the night, admiring the moon and stars over the Atlantic

Ocean. When he got home, he looked after the pets and turned off the downstairs lights. Sheila was in bed reading, and he slid in beside her and grabbed his book. Half an hour later, she turned off her light and he followed suit.

Minutes after that he was pleasantly floating along in his sleep when he woke up, again in a dream. And Harvey Brenton was back. But this time he looked a little worse for wear. His body seemed to be decomposing. Windflower stared at Brenton.

"Yeah, this was only temporary," said Brenton. "You start losing your good looks the longer you stay over on this side," he said with a cackle.

Windflower looked around. No stadium and no flashing scoreboard this time.

"Pretty boring, eh?" said Brenton. "But I have something else to show you." With that, Brenton pointed ahead of him, where the room seemed to open up wider. "Follow me," he said.

Windflower walked behind Brenton as they came into a large open area. Windflower recognized it as the L'Anse au Loup T, a narrow strip of land just outside Grand Bank that jutted out into the ocean in the shape of that letter. It was one of his favourite places. His Uncle Frank had said it was a powerful place, too. A place where secrets were revealed.

Windflower walked behind Brenton, right up to the edge of the water. When he got close, the ocean rose up and splashed him all over. When he was rubbing his eyes from the salt water, he could hear laughing. Harvey Brenton, for sure. You couldn't forget that cackle. But there was another laugh.

As he opened his eyes, he could see a large, fat harp seal.

"That was a good one," said Brenton.

"Thank you," said the seal. Windflower was not surprised at a talking seal. Animals and birds often talked in his dreams.

"I suppose you're some human in a seal form come to visit me and give me advice," said Windflower.

"Nope, just a seal," said Harvey Brenton. "If not, that's a pretty good suit," he said to the seal.

"It's a wetsuit," said the seal, and it started to laugh again. When Brenton joined in, Windflower got perturbed.

"Listen, it's been a long day," he started.

"Touchy old bugger, isn't he?" asked the seal. "You'd think he'd want our help."

Brenton nodded in agreement. "They don't understand."

"You can leave anytime you want," said the seal. "Just click your heels together and you'll be back in bed."

Windflower looked at the seal and then at Brenton. They looked serious. But as soon as he put his feet together, they both started laughing hysterically.

"Maybe you'll end up in Kansas," spurted Brenton through his laughter. "That was a great one."

"Gets them every time," said the seal. "Like the cat says, they're pretty dumb. Him especially."

"You know my cat, Molly?" asked Windflower.

"We know all the cats," said the seal. "They have nine lives."

"Is that true?" asked Windflower. He didn't wait for an answer because the laughter would have drowned it out. Now he was getting upset. He remembered to breathe and calm himself. "Do you have something for me?"

"Well, now that you ask," said the seal. "I have a riddle for you. Solve the riddle, and I'll answer any question you may have."

"Okay," said Windflower.

"On land. Not sea. I may have eyes, but I cannot see. I may be crisp or crinkled. I may be hashed or mashed. Red is my favourite colour."

"PEI potatoes," said Windflower. "They love the red soil on the island."

"Too easy," said Harvey Brenton. "You should have asked him one of Gollum's riddles. They never get those."

Windflower tried to interrupt and ask his question, but the bickering only grew louder. He kept trying until he could feel himself start to fade and then woke up again in bed with Sheila.

That was weird, he thought. But all good news as he snuggled into his wife. Either it was just a dream, and I can forget about it. Or I really do have a talking seal that I can ask a question of. If I can ever find it again. He gave up wondering about all that and let himself float back off to sleep.

Eddie Tizzard was getting ready to go to bed too. Hughie was fast asleep in his crib, and Carrie wouldn't be home from work 'til well past midnight. He turned out all the lights save one and went into the bedroom. Then his cell phone rang. It was the doctor from the hospital.

"Sorry to let you know that Diane Forsythe passed about an hour ago," said Doctor Savage. "I would have called earlier, but the paperwork."

"I know all about that," said Tizzard. "Her family has been notified, but I will pass the information along."

"I guess you should also know that Diane was pregnant," said Savage. "The embryo didn't survive either. Thought someone should know."

"Thanks," said Tizzard. "Good night."

That was an interesting twist. He called Majesky's number and left him a message. Then he called in to work to pass along the information. He asked the duty officer to check the protocols for an officer who died on duty. He thought he remembered one of the first things was to lower the flag outside the detachment. He told the officer if that was the case to make it happen. Somehow, that made him feel a little better as he went to bed, knowing that they were at least honouring the untimely passing of Inspector Diane Forsythe.

10

Windflower woke bright and early on Sunday morning, refreshed despite his crazy dream. He laughed to himself as he let Lady out the back door and put on the coffee. No sounds from above, so he had a few precious moments by himself. Later, Sheila would take Stella to church with her. Amelia Louise was currently under temporary suspension from that activity due to poor past performance. Sheila said that she might try her younger daughter out again around Christmas.

In the interim, Windflower would take her on his morning run, putting her in a carrier on his back. She was almost getting too big for that, but neither father nor daughter seemed to want to let that go. It was a special time for Windflower, and he thought that Amelia Louise felt the same. But for now, it was just Windflower, alone. Except for a pair of eyes gazing at him from the corner of the kitchen.

Windflower's relationship with Molly was, and he struggled for the word, difficult. Truth was he was kind of afraid of cats. His Uncle Frank had said that cats in dreams represented our feminine side, and since Molly had showed up in one of his dreams, maybe Windflower was actually afraid to show that side of himself. I'm not afraid, thought Windflower. He looked at Molly, and she stared a hole back at him.

Undeterred, he knelt down and called her to him. Reluctantly and very slowly, the cat came towards him. When she got close enough, he reached over and stroked her back. He had seen Sheila do this before and figured why not give it a shot. At first, the cat's back arched and it looked like she might pounce. Then she realized that he was actually going to pet her, and she relaxed and let him do his job.

A couple of minutes later, when Windflower stopped to go let Lady back in, Molly sauntered away, purring. Maybe she just said thank you, thought Windflower. Although when he looked back over again, the cat was once again completely ignoring him.

"I need more practice," he said to Lady as she sat patiently waiting for a treat. He gave her a Milk Bone and once again had made a friend for life. Cats looked like they might take a little more work. He sat for a few minutes and enjoyed his coffee until he heard two sets of feet running back and forth across the upstairs floors. He went to get the girls before they woke Sheila and brought them downstairs for breakfast.

Sunday morning waffles were a family tradition in the Windflower household, and he mixed up the batter and cut some fruit for the girls while they waited for Sheila to get up.

Eddie Tizzard had somewhat the same idea this Sunday morning. He and Hughie were making pancakes. Actually, he was trying to stir the batter, and Hughie was getting handfuls of it all over him. By the time Carrie came out of the bedroom, the baby and the table were a disaster area. She laughed at them both and took Hughie off the table. "I'll give him a bath while you clean this mess up."

Tizzard was almost finished cleaning everything and was ready to start the pancakes when his cell phone rang. He almost let it go to voice mail but at the last second picked it up. He was glad he did. It was Repa Sanjay, and she sounded frantic.

"He's gone," she said. "He took the dog out this morning. The dog came back, but he did not return. They gave me your number at the detachment. I am so worried. Nothing like this has ever happened before."

"Okay, I'm sure there's a perfectly good explanation," said Tizzard. "Tell me again what happened."

The woman ran through the series of events again.

"Maybe he had to go to the clinic," said Tizzard. "Have you called over there?"

"Yes, yes, yes," said Repa. "He's not there, and he would not go without telling me. "Vijay is very good about that. He never wants me to worry."

Now Tizzard felt a tinge of worry, too. But he didn't want to pass that along to the woman. "I can be over there in an hour or so."

"Thank you so much. I really appreciate it."

When he hung up, Carrie came out of the bathroom with a laughing and much cleaner baby. "Who was that?"

"Repa Sanjay," said Tizzard. "She says that Doc Sanjay is missing." He ran through the story with Carrie while he started the pancakes. "I'm going over there when I finish breakfast."

"Why don't you call Windflower?" she asked. "I'm not saying don't go. But he's right there. If you're going to be a big wheel, you have to start delegating."

Tizzard laughed as he served up the first batch of pancakes. "My dad says that 'big shots are only little shots that keep shooting.'"

"I think that's Mark Twain," said Carrie.

"Yeah, another one he probably got from my dad," said Tizzard. Carrie rolled her eyes, but he continued to wolf down his pancakes and then went to the living room to call Windflower.

Windflower had just finished his breakfast and was cleaning up. He looked down at his buzzing cell phone. "It's Eddie Tizzard," he said to Sheila as he walked outside to take the call.

"Good morning, Eddie."

"Morning, Sarge," said Tizzard. "I have a favour to ask. I think something may have happened to Sanjay." He told Windflower about the call from Repa.

"I can take a run over to her house," said Windflower.

"Great," said Tizzard. "I'm coming over soon. Thanks."

Sheila and Stella were upstairs getting dressed for church, and Amelia Louise was still lounging in the living room in her pajamas.

"Let's get you dressed," he said to Amelia Louise.

"Are we going for our run?" she asked.

"Yes, but first we have to visit Doc Sanjay's house," he replied.

"Why are you going over there?" asked Sheila, who had come down with Stella, both of them wearing dresses and bonnets.

"You look nice," said Windflower. "Eddie phoned me to tell me something is up with Sanjay. I'm going over to see Repa. Then we'll go on our run."

"Is everything okay?" she asked. Then, realizing that was a pointless question to ask a police officer, or former police officer, she added, "Never mind. Call me if there's anything I can do."

Windflower smiled. "I will," he said as he kissed Sheila and Stella and went upstairs to move Amelia Louise along. He could hear the front door close and looked out the window at Sheila and Stella walking to church.

Amelia Louise was almost ready, and Windflower helped her choose her top and got her and his carrier out the door shortly afterward. He drove across the brook to the Sanjay house on the other side. He and Amelia Louise went in to see Repa Sanjay.

"Oh, thank you for coming," said Repa. "It's been hours now, and I don't know where he is."

"What time did you last see him?" asked Windflower.

"He went out a little after eight this morning. Skippy came back about an hour later. But no Vijay." The little dog's ears perked up when he heard Repa speaking as if he knew that she was talking about him. Repa petted him absentmindedly.

"Did he say anything before he went out? Was there anything strange or different going on this morning?" asked Windflower.

Repa thought about it and said, "No, I don't think so." Then she thought again. "Last night there was something. Vijay went out with Skippy, and when he came back, he said there was a strange car parked down the lane from the house. There were two men inside."

"Did he say anything else about them? Or the car?" asked Windflower.

"No, only that it seemed odd to have a car out there at that time of night," said Repa. "There's never anybody around here that doesn't live here."

"Well, that's something to check out," said Windflower. "Maybe some of the neighbours saw the car or the men inside. I'll let Tizzard know. Is there anything I can get you? Anything we can do?"

"No, just help find Vijay," said the woman. She was trying not to cry, but at this last sentence she broke down. Windflower kind of looked on, helpless. Amelia Louise, though, knew what to do. She went over to Repa and put her arms around her. The woman snuggled into the little girl and hugged her back.

Windflower tried to leave, but Repa insisted they stay for tea and a snack. She and Amelia Louise went into the kitchen and came back shortly afterward with a tea tray and a plate of cookies. At Repa's prompting, Amelia Louise came over to Windflower to offer him one. He took one that tasted like shortbread.

"It's so nice," said Windflower. "Sweet and salty at the same time."

"They're nonta biscuits," said Repa. "Vijay's favourites." With that she started to cry again.

Back in Marystown, Tizzard had finished his second helping of pancakes and was playing with Hughie while Carrie got dressed.

"What are you going to do about the inspector job?" she asked when she came out of the bedroom and took the baby from Tizzard.

"I didn't tell you, but Diane Forsythe died last night," he said. "I'm waiting to hear back from Majesky."

"Oh my God," said Carrie. "What are you going to tell him?"

"I'm not quite sure," said Tizzard. "Something else I found out last night, and you have to keep this to yourself, is that Forsythe was pregnant."

"That's interesting," said Carrie. "I didn't even know she had a boyfriend. You know, I've been thinking about you and the job, and I have some ideas if you want to hear them."

"Absolutely," said Tizzard. "We're a team."

"I think you should take it. At least temporarily," said Carrie. "But I also think that the next permanent inspector should be a woman. You know why."

"I do," said Tizzard. "If we don't have a woman leader, then nothing will change."

"Thank you, Eddie. I love you," said Carrie.

"I love you, too," said Eddie. His cell phone ringing jarred them both a bit. He looked down.

"Majesky?" mouthed Carrie.

"Windflower," said Tizzard. "Hey, Sarge, what's up?"

"You might want to send a couple of other guys," said Windflower. "Repa says Sanjay told her that there was a couple of guys hanging around their neighbourhood last night."

"Okay, I'll line that up," said Tizzard.

"And I just remembered something. Levi Parsons said there were two men at the B&B yesterday. They were looking for Robert Smart. Levi told them the body was at the clinic and they should talk to Doc Sanjay."

"Worth checking out," said Tizzard. "I'll talk to Levi when I get there. Anything else?"

"Not from me," said Windflower. "Repa is pretty upset."

"Tell her we're on it," said Tizzard.

11

Windflower hung up with Tizzard and went to give Repa Sanjay an update. No good news, but at least there would be more resources on the case to find her husband. Before… Windflower couldn't go there. But he knew that the first few hours were critical in finding a missing person. As time went by, the chance of them returning home safe got slimmer.

He gave Repa a hug and went to find Levi Parsons himself.

Eddie Tizzard called over to the detachment to request backup and headed out towards Grand Bank. His cell phone rang as he was leaving town. He put it on speaker and said hello. This time it was Superintendent Majesky.

"Thank you for the message," said Majesky. "I hear you had the flag lowered as well."

"I did," said Tizzard. "Is there anything else I should do?"

"There's a protocol book in the inspector's office," said Majesky. "I want you to look after the family and get someone else to organize a public service. I've got media relations working on a press release. And I'll come down for the service. The family may want to do something here or ship the body out. You can work that out with them when they arrive."

"Okay," said Tizzard. "I can do that. But I'm also dealing with a case in Grand Bank, Robert Smart. And Doctor Sanjay has been reported missing."

"Oh yeah, Smart. I've gotten some calls about him. Diamond smuggler," said Majesky.

"Sanjay called me yesterday to suggest that Smart may have swallowed some diamonds. And that may have caused internal bleeding," said Tizzard.

"Death by diamonds, that's a new one," said Majesky. "Did we recover the diamonds?"

"No, and that might be part of why Sanjay is missing," said Tizzard. "There's reports of people who knew Smart being in the area. We're going to do a foot canvass to see if we can get some more information."

"Okay, keep me posted on that," said Majesky. "You think about the inspector job?"

Tizzard took a big breath and dove in. "I can take it on in the interim, but I really think what you need, we need, is a female lead in Marystown."

"Why do you think that?" asked Majesky.

"It's time," said Tizzard. "Forsythe talked to me the evening of the accident. She asked for my help. Some people were making it tough on her. If you don't appoint another woman, they might believe they're winning. You, we, don't want that."

"Agreed," said Majesky. "Okay, let's move ahead appointing you as acting inspector, and I'll get the paperwork moving on the staffing. Anything else?"

"I guess you should know that Forsythe was pregnant," said Tizzard. "The baby died in the accident. I'm not sure what to do with that information."

"Keep it to yourself for now," said Majesky. "Let me know about Sanjay and the diamonds."

That didn't sound quite right to Tizzard as he stared at the blank cell phone. But he had more than enough to occupy most of his brain as he sped towards Grand Bank.

Windflower dropped Amelia Louise back at home, where Sheila and Stella had just returned from church. "I hate to do this, but Doc Sanjay is missing, and I've got to help out." He handed over Amelia Louise, kissed Sheila and ran out the door again. Sheila knew better than to try to stop him when he was on a case.

"Call me," she yelled after him.

Windflower's first stop was the B&B. Beulah was there, cleaning the room of their last guest who'd departed that morning. She said Levi had left earlier with his friend. That would be his boyfriend, Christopher, thought Windflower. People in this small town, like Beulah, didn't really mind that Levi was gay. But they couldn't go as far as to say boyfriend or girlfriend about a same-sex relationship. Levi didn't really care, and neither did Windflower. He was more interested in getting information than a relationship status update.

He drove over to Levi Parsons' house and his cute two-tone Mini was in the driveway. Levi still lived with his parents, and his father Jerimiah greeted Windflower from his garage, where he was tinkering with an old pickup truck.

The father, once a fundamentalist Christian, had come to accept his son's sexuality after a bitter struggle. At the end, he told Windflower that it was more important to love his son than whatever anybody had to say about it. Today, the pair were as tight as thieves, and that was evidenced by the fact that Levi and Christopher were sitting having a late breakfast at the kitchen table.

"You want some, Sergeant?" asked Levi's mother, Charlene.

"No thank you, ma'am," said Windflower. "I just need a word with Levi."

Levi followed Windflower out to the backyard.

"What's up?" he asked.

"Tell me again about the men you saw at the B&B last night," said Windflower.

"Not much more to tell," said Levi. "They were big guys. Looked kinda mean to me. About your height. The muscular guy had a tat on his neck."

"A tattoo?" asked Windflower.

"Yeah, it was really cool," said Levi. "A pair of wings. One on each side."

"Did you see their car?" asked Windflower.

"I just saw it from behind. It was a four-door. White. Maybe a Toyota. That's about it," said Levi.

"Don't suppose you saw the license plate?" asked Windflower.

"Out of province," said Levi. "I don't know where it was from. Blue license plates."

"Anything else?" asked Windflower.

"Nope," said Levi. "What's going on?"

"I'll fill you in later," said Windflower. "Thanks."

He said goodbye to Charlene and Christopher and waved to Jerimiah Parsons as he drove away. He went around the corner and called Tizzard.

"Here's what I've got," he said.

"Great," said Tizzard. "That will help with the canvass. License plate could be Nova Scotia."

"Or Ontario," said Windflower. "Remember, they switched to blue from the old white ones."

"Yeah, and then they switched back because you couldn't see them at night," said Tizzard.

Despite the seriousness of the situation, both men chuckled at that bit of government incompetence. The levity didn't last long.

"Do you want me to help with the canvass?" asked Windflower. "I'm happy to help."

"No, I think we're good," said Tizzard. "Besides, you're not on the job until tomorrow."

"Okay, I'll check in again with Repa," said Windflower. "Even better, I'll get Sheila to do it."

"Good plan," said Tizzard. "I'll let you know if anything comes up. And you should probably know that I'm taking the inspector role, just temporary 'til they find somebody permanent. Diane Forsythe died overnight."

"I'm sorry about that last bit of news," said Windflower. "But I'm happy for you. It's a great opportunity. Good for you and good for the Force."

"I'm glad you think so," said Tizzard. "If it's okay, I might check in with you on stuff."

"Sure, I'd be happy to, Eddie," said Windflower. "Let me know as soon as you hear anything."

12

Windflower hung up with Tizzard and headed back home. Sheila was almost immediately on the phone with Repa. Windflower helped the girls with the puzzle that Sheila had laid out on the kitchen table.

"She wants me to come over," said Sheila.

"I'll look after the girls," said Windflower. "Maybe we'll go on an adventure."

"I love adventures," said Stella.

"Me too," said Amelia Louise.

"Call me," said Windflower as Sheila grabbed her purse and headed off.

"What's our adventure, Daddy?" asked Stella.

"Will there be snacks?" asked Amelia Louise.

"Well, we'll go on a hike," said Windflower.

Both girls groaned.

"To an abandoned village," he added.

The girls' eyes brightened.

"And can we have ice cream?" asked Amelia Louise.

"We'll have ice cream on the way home," said Windflower.

That led to a round of happy dances involving the girls and Lady. Molly looked suspiciously at this activity with a bit of a sneer, as if to say how dumb could some creatures get. Windflower noticed this and made a point to go over to her and give her a little rub on her head. At first it felt like Molly was only tolerating this intrusion, but after a while she started to purr and allowed him to stroke her back.

"Maybe this is the beginning of a beautiful relationship," Windflower said out loud. But Molly glared at this last remark. "Or maybe just baby steps." By now, the girls had their running shoes on and were gathering up their knapsacks for the adventure.

"C'mon, Daddy," said Stella as she and Amelia Louise pulled him along and out the door to the car.

"Where are we going again?" asked Stella.

"We're going to Point Crewe," said Windflower. "It's a small little place right on the ocean. Years ago, people lived there and went to church and school just like we do right here."

"But there's nobody there now?" asked Stella.

"Where did they go?" asked Amelia Louise.

"They all moved to other places," said Windflower. "I really don't know why they left. Maybe they didn't like living all by themselves so far away from everybody else."

"Maybe they wanted to make new friends," said Stella.

We could all use some more friends, thought Windflower as they drove out of Grand Bank and down into Fortune. About half an hour past Fortune, he turned down a narrow path beside the sign that said Point Crewe. He looked for the trail that Herb Stoodley had told him about, and soon the three members of the Windflower family were walking down the wooded trail. Well, he was walking. The girls were skipping and pausing to pick a few of the wild raspberries along the way.

He'd brought some water and a cut-up apple in his carrier that he brought on his back for the eventuality of Amelia Louise seeking a ride. The trail was relatively calm and peaceful until the girls and Lady spotted a rabbit trying to run across the path. That brought a whole new level of joyous chaos to the once tranquil scene.

After the futile rabbit chase, there was more excitement ahead as the water from a nearby pond had run down and crossed the path near a side road that separated the trail from the ocean. Large pools of shallow water lay ahead, and Lady and the girls ran to check it out. Before Windflower could get there, Lady was in the water, and the girls were taking off their shoes to wade across. He started to try to stop them, but their squeals of delight were too much. He removed his shoes and joined them.

After the water, they stopped on a large rock to have their snack and then moved farther down the trail. Now the ocean came into view along with the remnants of what must have been the settlement of Point Crewe. And that view was magnificent. There was a beautiful long beach and several concrete slabs that might have been a school or a church. If one scavenged deeply beneath the soil that had long been covered over from when there were houses and people living in them, you would likely find hundreds of relics of the folks who inhabited this place.

Now, all that remained were memories and the ocean. And of course, the eternal wind. If Windflower closed his eyes, he could see men dragging their boats onshore and women tending the fish flakes where they dried the cod their sons and husbands had scooped from the sea and deposited on the beach. He could hear a church bell ringing and children laughing. When he opened his eyes, it was Stella and Amelia Louise laughing as they ran towards him with shells they'd found near the water.

He examined them as the buried treasure that in fact they were and tucked them in his carrier for safekeeping. They all sat on the beach rocks for a few minutes to catch their breath and then headed back up the trail to the car. Windflower had promised ice cream, but his two little munchkins fell asleep in the car on the way home. When he arrived, they woke up just in time to greet their mother, who was sitting on the front steps.

"You okay?" asked Windflower.

"I am, but Repa is most certainly not," said Sheila. "She's a wreck. I'm going to go back later and bring her some food, but her kitchen is already full from people dropping things off. I saw Eddie, by the way."

"Any news?" asked Windflower.

Sheila shook her head. "I'm not sure he'd tell me anyway."

"I'll give him a call," said Windflower.

"So, where have you guys been?" she asked the girls.

"We went to a bandoned village," said Amelia Louise.

"That means there were no people there," added Stella. "We think they may have gone looking for new friends. Do you want to see our shells?"

While Sheila examined their discoveries, Windflower went inside and phoned Tizzard.

"Hey, Sarge," said Tizzard.

"Anything from the canvass?" asked Windflower.

"Well, there was a car parked along the road here last night. A white car with Ontario license plates. One of the neighbours saw it. Thought it might be a Buick. Said they saw people inside, maybe two of them, but no description."

"Anybody see anything this morning?" asked Windflower.

"Not yet," said Tizzard. "Not many people up early Sunday morning. But we'll keep at it."

"What does your gut say?" asked Windflower.

"Not good," said Tizzard. "Sanjay wouldn't have wandered off on his own. I have a feeling that this might be about Smart and those diamonds."

"Do we know where they are?" asked Windflower. "When I talked to him, I told them to put them somewhere safe."

"Maybe at the clinic?" said Tizzard.

"I'll meet you over there," said Windflower.

Windflower left Sheila and the girls and drove to the clinic to meet Tizzard. When he got there, he walked to the back where Doctor Sanjay had his office and examination area. Even though he was no longer practicing or officially the coroner, they still let him have this space to continue his forensic work and to do the occasional autopsy that a family might require.

He walked around the office and peeked into the examination area, but there was not really anywhere to hide anything in those spaces. He was opening all the cupboards when he heard Tizzard come in.

"Anything?" asked Tizzard.

"Nowhere in here to hide anything," said Windflower.

"Our guys have been here already," said Tizzard. "There were two men here last evening looking for Sanjay. The overnight nurse is gone home, but I've sent someone over to her house to interview her. Maybe she can give us a better description."

"There's security cameras, too," said Windflower.

"You're right," said Tizzard. "They no longer have a security guard, but they do have cameras."

"I think I remember there's a room near the front where they have a monitoring station," said Windflower.

13

Tizzard got the key from the on-duty nurse and opened the little room marked *Security*. It had a desk, a few orange vests, some pylons and a couple of filing cabinets. Above the cabinets were three screens. One showed the back entrance, one the parking lot and the other the front entrance.

Windflower sat at the desk and looked at the blinking equipment. "I have no idea what all this is or how to access the tapes. I wish we still had Smithson." Rick Smithson was the technical wizard of the Grand Bank RCMP detachment. That's when he was here and they actually had a detachment. Budget cuts had forced the closure and Smithson transferred out to Manitoba to be closer to his family in Ontario.

"We don't have Smithson. But we do have Betsy," said Tizzard.

"We do indeed," said Windflower. "And I'm sure she can operate this equipment." He opened his cell phone and called Betsy.

"Sorry to bother you at home on Sunday, but we need your help," said Windflower. That was all Betsy Molloy had to hear.

True to her word, she was there in ten minutes.

"Can you take us back to yesterday afternoon?" asked Tizzard.

"No problem," said Betsy. Five minutes later she had all three screens paused and started rolling them back in rapid fashion. Almost nothing from the back entrance camera. Next was the parking lot camera. As it started to get dark, they lost most of the screen, but as they kept watching, something came out of the shadows. It was two men walking towards the clinic.

"Stop it there," said Tizzard.

Betsy stopped the tape, and all three of them peered at the screen. It was still pretty dark and blurry.

"Can you make it bigger?" asked Windflower.

"Sure," said Betsy and enlarged the picture. It was still hard to see, but one man clearly had signs of something on his neck.

"It's the tattoo," said Windflower. "You can just make out one side. See the wings."

"I can," said Tizzard. "Betsy, can you go to the front entrance tape now? At the same time as we are now on this screen."

Betsy moved to the front entrance camera just before the time on the last screen. As they all watched, the two men came into sight again. This time their faces were clearly visible. And so were both sides of the neck tattoo. Betsy stopped the tape without asking. "You want a screen shot of this?"

"Betsy, you are the best," said Tizzard.

"Flattery will get you everywhere," said Betsy.

"Can you go forward and see if we can see anything else?" asked Windflower.

Betsy rolled the tape onward, but there were no cameras inside the clinic, and while they eventually saw the two men leave, they disappeared quickly into the blackness outside the building.

"Thanks, Betsy," said Tizzard. "I'm sorry we won't be working together anymore."

Betsy smiled. "Thank you, Corporal. But I have a feeling we'll be working on some things. My Bob always says that it's a long road that has no turns."

"See you tomorrow, Betsy," said Windflower.

"That I'm really looking forward to," said Betsy. At Tizzard's direction, she emailed the saved screen shot to his office in Marystown and left them in the security office.

"Next?" asked Windflower.

"We've got enough to start identifying the men, assuming they are in the database, finish our canvass and then begin looking for the car," said Tizzard. "Standard police work."

"But not usual," said Windflower. "My first guess is that our two mystery men have Sanjay, and they want the diamonds."

"What's your second guess?" asked Tizzard.

"That he won't tell them where they are," said Windflower.

"Unless he handed them over already, and they have dealt with Sanjay," said Tizzard.

"I don't even want to guess at that scenario," said Windflower. "In any case, you don't have much time to find them, and, I hope, him. I'll let you get back at it. If you need me, I'm here."

"Thanks," said Tizzard. He watched his old friend walk out of the clinic, and after saying goodnight to the nurse at the desk, he was outside soon afterwards. He paused and looked around at the building where Doctor Sanjay had spent so many years in service. And for the second time in a couple of days, the non-religious Eddie Tizzard said a prayer. This time that they had whatever help was up there to find the good doctor. Before it was too late.

Windflower arrived home to the happy scene of his daughters and Sheila in the kitchen, laughing and making individual pizzas for supper.

"We made you a carnival pizza, Daddy," said Amelia Louise proudly.

"Carnivore," said Stella. "That means lots of meat."

"Excellent," said Windflower.

"Any news?" asked Sheila, hopefully.

"Not much, although you may have heard that there was a strange car in the area yesterday. Tizzard has some leads he's following up on," said Windflower. "But…"

Sheila nodded. "I know, it takes time. Anyway, supper is all ready to go. If you can set the table, we'll go over to Repa's and drop off her a casserole. We can put the pizza in when we get back."

"Are you sure everybody should go?" asked Windflower. "The girls could stay with me."

"It was her request," said Sheila. "Said it gives her something to look forward to."

This time Windflower nodded. He got that.

After Sheila and the girls had left, Windflower set the table as requested and went to the living room, where he picked up his book. Lady was at his feet as usual, but as he started to read, he could feel something coming up behind him on the couch. In one smooth motion, Molly lowered herself right onto his lap. This was different, thought Windflower, as he started to stroke the cat with one hand while holding his book in the other. And pretty nice, too.

Sheila was a little surprised to see Molly on Windflower's lap when she got home with the girls. "New relationship?"

"No, we've always been close," said Windflower. "Just getting closer now. How's Repa?"

"Not good," said Sheila. "I'm really worried about her. I don't know what she'd do on her own."

"Can we have our pizza now?" asked Stella.

"We're starving," said Amelia Louise. "Daddy promised us ice cream, but we never got none."

"That's because you fell asleep," said Windflower. "You snooze, you lose."

Amelia Louise threw a cushion at him. Stella followed her sister. Soon all three of them were rolling around on the floor with Lady frantically circling like some kind of crazy referee. Molly, of course, had resumed her stoic pose atop the couch and was so bored that she promptly closed her eyes and fell asleep.

14

Fifteen minutes later Sheila interrupted the festivities by calling them all to supper.

"Great pizza," said Windflower. "Who made it?"

Stella raised her hand. Amelia Louise raised both of hers.

"They both did," said Sheila, defusing the building civil war.

Windflower tried to eat slowly, and the piping hot pizza helped that, but he was still finished long before Sheila and the girls. He waited until it looked like the girls were nearly done.

"Well, I guess it's that time," he said, standing up and pushing his chair back from the table. He gathered up the plates while the girls shouted at him to tell them what he was talking about. "Your mother knows," he said, filling the dishwasher.

"What time is it, Mommy?" asked Stella.

"I think it's ice cream time," said Sheila.

To the great delight of two little girls, Windflower got the wagon and Lady's leash and led the parade to the dairy bar up around the corner. They were not alone. Maybe half of Grand Bank was out tonight, and most had decided on ice cream for dessert. That meant a bit of a wait for the soft-serve cones for the Windflower crew, but everyone was in good spirits.

Eddie Tizzard was tired but in good spirits as well, or as best as he could be with the spectre of the missing doctor hanging over his head. He was on his way home to Carrie and little Hughie and the prospects of a hot pot roast dinner awaiting him. His phone started buzzing as soon as he left Grand Bank, so he switched it to the on-car system. That meant he could talk and still get home to Marystown quickly. And there were lots of people who wanted to talk to him.

Media Relations wanted him to approve the statement about Diane For-sythe. Her old assistant, Terri Pilgrim, called to see if she could help. She'd heard through the grapevine that he was taking over. He got her moving on the ceremony that would need to be set up. And he asked her to go into his email and retrieve the picture of the two men in the screen shot. She would run them through the system.

He talked to Majesky twice, first to confirm he was coming to represent the Force and then to give him an update on Sanjay and the diamonds. It seemed to Tizzard that the superintendent was more interested in the missing diamonds.

His second to last call before he came into Marystown was from his canvass crew who were also on their way back. They'd managed to talk to the on-duty nurse. She noted the neck tattoos but also said that the other guy spoke in an accent. Not French, she'd said. Maybe Dutch or German. More information, thought Tizzard. Always useful.

His last call was from Terri Pilgrim. She'd managed to get the picture and had a match for one of the men. The neck tattoo guy was local, at least to Newfoundland. He was from St. John's. Ricky Barber had been in and out of jail forever, and the last notation on his file was that he was working as an enforcer with the mob in Hamilton, Ontario.

"Can you see if he has a car registered to him in Ontario?" asked Tiz-zard. "And can you send the picture through Interpol? The other man might be European. Can you also get Media Relations to put out a notice with the pictures, noting they are driving a white car? And call me if you get any hits. Anything."

When he finally reached home, the aroma of the pot roast in the oven nearly made him swoon. He kissed Carrie and swung Hughie high over his head. While Carrie started dishing up supper, he told her about his day. Then, before he sat down to supper, he did something he almost never did: he turned off his phone.

"Ah," he said. "It's good to be home."

"Are you sure you're ready for all that's coming at you?" asked Carrie.

"As long as I have you and our little man here, I can do anything," said Tizzard as he tasted the pot roast. "This is wonderful," he added after his first bite. "You make the best gravy, too." He poured a generous amount over his mashed potatoes. By now, Hughie had also dug into his dinner. Literally. He had his hands in his mashed potatoes and gravy all over his face. All of the Tizzards really enjoyed their supper that evening.

After supper, Tizzard put his phone back on, answered all his messages and finally had a few quiet moments with Hughie and Carrie before they put him down for the night. Both of them were in bed not long after. Carrie had a big day on Monday. She was going to Grand Bank to meet Windflower in her new assignment, and Tizzard had to go into work to figure out his new Inspector role.

He was thinking about that as he fell asleep. He was drifting along aimlessly in his dream world when he suddenly woke up. He didn't often have vivid dreams. But he was pretty sure that this was one of those times. That's because he was in some form of coffee shop or café, and sitting across from him was Doctor Vijay Sanjay.

"Doc Sanjay, are you okay?" asked Tizzard.

"'Clouds come floating into my life, no longer to carry rain or usher storm, but to add color to my sunset sky,'" replied the man in his dream.

"Where are you?" Tizzard asked.

"'You can't cross the sea merely by standing and staring at the water,'" said the man.

"Okay, I get it," said Tizzard. "You can only answer in quotes. Tagore, right?"

The man smiled broadly and sipped on his tea.

Tizzard thought about what he could ask and get an answer that might help him. But his brain was too foggy.

The man spoke again. "'It is very simple to be happy, but it is very difficult to be simple.'"

"That would be me," said Tizzard. "Simple."

"'A mind all logic is like a knife all blade. It makes the hand bleed that uses it,'" said the man. Then, as mysteriously as this dream had appeared, the man who looked like Doc Sanjay and the coffee shop kind of melted away like mist. Tizzard woke again in his bed beside Carrie. He was too tired to think about all he had just seen and heard. Maybe he could talk to Windflower about it tomorrow. For now, he needed some sleep.

So did Winston Windflower. He joined Sheila, who was reading her book in bed, and tried to follow suit. But he didn't make it very long and was quickly fast asleep. Tonight, at least, just sleep and no dreams that he could remember when he woke to peals of laughter from downstairs.

He went downstairs to find the girls were decorating Lady in the living room. The Collie was kind and patient, but even she was having a hard time with their latest plan hatched by the mastermind, Stella.

"We're making Lady into a float for the parade," said Amelia Louise.

"What parade?" asked Windflower.

"The one we're planning for next year's Grand Bank Day," said Stella.

"It's come back year," said Amelia Louise.

"Come Home Year," said Stella.

"That's what I said," said Amelia Louise.

"But it's not for a year," said Windflower looking at a forlorn Lady, who was draped with crepe paper from Sheila's craft room and had plastic roses stuck on her with masking tape.

"We needed to practice," said Stella.

"Let's practice cleaning this up before your mom gets up," said Windflower. He helped the girls clean up Lady and put away all the craft supplies they'd taken out. He got them each some fruit and turned on the TV for them to watch while he made the coffee. By the time Sheila came down, the scene was calm and tranquil.

"This is nice," said Sheila as Windflower handed her a cup of coffee. "What was all the noise about earlier?"

"Don't ask," said Windflower. "I'm going outside for a few minutes." He kissed her and let an anxious Lady out in front of him. He opened his smudge kit and laid it on the deck. Then he sat quietly and let the morning come to him. He closed his eyes and could almost smell the grass growing. He opened them and admired Sheila's handiwork in the flower garden. The roses were spectacular this time of year.

He mixed his medicines and lit them using a long wooden match. He watched as the smoke started to rise and curl around him. It was as if he didn't have to direct the smoke this morning. It already knew where the sacred medicines were needed. He could sense the smoke pooling around his heart and then up almost into his eyes. He blinked but knew the messages were to be compassionate and open, so he tried his best to keep his eyes unshut.

He paused for a moment when the smoke seemed to wane and reflected on his life and the morning he had been graced with. It was easy to find the prayers of gratitude for his family and good health. The second prayers were for Doc Sanjay and Repa. However this worked out, and he hoped for the best, this was an extremely difficult time for them both.

Windflower felt much better after his morning rituals. He always did. He called Lady and went back inside, where Sheila had bacon frying and was mixing up scrambled eggs.

"Big breakfast this morning," he said, grabbing another cup of coffee.

"It's a big day," said Sheila. "First day on your new job. Oh, I forgot to tell you. Uncle Frank called last night. He's coming on Tuesday. He said not to worry, he'd get the taxi if you were too busy."

"I'll call him back," said Windflower. "But first, I have to get cleaned up. Have to look good on the job."

While Windflower was having his pleasant morning and a very nice breakfast, Eddie Tizzard was already at work. One of the advantages was that now he had an assistant. He'd never had one before. But Terri Pilgrim was great. She'd broken in a couple of inspectors by now and was ready for Tizzard from the get-go.

She had his files on his desk when he got there and offered to get him a coffee.

"I'm going to Tim Hortons," she said.

"That would be great," said Tizzard. "Here's twenty bucks. Can you get me a large double-double and an everything bagel with cheddar cheese? And a raisin bran muffin, too," he added, thinking that this could be a long day.

"No problem," said Pilgrim. "You have a briefing at eight with the senior team and Superintendent Majesky at nine."

And so it begins, thought Tizzard, who was already feeling trapped behind this desk. He thought about Hughie and Carrie, and that made him feel a lot better before he dug into the stack of files that lay on his desk. Action, Info, Reading. Which to start first? Obviously, Action, thought Tizzard

By the time Terri Pilgrim had gotten back with his coffee and food, he'd managed to authorize only one of the requested actions. And that was for a day off for one of the sergeants. All the rest he had questions about. Terri smiled knowingly and went to get her notepad.

15

Windflower walked into the old RCMP detachment. The signage outside had been removed, and the Canadian flag was no longer flying. Inside, it looked almost exactly the same, except for some darkened areas that had been closed off. They wouldn't need all that space for just him and Betsy.

Betsy was more than happy to welcome him back. She already had coffee on and had brought in a tin of homemade muffins. "Blueberry," she said proudly. "My Bob picks the berries, and I bakes."

Windflower took one along with the proffered coffee. He took a bite of the muffin. "Excellent, as always."

Betsy smiled. "Thank you, Sergeant."

"I'm not a sergeant anymore," said Windflower.

"Well, sir," said Betsy. "You will always be a sergeant to me. And according to this contract with the municipalities, they call you Sergeant as well. So that's settled," she added, handing him the paperwork with his name outlined as Sergeant Winston Windflower.

Windflower laughed and refused another muffin. He signed the contract and passed it back to her. "What's on the agenda today?"

"You've got a meeting with Mayor Wilson this morning, and I just received a message that Constable Evanchuk is on her way over," said Betsy. "It's nice that she's going to be part of the team."

Carrie Evanchuk was thinking the same thing as she came over the rolling hills into Grand Bank. She'd dropped the baby off at the sitter's and was looking forward to seeing Windflower and Betsy again.

She and Windflower had a good working relationship, and she spent a pleasant few minutes catching up with him and Betsy. And of course, trying one of Betsy's muffins as they drove together in her cruiser to the Grand Bank Town office.

Mayor Jacqueline Wilson was Sheila's successor as mayor of the town, and she had been designated the lead in dealing with their new Community Safety Officer.

"Thank you both for coming," said Mayor Wilson. "I'm particularly pleased you're here," she said to Evanchuk. "I think it will make a much smoother transition with you and the RCMP involved."

"I'm happy to help," said Evanchuk. "But I'm really only here temporarily to help Sergeant Windflower get started."

"How do you see this unfolding?" asked Windflower.

"We're not really sure," said the mayor. "But we're hoping that you can focus on prevention and bring in the RCMP for the more serious stuff. Speaking of which, do you know anything about what's happening with Doctor Sanjay? The rumours are that he was abducted."

"I don't know any more than he is missing," said Windflower. "Carrie, do you know any more?"

"Just that I think they have identified two men as connected to this situation, and Corporal Tizzard, I mean Acting Inspector Tizzard, is leading the investigation," said Evanchuk.

"Oh, to replace the late inspector," said Wilson. "I don't even think I met her. What a shame."

"Yes, she was very nice," said Windflower. "I only met Inspector Forsythe myself on the weekend."

"It was a very busy weekend," said Mayor Wilson. "A man dead at the B&B as well. What do you know about that?"

"The man, Robert Smart, was a guest at the hotel," said Windflower. "I don't know much more than we discovered him deceased in his room. Doctor Sanjay was looking into the cause of death."

"So this might all be connected somehow?" asked the mayor.

"I don't know, ma'am," said Windflower.

Somebody who did know was Eddie Tizzard, who was in the middle of his meeting with his two sergeants and two corporals, the executive team. He was surprised at how little reaction there was to Inspector Forsythe being gone and him being the new inspector. He asked them what their priorities were for the week. The sergeants mumbled something about traffic management and the corporals said nothing. He realized they were waiting for him to tell them what to do.

"Okay," he said to the first sergeant. "You take charge of the traffic management issue and report back to me by the end of the week." He put the other sergeant to work with Terri Pilgrim to plan the memorial service. "I want everybody else that doesn't have a firm assignment to work with me on the Sanjay case. If he's around this area, we want to find him. And fast."

Just as he was letting them all out of the meeting, Terri Pilgrim came rushing in. "We got a tip from Whitbourne. Somebody spotted Baker, the guy with the tattoos. They think they were heading east."

"To St. John's," said Tizzard. He put one of the corporals on the case to talk to the people in Whitbourne and to get the local RCMP involved there. He was about to start calling the Royal Newfoundland Constabulary in St. John's, who were responsible for policing that area, when Pilgrim spoke up again.

"There's someone here to see you," she said. "Kirk Forsythe."

Her brother, thought Tizzard. "Can you call the Constabulary and give them an update on what we know? Ask them for a contact person and have them call me. Thanks."

Tizzard walked back to his office and saw a man who must be Kirk Forsythe sitting in a chair outside his office. He hated this part of the job.

"Mister Forsythe," he said. "I'm Eddie Tizzard. I am so sorry for your loss." He held out his hand.

Kirk Forsythe rose from his chair and took Tizzard's hand. "I still can't believe it," he said.

"Come into my office," said Tizzard. "You want a coffee or tea or something?"

Forsythe shook his head and followed Tizzard inside. Tizzard closed the door behind them.

"Someone said you saw what happened," said Forsythe.

This was always the way, thought Tizzard. They wanted to go through what happened, as if by understanding it better, they might be able to bring their person back. It was just part of the process. The one he hated. But that was his job today. He began by talking about the man's sister and his interactions with her. He lied and said that everyone liked and admired her. That was a small fib to maybe bring the family some relief. The other man seemed to appreciate it.

Then he talked about the nice dinner they had before the trip back to Marystown. People wanted to know all of that, too. It felt normal and real and maybe like they were still there. But then he talked about the accident. The really hard part. He left out the smaller details like Diane being trapped in the vehicle, because he knew the next question that was coming.

"Did she suffer much?" asked Kirk.

"I think she was unconscious on impact," said Tizzard. That was likely the truth. "She was alive but not moving when I got there just moments after, and I believe the doctor said they kept her in sedation."

"The doctor told me she was pregnant but lost the baby," said Forsythe. "I didn't know she was seeing anyone. Was she?"

"I don't know," said Tizzard. This time it was the complete truth.

At this last response, the two men sat in that uncomfortable silence that surrounds grief until Terri Pilgrim interrupted them to tell Tizzard that Superintendent Majesky needed to speak with him.

Tizzard was relieved and went outside to take the call. "I'll be right back," he said. "We can talk about arrangements."

16

Windflower and Evanchuk were finishing up their meeting with Mayor Wilson. He let Carrie go out while he spoke privately to the mayor.

"I have to go to St. John's tomorrow to pick up my uncle," he said. "Hope that is okay."

"Frank is coming back, that's great news," said the mayor. "By all means, go pick him up. Tell him I said hi."

Windflower thanked the mayor and went outside to meet Evanchuk. They were going to have coffee before she headed back to Marystown. Minutes later they were enjoying a cup of coffee and one of the Mug-Up's famous raisin tea biscuits, steaming hot and smeared with butter.

After their snack, they chatted about Windflower's new job.

"I'm thinking that I will do a check-in every week with the mayors of all the towns. And I'll spend at least half a day at the high school," said Windflower.

"That's good," said Evanchuk. "I'm still doing some of that at Marystown Central High. It helps that they can see you on a regular basis. Some of my best tips come after I've visited."

"What do you think about using social media?" he asked.

"Could be good," said Evanchuk. "I'd suggest Instagram. That's what the kids use."

"Can you help me set that up?" said Windflower.

"Sure," said Carrie. "You can get Betsy to help as well. She can post on a regular basis. All you need to do is take pictures."

"I can do that, I think," said Windflower.

"Okay, I've got to get back," said Evanchuk. "I'm there if you need me."

"Thanks," said Windflower. When Evanchuk had left, he called his uncle.

"Hello," said a sleepy voice.

"Oh, did I get you up?" asked Windflower.

"Yes, but that's a good thing," said Uncle Frank. "I got to get packing anyway."

"I was calling to let you know I can pick you up," said Windflower. "What time do you get in?"

"I'm driving down to Edmonton tonight," said Frank. "If all goes according to plan I'll be in St. John's around supper time. Six thirty, I believe."

"That's a long day," said Windflower. "Maybe we should stay in town overnight and come back on Wednesday morning?"

"That's fine by me," said Uncle Frank. "Aren't you going to talk to me about Harvey Brenton? And the seal?"

"That would be good," said Windflower. "What's the seal all about?"

"Even though they are often playful and cracking jokes, seals are actually pretty powerful animals. They can live on land or in the ocean. They remind us to listen to what you see and hear, both while awake and in your dreams," said Uncle Frank.

"What question should I ask the seal, if I ever get back there?"

"Someone's in trouble, right?" said his uncle. "Ask them who it is and how you can help. Now, I gotta go pack. See ya tomorrow."

"Goodbye, Uncle," said Windflower.

"Couldn't help overhearing," said Herb Stoodley, who'd come by to pick up the plates from Windflower's table. "Frank?"

"Yeah, he's coming into St. John's tomorrow night," said Windflower. "I'm going to pick him up."

"It'll be nice to see him," said Herb. "That reminds me. I have a CD for you. I have it in the kitchen. I'll give it to you on the way out."

"Super," said Windflower. "Listen, I wanted to ask you about something else. Me and the girls went down to Point Crewe the other day. What do you know about that place?"

"Not very much," said Herb. "There's some people around town whose parents or grandparents lived there. I heard at one time there were about fifty people there. But as far as I know there hasn't been anybody living there since the 1950s."

"Why did they move?" asked Windflower.

"Electricity," said Herb. "When the power came, they wouldn't run it down to the coast. So, people in Point Crewe and lots of other small communities had to move to other places with access to electricity. Some held on as long as they could, but they eventually gave up and joined their neighbours in other villages along the coast."

"That's interesting," said Windflower. "They had to give up their way of life to take advantage of progress. But I understand why they did it, for sure."

"Any news on Sanjay?" asked Herb.

"I haven't heard anything since yesterday," said Windflower. "Maybe I'll give Tizzard a call."

"Let me know if you have any news," said Herb. "I'll get that CD for you."

Windflower called Tizzard, hoping he might be free and have some news to report. But before Tizzard could answer, another call came in to Windflower's phone. It was a local number. He hung up with Tizzard's call and took the new one.

"Sergeant, it's Repa. Some man just called and said they have Vijay. He was talking about diamonds and how they had to find them or Vijay will be hurt. I am so worried."

"It's okay, Repa," said Windflower. "I'll be right over."

He paid and took the CD from Herb at the cash without even looking at it, mumbled a quick thank-you and ran to his car. A few minutes later, he was sitting with Repa Sanjay in her kitchen.

She was barely consolable and kept breaking into sobs as she told Windflower her news. But he managed to help her get through it, and when she was done, he asked her to make some tea. It might have sounded like a strange request, and he really didn't want any tea. But it would give her something comforting and familiar to do while he called Eddie.

He got Terri Pilgrim. "Inspector Tizzard's office."

"Good morning, Terri, it's Winston Windflower in Grand Bank. Somebody called Repa Sanjay demanding diamonds in exchange for Vijay. I need to talk to Tizzard."

"I'll go get him," she said.

Tizzard was on the line shortly afterwards. "I've been dealing with Diane Forsythe's brother. What's up? Terri said something about diamonds and Sanjay."

Windflower told him about the conversation with Repa.

"We've got a lead on the two men who were in Marystown. One of them is local, and we think they're either on their way or already in St. John's," said Tizzard. "I've been in contact with the RNC, and I'm waiting to hear back."

"What do you want me to do?" asked Windflower, feeling a little weird to be asking Tizzard that question. Usually, the shoe was on the other foot.

"Can you stay there with Repa?" asked Tizzard. "I'm going to get our tech people to tap her line so we'll be ready when the next call comes. And I'll send someone over to be on the scene for us. Is Carrie still over there?"

"She's gone back," said Windflower. "Might still be on the road. I can stay here. Maybe I'll get Sheila to come over, too."

"That would be good," said Tizzard. "I'm kinda swamped over here. Dealing with the brother was tough."

"I bet," said Windflower. "Good luck with that."

"Thanks," said Tizzard. "I'll call you if there's any developments on our end."

Tizzard called Carrie.

17

"**I**'m almost in Marystown," said Carrie. "And you want me to go back to Grand Bank?"

Tizzard explained the situation.

"Oh, okay," said Carrie. "I'll turn around. How are you?"

"At times like this, my dad used to say he'd been ridden hard and put away wet," said Tizzard. "I'm not sure who he stole it from, but that's exactly how I feel today. I just met with Diane Forsythe's brother. At least I could turn him over to Terri and Sergeant Murphy, who are planning the memorial service."

"Well, keep smiling and remember to breathe," said Carrie. "'Breathing in, there is only the present moment. Breathing out, it is a wonderful moment.'"

"That's wonderful," said Tizzard.

"From my meditation book by Thích Nhất Hạnh," said Carrie. "You should try it sometime."

"I've tried meditating, but I always fall asleep," said Tizzard. "Anyway, call me when you see Repa and give me an update."

"Will do, boss," said Carrie.

"I like that," said Tizzard.

"Don't get too used to that," said Evanchuk, hanging up and swinging her car back towards Grand Bank. She arrived at the Sanjay house at the same time as Sheila.

"Carrie, nice to see you," said Sheila. "I'm so glad you're going to be back here more often. Although I wish the current circumstances were better. How's little Hughie?"

"He's not so little anymore," said Carrie. "He's been crawling for a while and now pulling himself up on anything he can find."

"Uh-oh," said Sheila. "Once they get mobile, your life as you knew it is over."

Carrie opened the front door for Sheila, and they both went in the living room to find Windflower trying unsuccessfully to console Repa Sanjay. Sheila went directly to Repa, and Windflower motioned Evanchuk to come into the kitchen with him.

"Anything new?" asked Evanchuk.

"No," said Windflower. "I guess now we wait. Your new inspector said he was going to put a trace on the line here. So, if they phone back…"

"I got it," said Evanchuk. "Well, not much both of us can do here. If you want to leave, I can hold down the fort here."

Windflower nodded as Sheila came into the room. "Carrie will stay, and I'm going back home," he said. "Where are the girls?"

"They're at the Mug-Up," said Sheila. "Moira said she'd look after them for as long as I needed."

"Okay, I'll check in on them along the way," said Windflower.

"Have you heard anything else?" asked Sheila.

Windflower shook his head. "If the phone rings, try to let it go for a few times before letting Repa answer. That'll give our guys a better chance to track." He gave Sheila a hug and said a quick goodbye to Repa with a promise to return soon.

After leaving the Sanjay house, he stopped for a moment in his car and just let the events of the whole day, the past few days, wash over him. He realized he hadn't processed much of what happened. That was the old police officer in him. Deal with the crisis and leave your feelings out of it. Except this time was different. This was his friend, Sanjay. As he felt his emotions, he started to cry.

Surprisingly, that felt good. He could release his fears and anxieties about his friend and just feel love and compassion for Repa.

He went back into the house, walked over to Repa and gave her a hug. "We'll find him. And bring him home," he said.

"I hope so," said Repa, and she gave him very slight smile.

Then he walked out again. Evanchuk just stared at him, and Sheila followed him out.

"Thank you for doing that," she said. "I think it helps." She gave him a hug, which he gratefully returned.

"Uncle Frank says I have to let my feminine side out more," said Windflower. "I'm working on it. I called him, by the way. He comes in around suppertime, and I think we'll stay at the Holiday Inn at the airport and come back in the morning. If that's okay."

"Fine by me," said Sheila, still a little surprised at seeing more of this side of her husband. "I'll book your room."

One more hug and Windflower was on his way again, feeling much better about the terrible situation that was happening around him. Maybe I should cry more, he thought.

Eddie Tizzard didn't want to cry, but he did want to pull his hair out. He was only half a day into his new assignment, and already the place was in chaos.

"Is it always like this?" he asked Terri Pilgrim, who was coming into his office with more paper.

"No," she said flatly. "Sometimes it's worse. Can I speak frankly?"

"Sure," said Tizzard. "Go right ahead."

"Inspector Forsythe was trying to sort things out, but that was slow going and lots of resistance," said Pilgrim. "Before that, Bill Ford was a nice man, but he was only a caretaker. We haven't had anybody really running things since Inspector Quigley went to Ottawa."

"Advice for me?" asked Tizzard. "Frankly."

Pilgrim let out a long sigh. "This could take some time. You should probably make this call first." She handed him a message slip. "And we found the license plate of Barber's car. Ontario plates. Here it is."

Tizzard picked it up and looked at both papers. "Thanks. It's Carl Langmead, RNC. I know that guy."

"Great," said Pilgrim. "When you're ready, we can talk."

Tizzard nodded and called Langmead's number in St. John's.

"Langmead," came the voice over the phone.

"Carl, it's Eddie Tizzard in Marystown."

"I hear congratulations are in order, Inspector," said Langmead.

"Acting Inspector," said Tizzard. "And it may be a very short assignment."

Langmead laughed. "I hear ya. I was acting head of the section for a couple of months and will never do that again. How's my old buddy, Windflower? I hear he's out of the business."

"He almost escaped," said Tizzard. "But they roped him into helping out after they shut down the detachment in Grand Bank."

"Well, say hello to him for me if you see him," said Langmead. "You're looking for Ricky Barber?"

"Him and an associate," said Tizzard. "We got pics of them in Whitbourne and think they may be in your area. I got a license plate for Barber's car. Here it is."

"I'll put that out over our system," said Langmead. "White sedan, Ontario plates. Should stand out like a sore thumb."

"What can you tell me about Barber?" asked Tizzard.

"He hasn't been around here for a while," said Langmead. "But when he was, he was a terror. He was a hangaround with the bikers, did lots of odd jobs for them. Mostly muscle. But even the bikers couldn't handle him. Said he was unpredictable."

"He must be something if the bikers got rid of him."

"Got run out of town," said Langmead. "Not by us, by them. He was a mean one. Probably still is."

"You should know, the wife got a call looking to find something that they would exchange for the doctor," said Tizzard.

"Are there diamonds involved?" asked Langmead. "That was the rumour."

"Appears so," said Tizzard. "There's a dead man in Grand Bank who was found with a baggie full of them in his stomach. Unfortunately for him, the baggie broke."

"Why is there always something interesting going on down your way?" asked Langmead. "All we get are fights on George Street after three in the morning."

"Be careful what you wish for," said Tizzard. "Keep an eye out for Barber and his buddy, and let me know if anything shakes down."

"Will do," said Langmead.

Tizzard hung up with the RNC officer to find Terri Pilgrim waiting at his door.

18

Windflower drove to the Mug-Up and parked in front. He saw the CD on his front seat and took a look at the jacket. Mahler, Symphony #7, by the Bavarian State Orchestra. Looks interesting, he thought. He laid it back down and walked inside the café.

Amelia Louise and Stella were sitting at a table in the corner, colouring. "Come see, Daddy. Look how good we're doing."

Windflower went closer and told them both their work looked terrific. Moira Stoodley came out of the kitchen and said hi.

"They have both been very good girls," she said. "If it's okay with you, I was going to take them home, and they can help me make some date squares."

"I love date squares," said Windflower.

"Can we go?" asked Amelia Louise.

"Absolutely," said Windflower. "You sure it won't be too much trouble?"

"Not at all," said Moira. "The staff can look after this place. We'll head over as soon as Herb gets back."

Windflower stayed for a few minutes with Moira and the girls until Herb arrived. He helped Herb unload his supplies from his van.

"Thanks for the CD," said Windflower.

"You're very welcome," said Herb. "I think you'll like it. It was voted one of the best of the year."

"I'm sure I will," said Windflower as he took the CD. He was thinking about driving to Fortune to say hello to the mayor when he passed by the high school and saw a commotion in the parking lot. He stopped his car for a closer look.

There were about a dozen boys forming a circle with a few girls hanging around the edges. Inside the circle, two boys were stalking each other, and Windflower saw one of them lash out with his leg and kick the other boy in a place that would surely hurt. He crumpled to the ground. All of the circling boys cheered. But they quickly scattered when they noticed Windflower.

He went directly to the boy on the ground. The kicker tried to run away, but he called out to him. "Stay here," he ordered. The kicker stood perfectly still as Windflower talked quietly to the boy who was moaning, clearly in pain.

"You'll be okay," he offered as comfort. The boy in pain wasn't so sure. He threw up on the ground, just missing Windflower's shoes. The other boy started to slide away, but this time he was stopped by another man, someone Windflower recognized as Bill Wilkins, the vice-principal.

"What are you doing?" asked Wilkins as he stood in front of the kicker. "Morning, Sergeant. Sorry to greet you this way. How's Crocker?"

"He'll survive. Is recess always like this?" he asked as he heard the school bells ring and all the kids who were just outside the building started filing in.

"Sometimes it's worse," said Wilkins. "This is summer school, and we're near the end. Another week and we're done. Some of them have already had it."

"I can see that," said Windflower.

"In my office," Wilkins said to the attacker. "And you can meet us there, too," he added for the benefit of the injured boy, who was feeling well enough to stand up by now.

The two boys walked off separately and slowly towards the school entrance.

"Thanks for your help," said Wilkins.

"No problem," said Windflower. "I was driving by when I saw the fight."

"Some of it is just hormones," said Wilkins. "But some of it is kind of disturbing. Like they think they can solve their problems with violence."

"Maybe they need some alternatives," said Windflower.

"We try," said Wilkins. "But they've tuned us out. Too much like their parents. But they might listen to someone like you. Can you come back in September when the full school returns?"

"Maybe," said Windflower. "I bet it would be better if I had someone younger with me. Do you know Carrie Evanchuk?"

"Eddie Tizzard's partner?" asked Wilkins. "Isn't she in Marystown?"

"She is, but she's been assigned as my liaison," said Windflower. "I think she'd be great at this."

"Good idea," said Wilkins. "Come see me and we'll get you set up. The sooner in September the better."

"Will do," said Windflower. He went back to his car and watched Wilkins round up the last few stragglers from recess. He was almost in Fortune when his phone rang.

"There's been another call," said Sheila.

"I'll be right there," said Windflower.

Eddie Tizzard had gotten a call, too. He'd been sitting with Kirk Forsythe and Sergeant Devin Murphy, going over details about the memorial service for Forsythe's sister. He'd explained that they'd already had her cremated and that he would bring the ashes back to his family for their own private ceremony later on. In Marystown, they would have a flag-draped but empty casket, and there would be a full parade of local RCMP officers and others from across the country to show their respects.

Terri Pilgrim pulled him out of the meeting. "One of our tech guys called. There's been another call to Doctor Sanjay's wife. They have a recording."

"Were they able to trace the call?" asked Tizzard.

"He's on his way up. Jarrod Norbert."

Tizzard offered his condolences again to Kirk Forsythe and went outside, where a young constable was waiting for him.

"Norbert?" asked Tizzard.

"Yes, sir," said the constable.

"What have you got for me?" asked Tizzard.

"I have the recording on my phone if you want to hear it," said Norbert. Tizzard nodded, so Norbert turned up the volume and handed it to his inspector.

"We're getting tired of waiting," said a voice on the phone. Tizzard thought he detected a touch of V in the "we're" from the man. "We want the diamonds." Once again, Tizzard heard the V sound. "Do you have them for us?"

"No, no, I don't know anything about any diamonds. Please don't hurt my husband," Repa pleaded.

"You have twenty-four hours to comply," said the man on the phone. "Otherwise, we have no choice. And no cops. Any police and we're gone, and so is your husband. Got it?"

"Yes, yes," said Repa. "Please don't hurt him…"

Then the phone was dead.

"Did you track it?" asked Tizzard.

"We have a cell phone number. But it's a burner, which means they use it once or twice and then throw it away," said Norbert. "But we got an initial location. It's in St. John's. We relayed it to the RNC."

"Any news from them?" asked Tizzard.

"Not yet," said Norbert. "But I'll be surprised if they find anything. We can no longer track the GPS on that phone. It's likely been dismantled."

"Okay, thanks," said Tizzard. "Stay on this. It sounds like they'll call back at least once more."

Norbert took his phone and left. Tizzard felt his own phone buzz in his pocket. He picked it up, hoping it was his friend Carl Langmead from St. John's. It was Majesky.

"Yes, sir?" answered Tizzard.

"Have you got a date for the service?" asked Majesky.

"Looks like Thursday morning," said Tizzard.

"Great. I'll be there," said Majesky. "What's going with the Sanjay case? Did we find the diamonds?"

After Tizzard gave him an update, Majesky hung up without saying anything else. It sounded like his super was more interested in finding the jewels than the missing doctor.

Windflower had no such contradictions.

"We have to find him," he said when Tizzard picked up his call.

"Well, the good news is that it sounds like he's still alive," said Tizzard. "And we've got a day to find him. Sounds pretty likely he's in St. John's." He gave Windflower the same info he'd relayed to Majesky.

"I can help in there," said Windflower. "I'm driving in tomorrow afternoon to pick up Uncle Frank. I could go earlier if you think it would help."

"Maybe," said Tizzard. "Are you at the house?"

"Just out in front," said Windflower. "I wanted the latest before I went inside."

"Can you talk to Repa again about the diamonds?" asked Tizzard. "Majesky is bugging me about them, and I don't know why, but I have a feeling if we can find them, it might help us with Sanjay."

"Okay, I'll do that," said Windflower.

Windflower hung up and went into the Sanjay house.

19

Evanchuk greeted him at the door. "Have you talked to Eddie? Were they able to trace the call?"

"I think so," said Windflower. "It was from St. John's. They're working with the RNC on this. How's Repa?"

"Not good," said Evanchuk. "I'm not sure how long she can hold up."

Windflower went into the living room, where Sheila was sitting with Repa Sanjay.

"Oh, Sergeant, is there any good news?" Repa asked.

"Some," said Windflower. "I talked with Eddie Tizzard, and they were able to trace the call. They think it's from St. John's."

"Can they find the men who are holding Vijay? Can they find him now?" asked Repa.

"They're working on it," said Windflower. "I'm going to St. John's tomorrow to help them."

"You will find him and bring him back?" asked Repa.

"I will do my best," said Windflower. "I know that it is very hard, and you have been very helpful. But I need to ask you some more questions. It may help us find Vijay."

Repa nodded, so he continued.

"Do you remember if he said anything, anything at all, about the diamonds that people are talking about?" asked Windflower. "It's really important."

"No, nothing," said Repa. "Only about the car with the two men outside."

Windflower tried another approach. "If Vijay was to hide something around the house, where do you think he would put it?"

"Vijay would never hide anything from me. We've been married too long to hold secrets from each other."

Windflower persisted, even as he saw both Repa and now Sheila getting perturbed with his questioning.

"He must have had occasion over the years to hide something, maybe birthday presents for your children. In the shed out back, maybe?"

"No, no, not there. He was always afraid that the wild cats in the neighbourhood would get in there," said Repa. She stayed silent for a moment and then spoke again. "But one time I do remember that he had a special gift for one of the boys. It was something electronic he had ordered. He didn't want him to find it, so he took it to work with him. He said he had a safe place."

"Where was that, do you think?" asked Windflower gently.

"I don't know," said Repa and started to cry. Sheila wrapped her in her arms and let her sob. Windflower backed away and went to the kitchen.

Evanchuk followed him out.

"I think the diamonds are in the clinic," she said. "That would be his safest place."

"We already searched his office," said Windflower. "Nothing there. Have you searched the house?"

"Top to bottom," said Evanchuk. "Nothing in the shed either," she added, anticipating his next question.

Evanchuk and Windflower sat quietly for a few minutes, listening to Sheila trying to comfort Repa. Then Windflower spoke up.

"Maybe you're on to something," he said. "It must be the Clinic. But where?"

"What's the safest, most secure place there?"

"The pharmacy," said Windflower. "Let's go check it out."

They told Repa and Sheila they had to go check something out and raced to the clinic in Evanchuk's cruiser.

The duty nurse sent them to see the head nurse, Lucy Roebottom.

Nurse Roebottom explained how the pharmacy worked. They kept a limited supply of pain medication on hand, and it was stored under lock and key. She and the doctors on staff were the only ones who had access, and every entrance to the pharmacy unit had to be logged, as well as what medications were removed. Windflower asked to see the log.

The nurse led them down a corridor to an unmarked room. She unlocked the door and turned on the lights. There was shelving on the walls and a chart with notations for each of the medications. And there on the table was the logbook. Nurse Roebottom passed it to Windflower. He quickly scanned it and found what he was looking for: Doctor Sanjay's name and the time of his visit.

Windflower and Evanchuk managed to convince Nurse Roebottom to leave so they could do a thorough search. She reluctantly left them alone, but they could hear her nervous footsteps pacing the hallway outside. They started searching one side to the other, careful not to disturb or misplace any of the medications. Finally, Evanchuk pulled out a small plastic bag and waved it at Windflower.

"Got it," she said.

Windflower examined the bag. "Doesn't look like much," he said. "But I bet there's tens of thousands of dollars in this little bag."

The pair thanked Nurse Roebottom, who quickly did a scan to make sure everything looked okay and locked the door. Minutes later they were back in Evanchuk's cruiser outside the clinic.

"Let's call the boss," he said. He put Tizzard on the speaker.

Eddie was surprised to hear news about the diamonds so quickly. "You are good," he said to Windflower.

"Wasn't me," said Windflower. "It was your talented wife, Constable Evanchuk."

"I'll thank her personally later," said Tizzard as Evanchuk beamed beside Windflower. "Either way, I'm pretty happy. I think we should use the diamonds as bait to get Sanjay back safe."

"What are you thinking?" asked Windflower.

"When they call back again, which appears likely, we get Repa to tell them that she has found the diamonds but wants her husband back first before she hands them over," said Tizzard.

"Even if they'd agree, how do we manage that?" asked Windflower.

"Repa tells them she has a family friend who will bring them to St. John's. That person will bring a couple of diamonds as good faith. If they can see Sanjay alive, they will hand over the rest at an agreed upon time and place," said Tizzard.

"I'm starting to get the picture now," said Windflower. "This is pretty dangerous. For everybody. Sanjay and the family friend. Whoever that might be."

"We could try to get an undercover officer from the RNC to do it," said Tizzard.

"I have to talk to Sheila," said Windflower.

"And I have to talk to Majesky. If he doesn't bite, this is over," said Tizzard.

"Same on my end," said Windflower. "Give me a few hours. Nothing is likely to happen between now and then. Unless the RNC finds your guys first."

"Okay, let's check in later," said Tizzard. "Make sure you look after those diamonds."

"I'm going to enlist our secret weapon in that task," said Windflower. "Betsy Molloy."

20

"Let's go see Betsy," said Windflower. Evanchuk swung the car out of the clinic's parking lot and drove to the old detachment office. Betsy was happy to see them and even happier when she was given the package of diamonds for safekeeping.

"My Bob has a place that nobody has ever walked before but him," said Betsy. "He's got secret berry patches all over the countryside. He'll help me find a safe place for these things. You have nothing to worry about."

Both Evanchuk and Windflower felt exactly like that as they drove back to the Sanjay house.

"I'm going to leave you with Repa while I talk to Sheila," said Windflower. "Okay?"

"Okay," said Evanchuk.

The pair walked back into the house, which was much quieter and calmer since their last visit. "We've got some good news," said Windflower. "We found the diamonds, and they're in safe hands. Now, we need a plan to make an exchange for Vijay. But first Sheila and I have to do something." He motioned to Sheila to follow him out. "We'll be back soon."

Sheila looked puzzled but went with him to his car. He started it up and drove off.

"Are you going to tell me what's going on?" she asked.

"Let's go for a drive first," said Windflower.

Sheila still looked confused but settled in as Windflower drove out of Grand Bank and onto the highway. He drove about ten minutes and then took the gravel road turnoff to the L'Anse au Loup T. It was the same place where Windflower had met Harvey Brenton and that saucy seal in his dream.

Today there was a thin line of fog draped over the T, but he and Sheila could also see it starting to drift away, back out to sea. That was usually an omen the warm weather would continue. But nothing was guaranteed about the weather in these parts. He took Sheila's hand, and they walked down towards where the seals usually played. Windflower had a crazy idea that he might see his old seal buddy, but mostly he wanted to just get rid of as much of the negative energy that had been building up in and around him in the last couple of days as possible.

By the time they got to the end of the pathway and found a nice big rock to sit on, the sun was breaking through the fog. Another good sign, thought Windflower.

"I know you're going to talk about doing something stupid, dangerous or both," said Sheila. Windflower started to speak, but she put up her hand, the universal message that all men understood or ignored at their peril. He stayed quiet.

"And you've probably already made up your mind to do it," she added.

"I said that you had to agree," Windflower protested.

"In your head that just means you have to convince me," said Sheila. "But I appreciate that you didn't say yes right away. You didn't, did you?"

"No, no," said Windflower. "Can I ask you now?"

"Go ahead." Sheila folded her arms in a gesture that Windflower completely understood. He had to convince her.

He talked about Sanjay first. What a great friend he'd been to him and their family. Not much reaction from Sheila, but she didn't look cold. Her mood brightened a little when he spoke about Repa and how they had to help her.

"So, what are you planning to do?" she asked.

Windflower told her, and she stayed quiet for a couple of long minutes. Windflower knew better than to interrupt. He had made his best case and waited for the verdict from his jury of one.

"You know, we agreed that it was the best decision for you to leave the RCMP," she started. "I also know that you were getting burnt out. But the main reason was that we wanted you to come home safe every night and not to have to worry about that. For us, for our family."

She stayed quiet again. And once again, Windflower waited.

"I agree. For Vijay and Repa. One time only," she said. "I'm not happy, and I'll be worried sick. But I won't stand in your way. Let's go back."

She took Windflower's hand when he offered it, and they walked back to the car in silence. Not another word was spoken until they got back to the Sanjay house.

"I think it's the right thing to do," he said. "Thank you for supporting me."

"Just make sure nothing happens to you. Or I may have to kill you myself," said Sheila.

Windflower smiled and went to talk to Repa. She was nervous but happy to finally have something to do that might make a difference in getting her husband back. He got Evanchuk to sit with her to go over what she would say if and when the next call came.

Meanwhile, Tizzard had gotten an earful from Majesky on his plan for getting Doctor Sanjay released from the abductors.

"Maybe they'll find them in St. John's," he said. "Without us having to do anything stupid."

"And maybe they won't," said Tizzard. "We found the diamonds. They're in a secure place right now. And we have Windflower making the transaction for us." He almost added "what could go wrong" but wisely resisted.

After a bit more back and forth, Majesky agreed. With conditions. Both Windflower and the diamonds had to wear a tracking device. Majesky claimed to be interested equally in both. Tizzard wasn't so sure.

When they finished that discussion, Majesky asked again about the memorial service for Diane Forsythe. "How's her brother taking all this?"

"He's pretty broken up," said Tizzard. "They've already arranged cremation. He asked about the baby and if we knew who the father was."

There was silence on the other end of the line after this comment.

"You still there, Superintendent?" asked Tizzard.

"She told me she had artificial insemination," said Majesky finally. "She wanted to have a baby on her own. That's why I suggested she talk to you for support. That wouldn't have been easy, especially in Marystown."

Tizzard stayed quiet this time, waiting to see if there was more information coming. But nothing.

"We'll do our best to keep Windflower and the diamonds safe," he said when he couldn't take the uncomfortable silence any more. "We won't lose either."

"You better not," was all Majesky said before the line went dead.

He tried to call Windflower in Grand Bank, but Carrie jumped the queue.

"How's it going over there?" he asked.

Instead of responding to that question, Carrie made her own statement. "I want to go with him."

Tizzard started talking about how that maybe was not a great idea, but she cut him off.

"With all respect, sir, I am the one most familiar with this case, and anyone can come and take my place as babysitter over here. He needs someone to go with him that he trusts," said Carrie.

"Okay," said Tizzard. "But in my other role as parent, I now have to go organize my own babysitting."

"Thank you, Eddie," said Carrie. "I know you're worried about me going, but I'm not going to take any chances."

"To quote Superintendent Majesky, you better not," said Tizzard. "How is Windflower?"

"He and Sheila have worked it out, but I'll let him tell you himself," said Carrie. "Can you send someone over to relieve me in the morning? I'll stay overnight with Repa in case we get a call and then drive with Windflower to St. John's."

"Sure," said Tizzard. He and Carrie chatted a little about their day, and he told her what Majesky had said about Forsythe's baby.

"I still wonder who the father was," said Carrie. "She wouldn't have done this on a random basis."

"That is interesting," said Tizzard. "But I have a thousand things more pressing than that to deal with right now. I'll call you later."

21

Windflower had two pressing things of his own to deal with right now: his two daughters. He and Sheila had agreed he would look after them and get them supper while she stayed with Repa.

He picked them up from Moira and Herb's place. They had been making date squares with Moira and had two packages of still-warm treats. Windflower tried a square and said it was the best he'd ever had in his life. That made the girls happy, and they were even happier when he suggested getting take-out for supper.

Windflower called in their order, and when they arrived their order was ready, two small chicken and chips for the girls and fish and chips for Windflower. When he got home, he made a small garden salad that he divided up between them. Sheila would have been proud of the salad. The take-out food, not so much. He wasn't planning on mentioning the supper menu to her.

After supper, they had a square each for dessert, and Windflower suggested a walk around town with a special visit to the brook. The girls knew what that was for. It was duck-feeding time. They helped Windflower tear up half a loaf of almost stale bread, and soon they and Lady on her leash were walking around Grand Bank.

First stop was the wharf. There was always something happening there. Not as much as in the old days, when dozens of boats would line the wharf, and as many men would be loading and unloading supplies. This evening the attraction was at the far end, where a few boys and some not-so-young men were fishing off the dock. One of them had hooked a salmon, and they were discussing what to do with it.

They decided that the lucky fisherman should take it with him, and as they like to say in this area, they skedaddled away. That was because it

was technically illegal to fish or catch salmon without the proper license.
Which no fisher on the wharf possessed. But in the absence of the fishery
officer, one salmon was on its way to a freezer somewhere in Grand Bank.

Windflower did his best to ignore this situation. He didn't want to con-
done or ignore it. He didn't want to be involved, just enjoy his time with
his family. The fishermen, young and old, were quite happy to keep him
out of it, and he could sense their anxiety lessen as they made the turn
towards the brook.

The ducks were thrilled at the sight of the girls and the possibility of
a snack. Not so much with Lady, who Windflower kept tethered close to
him. The ducks quacked loudly as they scrambled for the scraps of bread
that Stella and Amelia Louise were frantically throwing in the water. Far
too soon for anybody's liking, the bread toss was over and the trio headed
home with Lady.

At the house, Windflower got a bubble bath ready and dumped both
girls in together. He could hear their splashing and giggling from downstairs, where he'd made a cup of tea and was sitting relaxing while the girls
enjoyed their bath time. That didn't last long. Eddie called from Marystown.

"Anything new?" he asked Tizzard.

"Nope. The St. John's people are still looking but haven't located them
or the car," said Tizzard. "Are you sure you want to do this?"

"I'm okay," said Windflower.

"Majesky is worried about you and the diamonds," said Tizzard. "Do
you have them?"

"In a safe place," said Windflower. "I'll bring them with me to St.
John's."

"Good," said Tizzard. "Carrie is coming with you. Insisted on it."

"That will be nice," said Windflower. "We'll get to spend some time
together."

"It's not a vacation. My wife and my best friend heading out into the
jaws of danger."

"It'll be fine," said Windflower. "Sheila has let me do it, but she's sworn
me to come back safely."

"Do you want a service weapon to take with you? I hope not, but you might need it."

"No, I've made up my mind on carrying a gun," said Windflower. "Unless I go back to the Force, which is highly unlikely, I've had my fill of guns. Who's my contact in St. John's, by the way?"

"Carl Langmead," said Tizzard.

"Carl? That is super news," said Windflower. "We go way back."

"Thought you'd be pleased with that. Anyway, I gotta go pick up Hughie. I'm on duty tonight. Carrie will stay over at Sanjay's house and pick you up in the morning."

"Me, too," said Windflower. "Mine are in the bath. I better go see what mess they've made up there."

"Winston, be careful," said Tizzard just before he hung up.

Windflower went upstairs to find soap and bubbles and water everywhere. But this really was good, clean fun. He got the girls out, dried and sent them to their bedrooms to put on their pajamas and to pick out a book each to read before they went to bed.

Stella, who could read by herself, brought back What's My Superpower? a fun and easy book about a little girl, Nalvana, who felt that all her friends had some special gift. Like a superpower. She loved this story, and Amelia Louise loved hearing it.

Not to be outdone, Amelia Louise had brought two books. The first was I Spy Animals, in which you had to find an animal that began with a specific letter. It was more of a game than reading, but it was the best Amelia Louise had to offer. Then she pulled out her second choice, Goodnight Moon. It was still one of both girls' favourites after all these years, and they both wanted to find the little mouse that was hiding in the pictures.

It was also the perfect book for cuddling and getting sleepy, and by the time Windflower finished, they were both ready for bed. He took them each to their bed and tucked them in. He gave them a kiss and turned out the big lights. Now, he could relax.

This time he got a full hour of sitting and reading his book until he heard the door open and Sheila came in.

"How did you make out?" she asked. "It's remarkably quiet around here."

"Guess I have the magic touch," said Windflower. "'It is a wise father that knows his own child.'"

"It's because you're so like them," said Sheila. "'Men from children nothing differ.'"

"We had a nice quiet evening, had supper, fed the ducks," said Windflower. "How are things over there?"

"Not good," said Sheila, throwing off her shoes and grabbing Windflower's cup of tea. "Repa is now on a knife's edge, waiting for the phone to ring. One of her sons is coming in the morning, so hopefully that will help settle her down."

"Carrie Evanchuk is coming with me to St. John's," said Windflower.

"She told me," said Sheila. "Eddie must be out of his mind."

"He's worried, but it is her assignment," said Windflower.

"This feels like we are back in the bad old days," said Sheila. "I've made my peace with this, though. 'Cause I know it's the last time, right?"

"Right," said Windflower, although not quickly enough to avoid a poke in the ribs. "Why don't you have your bath? I'll take Lady out one more time."

Windflower and the dog had a quick spin around the neighbourhood, and he was back home again soon after Sheila had gone upstairs. He followed her up, and before long he was in bed and asleep.

But as happened far too often for his liking these days, he was soon awake again in another dream. This time he was down by the wharf, and he noticed something happening down the near the end where the fishermen usually gathered. He went towards the commotion for a closer look.

22

His old friend the seal was back, and this time he was doing tricks to entertain a growing crowd on the wharf who cheered his every move. The seal spotted Windflower and motioned with his head that he should come towards him. Windflower, who'd been tricked more than once by the seal, slowly crept his way. The crowd parted to let him through.

That was when he saw that the crowd was actually cardboard cut-outs of people and that he and the seal appeared to be the only living, if you could call it that, creatures on the wharf.

"I know, it's pretty lame," said the seal. "But you gotta practice somewhere."

Windflower just shook his head, a bit befuddled about what exactly was going on. He shook himself more awake.

"I could splash you a little if that would help," said the seal.

"No thanks," said Windflower. "But you owe me an answer."

"Wow, a mind like a steel trap," said the seal. "Shoot."

Windflower thought how he could phrase the question to get the most information. The seal tapped his flipper on the wharf to urge him to hurry up.

"Where is Sanjay, and is he okay?" asked Windflower.

"St. John's," said the seal. "That technically fulfils my commitment, which was for one answer. But seeing as how I feel generous today, I can also tell you that he is not dead. Okay? That's pretty subjective."

The seal went to slip into the water, and Windflower called out, "Hey, wait, any chance of another question?"

"Always possible," said the seal. "But no guarantees. And don't bother asking. I know what the question is. We can read minds over here, remember."

"Okay," said Windflower. "Thanks."

The seal paused for a moment. "In the darkest of dreams, far from the water of life, in a cavern of living that flies."

"That's it?" asked Windflower.

But there was no reply from the seal, who slipped over the side of the wharf and into the water. Windflower watched as the seal dove and then came up again fifty feet from shore, bobbing in the water. Then as the seal disappeared again, he woke up in bed with Sheila.

Eddie Tizzard didn't have a lot of dreams but didn't get much sleep either. Hughie had a bit of a cough that kept waking both of them up. The baby finally went to sleep around three thirty and Tizzard soon after that. But the alarm at six was still pretty jarring. Not long after, he could hear Hughie starting to cough again.

He got up and changed Hughie and put on some coffee and a bottle of milk to warm up. He fed Hughie first, and once he was looked after, he put him on the floor in the living room and sipped his coffee. He was thinking about Carrie and how much he missed her when she called.

"How was your night with Hughie?" she asked. "Does he still have a cough?"

"Yeah," said Tizzard. "Kept us both up most of the night. He looks better than me right now, though." He laughed as Hughie crawled over to him and pulled himself up on Eddie's knee. He grabbed his phone and snapped a pic. "Sending you a text."

"He looks great," said Carrie. "Does he have a fever?"

Eddie checked his forehead. "Seems okay."

"That's good, because you can't take him to the babysitter's if he has a fever," said Carrie.

"That is good. I have to get into work. How were things over there?"

"It was quiet," said Carrie. "No phone calls. Repa was up most of the night walking around. I tried to sleep, but it was like having a ghost in the house. At least her son is coming today."

"Your relief should be there soon," said Eddie. "I told Windflower you'd pick him up. Carrie, I want you to be extra careful. Don't take any chances."

"I thought you were going to say something like don't do anything like I would do," said Carrie.

"I'm serious. Please be careful."

"I will," said Carrie. "I love you. Give Hughie a kiss for me."

"I will, and I love you, too," said Eddie. "Call me along the way to St. John's."

Eddie hung up and made himself and Hughie some oatmeal for breakfast. Most of the baby's breakfast ended up on him and his highchair, but Eddie cleaned him up, changed him and packed his bag for the babysitter.

Windflower had finished breakfast as well and was walking Lady while he waited for Carrie to come and pick him up. He'd already called Betsy and arranged pick up of the diamonds on the way out of town. The fog had burnt off with the sun this morning, and both man and dog were happy to be outside on this glorious day. Lady was busy checking out every bush they passed. Windflower was thinking about the riddle that that pesky seal had given him last night.

What did it mean? "In the darkest of dreams, far from the water of life, in a cavern of living that flies."

He was pondering that question, deep in thought, when he heard someone shout his name. It was Carrie.

"You almost ready to go?"

"Meet me back at the house," said Windflower.

Carrie was playing with the girls when Windflower arrived. That gave him a chance to grab his overnight bag, and he made sure he tucked the CD that Herb Stoodley had given him inside. It also gave him time to say a private goodbye to Sheila before hitting the road.

She held him extra tightly and made him swear again to come back safely.

"I will," said Windflower as he gave her one more squeeze and went out to see the girls. He carried them both out to Carrie's car with him, one on each arm. He kissed them both and sent them back to Sheila, who stood in the driveway, looking like she was trying not to cry.

He got in the car with Carrie, and they drove to Betsy's house, where she handed over the jewels. "Be careful," said Betsy. "I bet the people who are looking for them are not very nice."

Windflower thanked Betsy and put the diamonds into a zippered pocket in the side of the light jacket he was wearing.

"It must be hard," said Carrie when they started off again. "To leave the girls behind like that. I miss Hughie terribly, and last night was one of the few I've missed seeing him."

"Yeah, it's tough," said Windflower. "How did Eddie make out with the baby on his own?"

"Bit of a disaster," she said with a laugh. "Be good for him, though. He'll get to see how hard it is sometimes."

Windflower smiled at that thought. Their conversation was cut short when Windflower's phone rang. He looked down at the screen. "Private number," he said. "Must be a cop."

It was Carl Langmead from the Constabulary in St. John's.

"Winston, how are ya b'y?" said Langmead.

"I'm well," said Windflower. "I'm going to put you on speaker. I'm driving to St. John's with my colleague, Constable Carrie Evanchuk."

"Well, good morning to you both," said Langmead. "I just talked to the new inspector. He said to give you a shout. We found the car."

"That's good," said Windflower. "Any sign of our two amigos?"

"No, but it's their car. Registered to Ricky Barber, and his prints are all over it. And we've got a name to go along with the other guy: Frederik Bund. Dutch citizen but known throughout Europe as the diamond guy," said Langmead. "He's a former paratrooper with extensive military training. They call them Maroon Berets. We suspect that the two of them have other transport, borrowed or stolen, but unless they've headed back your way, they haven't left the city."

"Okay, thanks," said Windflower. "We're just on the road now. Be in town around noon. I'll call you then. Unless anything else happens."

"Great," said Langmead. "See you soon."

23

"At least we have confirmation they're in St. John's," said Carrie.

Windflower nodded. "Not much to do until we get there," he said as they moved into the open spaces outside of Grand Bank. "How about a little music?"

"I'd love that," said Carrie, glancing at the CD before Windflower took it out of the case. "Smithson was giving me a classical music education before he left."

"Yeah, he was training to become a professional musician before he settled on law enforcement. I kind of miss him," said Windflower as he put the CD into the player. A piece of paper fell out as he was doing that. He paused on the music and started reading the note.

"I should have known," he said. "It's from Herb. He's my tutor."

"What does it say?" asked Carrie.

"It's an explanation of the piece," said Windflower. "He always says that understanding the music and its origins will help you appreciate the music and the composer."

"It's Mahler, right?" asked Carrie.

"Yes," said Windflower, "Mahler's Symphony No 7. Written in the early 1900s, also known as the 'Song of the Night.' Mahler was already known as a great conductor, but this piece helped cement him as a first-rate composer as well. It had its premiere in September 1908 as part of the Diamond Jubilee of Austro-Hungarian Emperor Franz Joseph."

"Interesting," said Carrie

Windflower pressed "Play," and the music quickly filled the interior of their vehicle. He loved the slow movements at the beginning of the CD, with the harmonious violins leading the way. Later guitar and mandolin were profiled in a flowing serenade. And the last section featured trumpet fanfares and some kind of harp to create a magical, almost night-time experience.

Both he and Carrie were transfixed by the music and didn't even notice that they had traveled so far until the winding turns that indicated Swift Current came into view.

"That was amazing," said Carrie.

"It's a great piece," said Windflower as they arrived in the small community of Swift Current, fifteen minutes away from their pit stop in Goobies. Goobies was little more than a collection of gas stations and restaurants that served people coming and going from the Burin Peninsula to St. John's and all along the Trans-Canada Highway. But almost everyone stopped there to get gas and a snack for the road.

At the service centre, Carrie filled the car while Windflower went inside to get them coffee and a treat. He came back with two apple flips and two packages of Purity Jam Jams, the little jam-filled cookies he had developed an addiction to. Luckily, there were only two cookies in each package, so he had to savour his treat while Carrie got back on the highway to St. John's.

They were near what the locals called the Overpass, just on the outskirts of town, when Carrie's cell phone went off. She pulled over to the side of the road and turned on her roadside lights.

It was Brinkley, the constable from Marystown who had come to relieve her. She had briefed him on what to do if the phone rang at the Sanjay house and had left him with a script to help Repa get through the call.

"She was great," said Brinkley. "Calm and confident, like she'd done this before. She said she'd found the diamonds and would exchange them for the safe return of her husband. She said they were with a family friend who would make the exchange. She gave them Windflower's number."

"Excellent," said Carrie. "Have you talked with the inspector?"

"Yes, just hung up," said Brinkley. "He said to call you right away."

"Okay, thanks," said Carrie. "Let me know if anything else happens."

Windflower and Evanchuk didn't have to wait long for something else to happen. They were driving on the harbour arterial road on their way to downtown St. John's when Windflower's phone rang. He opened it and put it on speaker.

"I don't know who you are or what game you're playing, but you better not be screwing us around," said a man at the end of the line. "Have you got the diamonds?"

"Yes," said Windflower. "Have you got Sanjay? Is he okay?"

"He's okay," said the man. Windflower detected a slight accent. Maybe it's the Bund guy, he thought. "Can you come to St. John's?"

"Yes," said Windflower. "But I will not be giving you anything until I know that Sanjay is safe. Let me speak with him."

"I will call you again," said the man. "Do not waste my time or your friend will suffer for it."

With that, the phone went dead. "Let's call your inspector," said Windflower.

"So, we got the call," said Windflower when Tizzard came on the line. "It sounded like it might be Bund, the European diamond guy. He said he'd call back later. We're almost in town now."

"Good," said Tizzard. "Anything from Langmead?"

"Nope," said Windflower. "Other than they've found the car, abandoned. They think they have another vehicle. And they've confirmed it's Frederik Bund."

"Where are you headed now?" asked Tizzard.

"Maybe go to the hotel and check in if the room is ready. Then have lunch," said Windflower.

"I envy you that," said Tizzard. "I'm eating Tim Hortons at my desk again. Meeting with the Marystown mayor and council all morning and with Murphy on the memorial service. Can't seem to get out of my office."

"That's why they pay you the big bucks," said Windflower, laughing. "Listen, something's been bothering me. Why are Ricky Barber and Bund in St. John's? Why didn't they stay around the area where they were pretty sure the diamonds were, if that was their game?"

"Probably because it was too small and they'd be too noticeable in Grand Bank," said Tizzard.

"Fair enough," said Windflower. "But how are they getting out of St. John's? Out of Newfoundland. The airports are a no-go, and the ferries are going to be watched like a hawk."

"If they can't drive or fly, they'd have to go by sea," said Carrie. "Maybe they have a ride lined up to take them to Halifax or even farther."

"Yeah, that's possible," said Windflower. "Your wife is the smart one in the family."

"I agree with that," said Tizzard, and this time he was the one laughing. "Why don't you call Langmead and see if the RNC can spring someone to go check out boat rentals or charters?"

"Will do," said Windflower. "Feel like fish and chips, Carrie?"

"Now you're just being mean," said Tizzard. "I gotta go. Love you, Carrie."

"Love you, Eddie," shouted Carrie.

"I love you, too, Eddie," said Windflower, but the acting inspector was gone.

"To the hotel?" asked Carrie.

"Sounds good," said Windflower. "I'll call Langmead along the way."

"You should also line up some backup from the RNC," said Carrie. "I'll be here, but we might need support if there's an exchange."

Windflower gave Langmead the update, including a request for support.

"No problem," said Langmead. "I'll give you two of our finest. And if there's a swap, I'll be in the picture, too. I'll get them checking on the boat charter first, although I suspect it's a private deal. Most of the charters in St. John's are for whale-watching and short trips around the bay."

"Maybe suggest Kijiji," whispered Carrie, who was listening in. Windflower nodded.

"My capable sidekick suggests trying sites like Kijiji," said Windflower.

"Sure, we'll try that," said Langmead. "If they are going by boat it would have to be a fairly big one. The Atlantic Ocean is no place for a small pleasure boat. That might make finding the one they're planning on using easier, if that's the plan."

"Okay," said Windflower. "I'll call you when I hear more from Sanjay's keepers."

24

Carrie pulled the car up in front of the hotel and waited while Windflower checked in. Then she enquired about a room for herself.

"Might as well," she said. "I'm going to need to get out of these clothes, and I don't really want to stay at the RCMP house. We should go by there and get another vehicle, too. Don't want to be driving around St. John's in this cruiser." She was in luck. They had a room for her. Windflower went to his room to drop off his bag while she checked in.

He called Sheila as soon as he got into his room. She was happy to hear from him. So were both girls, who insisted on speaking with him as well.

Sheila was pleased to hear that there had been another phone call and that Windflower had made a connection with the men who had Doctor Sanjay. She was going over with the girls to visit with Repa later in the afternoon.

"Call me later this evening," she said. "And don't forget your promise."

"I'll be careful," said Windflower. "We've also asked for backup from the Constabulary."

"I like that, too," said Sheila. "Remember to pick up Uncle Frank at the airport."

"Will do." He hung up and went back to the hotel lobby. He almost missed Carrie, who was sitting right in the middle of the lobby. She was dressed in jeans and a sweatshirt and had her hair tucked into a Toronto Blue Jays hat. She also looked about nineteen, thought Windflower.

"You ready?" she asked. "I've got a car lined up in the White Hills. Wanna go pick it up?"

"Sure," said Windflower. They drove from the hotel near the airport to the RCMP complex in the east end of St. John's in less than ten minutes, down near Quidi Vidi Lake, where the annual regatta was held every year, and then up through the area called Pleasantville to the RCMP offices. Carrie went in and got the car while Windflower had a walk around the building.

He had no desire to go inside to visit. He'd been here for the first year of the pandemic, and just thinking about that made him a bit uneasy. He was by himself in town for most of the year on a security detail while Sheila went back to Grand Bank with the girls. He enjoyed the work, but a few visits home every month or so was unbearable. Carrie was out not long after with the keys to the perfect undercover car, a 2019 Dodge Challenger. At one time people called this type of car a muscle car. Windflower wasn't sure exactly what they called them these days, but when Carrie started it up and squealed out of the parking lot, he pronounced it pretty cool. She didn't disagree.

"The important thing is that we don't look like a cop car," said Carrie. But Windflower could tell that she was pretty pleased to have a cool car to drive around for a few days. Why not, he thought?

"Fish and chips?"

"I've been thinking about it ever since you mentioned it earlier," said Carrie. "Leo's?"

"How do you know about Leo's?"

"Eddie, who got it from Ron Quigley," said Carrie. "Said that Ron grew up in the neighbourhood."

"Ron told me that, too," said Windflower as they came across town from the RCMP offices in the east end. They drove up Military Road, past the great Basilica and up the narrow street that led to Leo's restaurant.

Ron Quigley had introduced the place to Windflower a few years back, and once he tried their fabulous fish and chips, he was a repeat customer whenever he came to St. John's. Leo's was a small family-owned diner with a couple of booths and a few tables. Carrie and Windflower slid into one of their booths. They both ordered fish and chips St. John's style, with dressing and gravy.

While they were waiting for their order, Windflower got them soft drinks from the self-serve cooler. Carrie wanted a Pineapple Crush, like an Orange Crush but with pineapple flavouring, while he took a Crush Birch Beer for himself. He loved the strange taste of this concoction, some weird combination of root beer and cream soda mixed together. If Windflower was to tell a Newfoundlander what it tasted like, he would probably say it was "sum good, b'y."

Their lunch was sum good, too. The fish tasted fresh and delicious, and the fries were perfect. The crumbly dressing soaked up the gravy and went great with the deep-fried fish and French fries.

As they basked in the glow of very full bellies, they sipped on their drinks and sat for a moment to relax.

"Ron told me he used to live just up the road from here on Mayor Avenue," said Windflower. "He said this area was known for pubs and fish and chip shops. His family loved Leo's and would have it almost every Friday. He told me the fish was so fresh back then that they would see the local fishermen drop it off in the morning at the back door."

"It's still pretty fresh," said Carrie. "What's next?"

"Let me call Langmead," said Windflower. "If he's in, maybe we can drop in to see him. The RNC is just around the corner."

Langmead was in, so they left their car and walked over to the RNC building on Fort Townshend, which Windflower explained to Carrie was originally the site of the headquarters of the British garrison in the territory of Newfoundland, back in the late 1700s. They passed by the new Provincial Museum called The Rooms.

"Have you ever been inside?" asked Carrie.

"A couple of times with Sheila and the girls," said Windflower. "It's an amazing place with thousands of works of art and so much information on the history of this province and this part of the world. And they have a café overlooking the harbour, which has the best seafood chowder ever."

"Might have known you'd know where the best food is," said Carrie as they passed by the Tim Hortons that was most conveniently located near the entrance to the Royal Newfoundland Constabulary headquarters.

Carl Langmead met them at the door and led them upstairs to his office. "You guys are looking good, a little casual today."

"Undercover," said Windflower. "And much more comfortable. So, you have anything new for us?"

"Not really," said Langmead. "Although I've got our marine unit scouring the local harbours to see if they can find out anything about a rented boat."

"You have a marine unit?" asked Carrie.

"Yeah, it's been around for a while," said Langmead. "Been going since the 1800s. During the First World War they helped monitor the waters for spy activity in the Labrador Sea. Today, they work with the Coast Guard and Search and Rescue to help ships and mariners who get in trouble close to shore. They even have to rescue a few tourists every year when they climb down on the rocks and get stuck there."

"So, they have a boat?" asked Windflower.

"I think a thirty-footer," said Langmead. "But don't quote me. I'm strictly a dry land person."

"Anything else?" asked Windflower.

"Not much," said Langmead. "I've got everybody asking around Barber's old hangouts to see if anything comes up, but nothing yet."

"Okay, well it's good to see you. We'll call when we get the next message," said Windflower.

He and Carrie left the RNC building and walked back to their car. "Let's go for a drive," said Windflower. Carrie drove back near the Basilica and took the first street that took them straight downtown. A couple of turns later they were driving along the waterfront. There was a supply boat and a couple of fishing boats, but apart from the whale-watching ships, the harbour felt eerily quiet.

"I remember it being busier than this when I was here before. As someone from a land-locked province like Saskatchewan, I loved seeing them all," said Carrie.

"Yeah, the traffic comes and goes," said Windflower. "Part of what's missing is the big cruise boats. They would take up half this side of the harbour. But it's still pretty nice to be by the ocean. Feels peaceful."

"Where next?" asked Carrie as they went past the container port.

"On a fine day, Cabot Tower please, driver," said Windflower. "Just go back up on Duckworth Street and follow it to the end."

25

Carrie followed the directions, and soon they were at the base of a very steep hill. They climbed it slowly, passing the Geocentre and the old Battery Hotel, which was now a dormitory for the university. They passed many walkers, joggers and runners who were on their way up or down the hill. The ones going up were more cheerful. The ones coming down looked relieved and exhausted.

"I can't imagine running this hill," said Carrie.

"I have done it before," said Windflower. "It takes training, and it's as hard as it looks." They passed the Visitors Centre and parked in the nearly full parking lot. They got out of their car and walked to the ocean side to take in the view.

"This is incredible," said Carrie as they gazed out onto the ocean that seemed to go on forever.

"It's pretty nice," said Windflower. "I'm glad we had a nice day. It kind of makes you want to go out to sea, doesn't it?"

Carrie nodded, and they walked around the area, taking in all the views, including overlooking Pleasantville and the RCMP headquarters and a stunning view of the harbour from this height. They walked over to Cabot Tower, the most prominent landmark in St. John's, and read about the history of this location.

Cabot Tower had been built in the late 1800s to commemorate Queen Victoria's Diamond Jubilee and the four hundredth anniversary of John Cabot's voyage to discover the New World. At first it was used for flag signalling for both the military and local merchants who got early notice that their supplies were coming. But its main claim to fame was when Guglielmo Marconi received the first transatlantic wireless signal there in 1901. It was the beginning of the telegraph and a new age in communication technology.

"That's amazing," said Carrie. "Without Marconi we might never have had cell phones."

"I'm not sure that's real progress," said Windflower.

Carrie laughed, and the pair went back to their car and began the sharp descent. They were near the bottom when Windflower's cell phone rang. They both jumped, thinking it was the men who had Sanjay. But it was Carl Langmead.

"What's up, Carl?" asked Windflower.

"We've found one of the men we were looking for," said Langmead.

"Which one?" asked Windflower. "Did they tell you anything?"

"Unfortunately, Ricky Barber isn't able to speak. He's dead," said Langmead. "Someone came across the body this morning in a wooded area down in Logy Bay, near the Marine Lab."

"Any witnesses or signs of our other friend?" asked Windflower.

"Nope," said Langmead. "Somebody out walking their dog came upon the body just off the road. I haven't been down there, but our guys say it looks like he may have been dead and deposited there. Looks like a lot of evidence of dragging around the bushes."

"How did he die?" asked Windflower.

"Shot," said Langmead. "Likely at close range, according to the people on the scene. But we'll have to wait for forensics to be sure."

"Wow," said Windflower. "Thanks for letting me know."

"What do you think this means?" asked Carrie after Windflower had hung up.

"Hard to say," said Windflower. "It can't be good news. But let's hope it's not bad news for Sanjay."

The pair was silent as Carrie drove back to the hotel. "Can you call Eddie and give him an update? Then, take a break," said Windflower. "We have to pick up Uncle Frank in a couple of hours, and we have no idea what's coming our way later today."

Carrie stayed in the car to make her call while Windflower went to his room. He called Sheila. He needed to get some sense of normalcy back. He got that and more. Stella answered the phone. That was her latest thing. She was always practicing what she called her "telephone voice."

"Good evening. This is the Windflower and Hillier residence. How may I help you?" said Stella.

"Wow, you sound like a professional," said Windflower. He could hear another voice in the background.

"I wanna do it," said Amelia Louise. "It's my turn."

Windflower heard a thud, and then a scream, and then Sheila's voice loud and clear. "Stop it. Go to your rooms."

He could hear protests, but soon after nothing. Sheila came on the line. "Sorry about that. The usual competition. Can't seem to break them of this one. But I will eventually. How are you?"

"I'm fine," said Windflower and told her about his day.

"That all sounds very nice," said Sheila. "Except for the part about the dead man. Will it affect getting Doctor Sanjay back?"

"I hope not," said Windflower. "Anyway, I just wanted to check in. Good to hear that everything is the same back home."

"'A baby is an inestimable blessing and bother,'" said Sheila. "We have two blessings."

"And sometimes two bothers," said Windflower. "Nice Mark Twain quote, by the way. Here's another one that Eddie told me, although I think he claimed his dad said it first. 'My mother had a great deal of trouble with me, but I think she enjoyed it.'"

"That sums it up pretty good," said Sheila. "Say hello to Uncle Frank for me. And be careful, Winston."

"I will. Love you, Sheila," said Windflower.

"I love you, Winston," said Sheila, and she was gone. Windflower lay on his bed and turned on the TV. Instead of watching the baseball game, he almost immediately fell asleep. Only to find not long after that, he was in a dream.

26

This time he woke back in his own bed in their house in Grand Bank. He could hear the children playing downstairs and Sheila trying to quiet them. He called out to Sheila, but there was no answer. He tried calling louder, but still nothing. He was getting exasperated when he saw Molly sitting on the bed.

"They can't hear you," said the cat. "It's a dream, remember."

"Oh, yeah," said Windflower. "What are you doing here?"

"Is that any way to treat an old friend?" asked Molly. "I thought you were trying to get along better these days."

"I am," said Windflower. "Sorry, I'm glad you're here." He thought for a moment about what to say next.

"That's okay, take your time," said Molly. "As you know, I like a leisurely pace. When you have nine lives, you realize that there's no rush to get anywhere."

"Do you really have nine lives, cats, I mean?" asked Windflower.

"I'll tell you a secret," said Molly. "We all do. Even you. But sometimes, like Harvey Brenton, you get a time out for bad behaviour. But listen, why don't you ask me about what's on your mind? You know I can hear your thoughts, right?"

"I do," said Windflower. "I really want to know where my friend, Sanjay, is."

"Well, the seal did tell you."

"What do you mean?" asked Windflower.

"The riddle," said Molly. "I know he's a trickster, and it's hard to believe what he says all the time, but he did tell you. How did it go again?"

Windflower thought for a second and remembered. "In the darkest of dreams, far from the water of life, in a cavern of living that flies."

"Okay, then, let's break that down," said Molly. "Clearly the darkest of dreams means a very quiet and secluded place, away from traffic and people likely. The water of life must be the ocean. And what do you think the cavern of living that flies is about?

Windflower looked stumped. "Give me a clue."

Molly gave a great sigh. "Where are you picking up your uncle?"

"The airport terminal," said Windflower. "Sanjay is at the airport?"

Another sigh from the cat. "No. Not at the airport. But maybe near the airport."

"Well, that narrows it down," said Windflower. "Thanks."

"You know how to thank me," said the cat. "Salmon. Anytime you like." She then jumped down off the bed and started to saunter off. Windflower tried to get up, and when he did he was back at his hotel in St John's. His cell phone was ringing.

"Ready to go to the airport?" asked Carrie.

"I'll be right down," said Windflower, waking up a little groggily and wondering if what he just heard in the dream world was really true out here. Maybe he'd talk to Uncle Frank about it.

Carrie dropped him at the arrivals door and drove around the lot while he went inside. Uncle Frank's flight had arrived, and when Windflower got to the arrivals area, the passengers were coming down the escalator. One of the last was his uncle, who when he saw Windflower gave him a smile and a wave.

The men embraced at the bottom of the escalator.

"It's so nice to see you, Uncle," said Windflower. "We've all missed you."

"Nice to see you, too, Winston," said Uncle Frank. "Are you by yourself? Where's Sheila and the girls?"

"They're still in Grand Bank. But anxious to see you," said Windflower. "I came in early. I had some business. Carrie Evanchuk is with me."

"Oh yes, Eddie's wife," said Uncle Frank. "Nice girl."

The men stood by the luggage carousel and chatted while they waited for Uncle Frank's suitcase.

Windflower told his uncle about his latest dream. "I know they're important messages, but are they real? Like for out here?"

"Our people have always believed that the dream world is as real as this one," said his uncle. "There are too many things that cannot be explained just by what we see or hear. Dreams are real, and they give us information that we have to interpret, discern, the same way we take other information, like the weather forecast. What does a fifty percent chance of precipitation mean anyway? To me it says I should probably take an umbrella, just in case."

"So, I should take the information I get from a dream and test it?" asked Windflower. "Against what?"

"Use your intuition," said Uncle Frank. "It is a gift from Creator that we've let slip in this crazy Google world where all the answers seem to be at your fingertips. But that is not all there is. What does your gut say?"

"I think Sanjay is out here somewhere, near the airport," said Windflower. "It feels right."

"Then act," said his uncle. "To believe something and not act upon that belief is always a mistake. Now, there's my bag," he said, pointing to a battered old brown suitcase.

Windflower grabbed the bag off the carousel, and he and Uncle Frank walked outside to meet the waiting Carrie.

"Now this is what I call traveling in style," said Uncle Frank, going to Carrie to give her a hug.

"You give the best hugs," said Carrie. "Nice to see you."

"When you get old like me, it's all I have to offer any more," said Frank. "I used to have a car like this. A '73 Barracuda. I could get myself in a lot of trouble just riding around by myself," he said with a chuckle. "Don't suppose I could drive?"

"You get in the front seat, Uncle," said Windflower as Carrie looked like she just might hand over the keys. "I'll get in back. Let's go to the hotel and get you checked in before you get us all in trouble."

Uncle Frank was at hotel reception when Windflower's cell phone rang. Unknown number.

He stepped outside and sat on the bench in front of the hotel. "Hello."

"Are you in St. John's? Have you got the diamonds?" asked the man on the other end of the line.

"Is Sanjay okay? Can I talk to him?" asked Windflower in return.

"I ask the questions," said the man.

"Yes, I'm in St. John's. But I'm not handing anything over until I know he's safe," said Windflower.

"He's fine," said the man. "I want you to meet me and drop off the diamonds. Then I will tell you where he is."

"I need to see him first," said Windflower.

"How do I know you have the diamonds?" asked the man. "You could just be a cop."

"I'm not a cop," said Windflower, telling the truth. "How about we arrange for me to give you a sample in return for letting me see Sanjay? It's not like I can really trust you either."

He could hear the other man thinking. "Okay. Do you know Bowring Park?"

"Yes," said Windflower.

"Go there and leave something for me by the Peter Pan statue. And no games. I'll be watching. If I see or hear anything strange, the old guy gets it. No cops or he's dead."

"Got it," said Windflower. The line went dead.

27

Windflower went back inside.

"Are you hungry?" he asked Uncle Frank, who was sitting with Carrie in the lobby.

"Yes, b'y, I could eat," said his uncle.

He got a room service menu from the front desk, and Uncle Frank chose the pan-fried cod with mashed potatoes. "I try to eat fish at least once a day when I'm in Newfoundland."

"Great," said Windflower. "You go to your room, and I'll put this order in for you. Carrie and I have to go out for a little while, but we'll be back. Okay?"

"Perfect," said his uncle. "See you soon."

Uncle Frank went up the elevator to his room, and Windflower and Carrie went outside. He told her about the phone call.

"I'll call Langmead along the way," he said.

"So, I'm going to Bowring Park," said Windflower when he reached Langmead.

"Okay, I'll have guys at either exit. Undercover and well hidden. I'll come over, too. I'll be in the hospital parking lot. Why don't you meet me there?"

Ten minutes later, Windflower spotted Langmead's car at the hospital across the street from the park. He got out of their car and sat in the front seat with Langmead. The RNC officer was wearing a t-shirt and had a ball cap on.

"Casual day at work?" asked Windflower.

Langmead smiled. "We've got eyes on either end. But there's lots of people around. It might be hard to spot your guy. We'll hang around for a few hours and see what shows up."

"I'm going to leave him two diamonds in this hotel key envelope. He said to leave it by the Peter Pan," said Windflower.

"Probably the most popular spot in the park," said Langmead. "But I'll be on foot and find a spot to observe it."

"Okay," said Windflower. "I'm going to get Evanchuk, and we'll play tourist. Then I'll lay it under a stone near the statue. After that, we're just going to go back to the hotel and wait for you. Unless you want us to hang around?"

"No, I think it'd be better if you left," said Langmead. "Might spook our guy. And we can handle this end of it."

Windflower got out of the car and motioned Carrie to come with him. "We can leave the car here. Have you ever been to Bowring Park?"

"No, but I'm looking forward to it," said Carrie as they walked across the street and joined the many couples and families who were planning on enjoying the park today.

"There was a farm here one time," said Windflower. "Then it was bought by the Bowring family on the hundredth anniversary of being in business in Newfoundland. They donated it to the city in 1911."

"You know a lot about it," said Carrie.

"Only what Wilf Pittman told me about it," said Windflower. "He was my neighbour when we lived in St. John's. The girls love this place."

"I can see why," said Carrie. "It's magical."

"Their favourite part is the duck pond, right down there," said Windflower as they came near that area. "And of course, Peter Pan."

He and Carrie walked towards the statue but couldn't get too close because there were some kids playing and climbing on and near it.

They sat on a nearby park bench. "You notice anyone following us?" asked Windflower.

"No, but why would there be?" asked Carrie. "Nobody knows you're the one with the diamonds."

"True," said Windflower. "Can't be too careful, though."

When the children playing near Peter Pan had finally been pulled away by their parents, Windflower went up to the statue and pretended to read the plaque. He pointed it out to Carrie, who read it out loud while he laid the envelope under a stone and placed it up against the statue.

"In memory of a dear little girl who loved the park, Betty Munn," read Carrie.

Windflower tried to casually look around and saw a couple approaching. "Do you know that little girl was the granddaughter of Sir Edgar Rennie Bowring?" he asked Carrie.

"No, I did not," said Carrie as they started to move away, saying hello to the couple who was coming in for a closer look.

"She drowned in 1918, and Bowring commissioned a duplicate of the Peter Pan statue that stands in Kensington Gardens, London, in memory of his granddaughter."

"You are a fount of Bowring Park knowledge," said Carrie as they slowly left the park, trying as hard as they could not to look behind them.

"Are we sticking around?" she asked.

"Not required," said Windflower. "We have to rely on the Royal Newfoundland Constabulary."

They went back to the hotel, and Windflower checked in on Uncle Frank. He knocked on his door but got no answer. He was going to knock again when he heard the distinct sound of snoring from inside the room. Windflower smiled and went back to the lobby, where Carrie was on the phone. "Eddie," she whispered as she passed him the phone.

"Now we're just waiting," said Windflower. "Did Carrie tell you that Ricky Barber is dead?"

"She did," said Tizzard. "Have you confirmed that Sanjay is alive?"

"That's the big question," said Windflower. "Although if the objective is to get the diamonds back, that's his only card, isn't it?"

"I hope so," said Tizzard. "Keep me posted."

"Supper?" Windflower asked Carrie.

She nodded, and they walked into the restaurant. Windflower ordered the fried fish but was disappointed it didn't come with scrunchions, the little pieces of fried salt pork that often came with the fried fish, or they certainly did when Windflower made fish. But it was passable. They waited for news from Langmead or the guy who had Sanjay.

Langmead was first, and Windflower left the restaurant to take the call outside.

"He slipped away," said Langmead. "We spotted him too late. He was jogging and was going for the package but must have spotted us and took off across the park. He must have gotten out through the bushes somewhere. In any case, he's gone. But at least we still have the package."

"Shoot," said Windflower. "I guess we'll have to see if he comes back."

"It feels awful to screw up like that," said Langmead. "And we don't really have any leads either."

Windflower thought for a second, hesitated, and then decided to jump in. "Do you ever follow your instincts?"

"Yeah, sure," said Langmead. "Many times all we have is a hunch. We try it, and if it works, great. If not, we do something else."

"I have a hunch that Sanjay is somewhere around the airport," said Windflower. "But in a wooded area."

"Why do you think that?" asked Langmead.

"I dunno," said Windflower. "My instincts."

This time Langmead did the thinking and the hesitating. "Why not? There's a lot of new housing out in the Airport Heights area. It comes right up against the woods. Worth a look, I guess. Maybe have my guys take a drive around. See if they see anything unusual. Undercover. On the q.t."

"Maybe we're looking for short-term rental or an Airbnb?" said Windflower.

"Now, that's brilliant," said Langmead. "Okay, we're on it."

28

Windflower went back into the restaurant and ordered dessert. But he didn't get to eat half of his blueberry pie before his cell phone rang again. Unknown number. He picked it up right away and said hello.

"Winston, is that you?" asked Sanjay.

"Doc, are you okay?" asked Windflower.

"He's fine," said the man who took the phone from Sanjay. "But enough screwing around. Here's what we're going to do."

Windflower listened as the man outlined his plan. Windflower was to leave the diamonds at a location near the old Memorial Stadium. He knew that place well. It was near Quidi Vidi Lake and had been on his way to work when he was in St. John's. It was no longer an arena. Years ago, it had been converted into a supermarket.

"But what about Sanjay?" asked Windflower.

"I'll tell you his location once the diamonds have been recovered," said the man. "And no more cops. The locals are too stupid to catch me anyway, but I don't want to see them around anywhere. I would take that as a sign of bad faith. Your friend will pay the price."

"I can do it, but we do it together or not at all," said Windflower. "I need to see Sanjay."

"He'll be there when you arrive," said the man. "No cops or we're done."

"When is this going to happen?" asked Windflower, but the man was gone.

He gave Carrie the information and asked her to call Tizzard. He would phone Langmead.

"That was fast," said Langmead.

"We get another chance," said Windflower. "We'll have to be more discreet moving forward."

"Got it," said Langmead. "I'm just looking at the map of that area of town. There are limited openings to get in and out. It will be easy to cordon off all those possibilities once we know exactly where it is. I'm going to call in some more guys and have them on standby."

"This guy sounds like a pro," said Windflower. "I know you know, but we can't take any chances until we know Sanjay is safe."

"Understood," said Langmead. "We'll have a soft perimeter and get him on the way out. Once we have Doctor Sanjay, we can grab Bund. You don't seem as worried about the diamonds."

"I'm not," said Windflower. "I'm no longer a member of the RCMP. I'm a private citizen."

"Be careful," said Langmead. "He's likely killed before, and he will do it again."

"Don't worry," said Windflower. "I lost my hero complex a long time ago. I just want my friend back. And I have what Bund wants."

Windflower and Carrie went to their respective rooms to await the next development. He tracked by Uncle Frank's room again, but there was only more snoring coming from inside. Good, thought Windflower, he'll get some rest and be none the worse for whatever might happen this evening.

He phoned Sheila and got to say goodnight to the girls. Sheila didn't bother asking him to be careful again. That was implicit in her voice as she talked about her day with the girls and their plans to go to the beach at Golden Sands tomorrow.

"I hope the weather is nice," said Windflower. "I love that place. Nice soft sand, and the water is so shallow, you don't have to worry too much about the girls."

"Yes, it should be nice," said Sheila. "Anyway, I'll let you go. Call me later tonight. Whenever it's over. I just need to hear your voice."

"I will," said Windflower. After hanging up with Sheila, he tried to watch TV, but he was too anxious.

Carrie was having the same experience. He met up with her in the lobby. "Let's go for a spin in your new toy," he said.

Even though they were both nervous, that helped to shake up their mood as Carrie drove them all over town. They went down towards the

RNC building and got stuck in the traffic from a concert that was happening in Bannerman Park.

"Do you know anything about this park?" asked Carrie while they were waiting.

"Not too much," said Windflower. "I only know they have a great skating rink here in the winter called The Loop. That's where we discovered Stella is actually a pretty good skater."

"Wasn't she in figure skating last year?"

"Yes, she did the CanSkate program last year, but this year she'll be in the junior program with the Ice Crystals," said Windflower. "She's pretty excited. But let me look up Bannerman Park. Now you've got me curious."

Windflower scrolled on his phone until he found what he wanted.

"Wow, there's lot of history here," he said. "The Park is named after Sir Alexander Bannerman, who was the governor of the Colony of Newfoundland. In 1864 he gave permission to establish the park and ordered the land to be provided. Through the years it has been a tent city when St. John's had its great fire and the scene of a major riot when the government was situated in the Colonial Building, just back there."

"Interesting," said Carrie as the traffic started to move. They drove along until they came to the Tim Hortons in front of the RNC. Windflower jumped out and got them both a coffee. They continued the drive all along this road, which was changed from Military Road to Harvey Road and then Lemarchant Road and then Cornwall Avenue before finally becoming Topsail Road.

"Why do they do that?" asked Carrie. "Keep changing the name of the road?"

"Who knows?" asked Windflower. "Maybe they just kept building more pieces on. At one time all there was of St. John's was down near the water and on the hills coming down to the harbour. Everything up here is relatively new."

They went all the way out Topsail Road and turned down near Bowring Park, which was now almost completely in darkness. Then they took the Harbour Arterial Road back downtown. It was a beautiful clear night, and they could see the Waterford Valley and the small river that ran beside it. As they came closer to downtown St. John's, the lights of the city came into view, and there was a lot more activity with people out for dinner or drinks at the numerous bars in the famous George Street area. They were making the turn for home from the harbourfront when Windflower's phone rang.

29

"Listen carefully and follow these directions exactly," said the man that Windflower was pretty sure was Frederik Bund. "I know you used to be a cop but aren't right now. Correct?"

"That is correct," said Windflower. He motioned to Carrie and mouthed "Langmead." She called the RNC officer, got him on the line and nodded to Windflower. He put his phone on speaker.

"And you probably know who I am, too," said Bund. "Although that matters little. You and I are here to do business. One transaction and we're done. Got it?"

Windflower didn't feel the need to respond. Bund continued talking.

"Number one, no cops. I see cops and I'm gone, and so is your friend. Number two, I want you to drive me somewhere once we make the connection. Can you do that?"

"Yes, I guess so," said Windflower.

"Three, I will meet you at the location and leave the doctor in the car. He's in the trunk. You'll have to trust me," said Bund with a slight laugh.

"I don't think so…" Windflower started, but Bund cut him off.

"This is the way it will work, yes or no?" asked Bund.

Windflower thought for a second. "Okay."

"Good," said Bund. "The Avalon Mall parking lot. Half an hour. I'll be in a dark blue Malibu."

Windflower kept staring at the phone, but that was the end of the call.

"You get all that?" he asked Langmead.

"Yeah, gives us time enough time to recalibrate," said Langmead. "Although that location is harder to secure without being seen. But maybe that's why he chose it. Where are you now?"

"We're down near Quidi Vidi Lake," said Windflower.

"Swing by here. I have something to give you," said Langmead. "I don't like the part of the plan where you go with him. But a GPS tracker will help. Are you okay with doing this?"

"I'm okay," said Windflower. "We'll come by and pick that up. Can Evanchuk go with you?"

Carrie was shaking her head beside him.

"Sure, she can ride with me," said Langmead. "Not as nice wheels as hers, though."

"See you soon," said Windflower.

"I want to go with you," said Carrie. "That's why I came here."

"Too dangerous," said Windflower. "For all of us. You can be my eyes and ears. I'm counting on you."

"I don't like you going with him either," said Carrie. "But I get it. It wouldn't make Bund happy to see me show up."

"Okay, let's get the tracker," said Windflower.

They drove quickly to the RNC building, where Langmead was waiting, still dressed in his casual clothes. He had another uniformed police officer with him. "This is Hickey," he said. "He'll hook you up."

Hickey smiled at Carrie and Windflower and then climbed under their car with a small square GPS tracking unit. He screwed it into a small bracket that he somehow attached to the bottom of the car. When he got up, he grabbed the tracking monitor out of a nearby box and turned it on. It blinked green and then flashed their location. First, in longitude and latitude and then *Harvey Road and Parade Street St. John's, Newfoundland and Labrador, Canada.*

"You're all set," said Hickey as he passed the monitor to Langmead.

"Thanks," said Windflower.

"Okay, we're just getting up in position," said Langmead. "We have unmarked cars around a little way along all four possible exit routes, and more regular cars in back-up out of sight. Plus, we can track you now. And me and Carrie will be in the parking lot with you."

"Good," said Windflower, who was starting to get nervous. He couldn't even look at Carrie, who appeared like she was going to cry. "Sounds like we have a plan. Let's get Sanjay back."

Carrie handed him the keys and watched silently as he drove away. She got into Langmead's car and followed a discreet distance behind.

Windflower drove across town and up Freshwater Road until it turned into Kenmount Road. He could see the large Avalon Mall from a distance, and when he got closer, he turned into the first entrance. The mall was closed, and that meant there was only a scattering of cars in the parking lot. He scanned it quickly, but there was no blue Malibu. He parked and stood outside, waiting. He saw Langmead's car come into the same mall entrance and keep on driving towards the main doors and then stopping in the lane closest to the door as if he were picking someone up.

As Langmead moved away from the doors, Windflower saw the car he was looking for enter the parking lot from the other side and drive right towards him. The Malibu parked beside him, and a man got out.

"Windflower," said the man. "Got my diamonds?"

"I do," said Windflower, patting his jacket. "But first, Sanjay."

Bund smiled and went to the trunk of his car. He opened it. Vijay Sanjay was lying inside with his hands and feet bound with rope. He had tape over his mouth but was clearly trying to speak to Windflower.

"Sanjay," said Windflower.

Bund shut the trunk quickly. "The diamonds," he said, holding out his hand.

Windflower reached into his pocket and handed over the plastic bag. Bund took a quick look and smiled again. "The keys."

Windflower passed over the keys and went to get into the passenger side.

"No," said Bund, opening the Challenger's trunk. "In here." The man opened his jacket to show Windflower the gun tucked into his waistband. "Let's go."

Windflower hesitated for just a second and then climbed into the trunk. He felt it slam closed and then almost total blackness. The car started and moved quickly after that. Windflower could tell they were going pretty fast and guessed they were on a highway, maybe heading out of town. Then he felt the car veer sharply, and he was thrown from side to side. He tried to hang on to the sides of the trunk, but that was futile. The car slowed dramatically, and the road they were on became super bumpy. Then it stopped, and he waited for what would happen next.

Bund must have turned off the car, because for a moment it became super quiet. Then Windflower heard another car start up and then move away until he couldn't hear anything at all. He lay there in the dark for what seemed like forever until he heard voices. Finally, the trunk was popped open. From inside the car. He blinked at the light.

"Sarge, are you okay?" he heard. It was Carrie, and beside her was Langmead.

30

"I'm okay," said Windflower. "A few bumps and bruises, but I'm fine. But where's Bund? Is Sanjay all right?"

"They said Sanjay was fine but are taking him to the Health Sciences to check him out. He was asking about you," said Langmead. "Bund is gone, and unfortunately our GPS is here."

"How did he get away?" asked Windflower, stretching and starting to feel the impact of the recent bumps he had endured in the trunk of the car.

"He had another vehicle," said Langmead. "We had him under watch on the highway, and then he took this side road that has no exit. But it looks like he walked over to the other side, where he had either a car or somebody waiting for him."

"Sounds like he had help," said Windflower, coming out of his grogginess. "How would he even know this side road was here?"

"Agreed," said Langmead. "I've already asked our people to go back over Barber's contacts and the ones they have inside the bikers. And our canvass has started in Airport Heights. We did get one break, though."

"It'll be good to have some good news," said Windflower. "Especially since I have to tell Tizzard and eventually Majesky that the diamonds are missing."

"We think we've found the boat Bund plans to leave on. A guy has leased his boat for two months out in Petty Harbour. Said the guy paid cash and left a credit card as a deposit. The name on the card was Richard Barber."

"That's good," said Windflower. "Your guys are on that?"

"Yes, both on land and the Marine Unit," said Langmead.

"Carrie, can you call HQ and tell them to alert the RCMP coastal boat?" said Windflower. "Make the connection with the RNC."

"I don't think they have a cruiser anymore," said Carrie. "Cost-cutting. Now all they have are a couple of inflatable boats. But I'll make the call. I have to see if they have an extra set of keys for the car. Bund took them with him."

"How did you get into the trunk?" asked Windflower.

Langmead pointed to Evanchuk.

"It's an old farmer's trick from Saskatchewan," said Carrie. "All you need is a flat-head screwdriver, which our friend from the RNC had in his car. If you can get in the car, you unbolt the back seats and take one out. There's a metal bar inside and then a box you have to turn clockwise. Then you're done."

"I'm impressed," said Windflower. "I guess we need a ride downtown."

"I'll have a car and driver at your service," said Langmead. He went to his car, and within a few minutes an RNC cruiser was there to pick them up.

"I'm going to stay and make sure we don't miss anything," said Langmead. "Davis will help take you wherever you want to go. Probably to bed after all this excitement."

"I could certainly use a hot bath," said Windflower. "But we should go see Sanjay at the hospital and then call the family."

"We also have to call Eddie," said Evanchuk.

"I'm not looking forward to that," said Windflower. He called Tizzard's number.

"So, what's going on?" asked Tizzard.

"Do you want the good news or the bad news?" asked Windflower.

"Uh-oh," said Tizzard. "You lost the diamonds. Tell me you didn't lose the diamonds. Majesky will have our... You know what he'll do."

"The good news, since you asked, is that Sanjay is okay. We're heading over to the Health Sciences to check in with him," said Windflower. "And I didn't get shot. Although I did have a very uncomfortable trip in the trunk of a car."

"I'm glad that Sanjay is okay and that you didn't get killed. Sheila might have killed me if you did. Sorry to be crass, but what about the diamonds?" asked Tizzard.

"They're missing, for now," said Windflower. "I guess they're not really missing. Frederik Bund has them, to be exact."

"Does that mean you have a plan to get them back?" asked Tizzard. "Give me a lifeline here."

"Langmead and the RNC are on it," said Windflower. "They had everything covered, but it looks like Bund has another assistant. They have a handle on a boat that was leased to Ricky Barber, and they are actively looking for whichever local is helping Bund. So, I think they have a good chance of getting both Bund and the diamonds."

"Thank you, Pollyanna," said Tizzard. "It's not much, but I'll give it to Majesky. He may want to talk to you."

"That's fine," said Windflower. "I'm happy to talk to the super. I don't work for him anymore, remember?"

"I may not be either after this," said Tizzard. "Can I speak to Carrie?"

Windflower handed over the phone, and Carrie said goodnight to Tizzard just as they were pulling into the Health Sciences complex, the sprawling medical centre just across from the university.

Davis dropped them at the main entrance and told them he'd be waiting near Emergency when they were ready to leave. Sanjay was still in observation, so they walked to that area where an RNC constable was sitting on a chair in the waiting area. He pointed them towards the duty nurse. She looked at them strangely at first and told them no visitors were allowed. Carrie's badge helped change her mind.

31

Sanjay was lying in bed. He had an intravenous tube and seemed to have a few bruises and cuts around his head and face that had been treated. But he looked comfortable, and at first Windflower thought he was sleeping. He motioned to Carrie that they should leave when Sanjay spoke up.

"Winston, you're here," he said.

"I am indeed," said Windflower. "How are you, my friend?"

"Oh, and the lovely Carrie is with you," said Sanjay. "I am okay. Continuing to grow old, which certainly beats the alternative."

"I won't question you too much about your ordeal," said Windflower. "The Constabulary may have more on that later. But I have to ask about anybody else who might be around with Bund."

"At first there was only that Barber fellow," said Sanjay. "A brute, if there ever was. Then he wasn't around anymore. I could hear him and Bund arguing sometimes."

"What were they fighting about?" asked Windflower.

"It wasn't clear," said Sanjay. "They were always at it, as my mother used to say. I was just happy that he went away. I am assuming it wasn't a voluntary departure."

"No," said Windflower. "Did you see or hear anything else?"

"I was blindfolded, so I didn't see anybody or even where I was. But I thought I heard an airplane fly over."

Windflower took a quick glance at Carrie to see if she was paying attention. She nodded and marked something down in her notepad.

"And I'm not sure, but I think one of the other men was called Mitch," said Sanjay. "Sorry I can't be of more use."

"That's great," said Windflower. "Very helpful. Have you talked to

Repa yet?"

"No, I was waiting for the nurse to come back."

"Let's do it now," said Windflower. He called Repa's number.

"Hello," said a man's voice. Windflower thought he recognized him as one of her sons.

"Is that Anil or Palish? It's Winston Windflower."

"It's Anil. Do you have word on my dad?"

"I'm with your dad right now at the hospital. He's safe. Is your mom there?"

Seconds later, Repa was on the line, and Windflower passed the phone to Sanjay.

"Yes, yes, I am. No, no, I have not been badly injured. They just want to examine me. But I am okay. Don't worry. What is Anil doing there?"

Sanjay listened to his wife for a few more minutes and then handed the phone back to Windflower.

"Oh, Sergeant, I am so happy," said Repa. "Thank you for saving my Vijay."

"I didn't do very much, but I'm happy he is safe and sound," said Windflower. "Hopefully, he'll be home with you soon."

After Windflower had hung up, Sanjay said, "Thank you, Winston. And you too, Carrie. I know that you have risked your own safety to help me. I will never forget your assistance. As my beloved Tagore would say, 'You can't cross the sea merely by standing and staring at the water.'"

"That is true, but we were just doing our jobs," said Windflower.

"I am very happy that both of you came to save me," said Sanjay. "Can you do me one more favour? Will you ask them when I can go home? Repa and my son will be anxious to see me, as I them."

"Sure," said Windflower. "We have to make some calls, and we'll be back soon."

"Can you see if you can get an update for Sanjay?" Windflower asked Carrie. While she went to do that, he called Langmead.

"Sanjay says that he thought he heard an airplane," said Windflower. "And he thinks the guy helping Bund may be called Mitch or something like that."

"Both useful tips," said Langmead. "We've got the boat staked out, and the marine unit is on standby. I'll pass along the name to the team looking for Bund's local connections. We'll see what shows up there. And we're still going door to door in Airport Heights."

"Good," said Windflower.

"And I'm sending your car over. It should be outside when you're ready to leave," said Langmead. "You must be exhausted. Go back to the hotel and get some rest. I'll call if anything breaks."

Windflower hung up as Carrie was coming back into the area. "They're going to hold him overnight and let him go in the morning. Just as a precaution," she said.

"Go give him the good news," said Windflower. "I have to call Sheila."

Sheila was in bed but relieved to hear that Windflower was okay. He didn't bother her with his ride in the trunk of the car. No point upsetting her. And she was more than happy with the news about Sanjay. "Does Repa know?"

"We just talked with her," said Windflower. "Everybody's pretty happy around here." Everybody but Majesky, he thought. But he didn't want to burden Sheila with the loss of the diamonds either.

"How's Uncle Frank?" she asked just before they said goodnight.

"He was sleeping when we left," said Windflower. "I'll go check on him when we get back to the hotel."

Their driver, Davis, was standing guard on their Challenger when they came out of the hospital. "Thank you, Constable," said Windflower. "Your work here is done."

Davis gave a mock salute and went back to his RNC cruiser. "I wonder how Uncle Frank is making out?" asked Carrie.

"He's probably still sleeping," said Windflower.

That would not be the case. When they arrived at the hotel, Uncle Frank was sitting behind the reception desk, eating from a bucket of fried chicken with the night clerk.

"Mary Brown's," said Uncle Frank. "You want some?"

Windflower shook his head and laughed. "You've already made a new friend, I see."

"Clark is the best kind, b'y," said his uncle. "And Mary Brown's delivers here. Did you know that?"

"I did not," said Windflower. He did not have any more time to be educated by his uncle on the intricacies of Newfoundland fried chicken because his cell phone rang. A Halifax number. He knew who that was: Superintendent Wally Majesky.

32

"Superintendent," said Windflower as calmly as he could and awaited the avalanche of abuse that he was sure would follow. Much to his surprise, Majesky was almost as calm as he was.

"I hear that the diamonds were lost in your last encounter," said Majesky.

"Yes, sir," said Windflower, reverting to his old RCMP style. "It was unfortunate, but we did manage to release the hostage without any injuries."

"I heard that," said Majesky. "Congratulations."

Windflower was now both surprised and suspicious. "Excuse me. Is there something I should know?"

"I am only going to tell you, and you have to promise to keep it secret," said the superintendent. "The diamonds you lost are fake. We received the news from Interpol that Robert Smart was actually working for them, trying to ensnare Frederik Bund."

"What?" asked Windflower. "But Smart died from internal injuries. We checked his pulse. The paramedics pronounced him dead. Doctor Sanjay?"

"Smart was pretending to be dead," said Majesky. "He took sedatives that slowed his whole nervous system and then sat for a long time in a cold bath. He appeared dead. Sanjay, of course, could tell the difference, but he was in on it the whole time."

"That's crazy," said Windflower. "Smart actually did that?"

"Apparently, it's not his first time," said Majesky. "But I can assure you that he is alive and well and on a flight to Geneva right now to meet his handlers."

"Sanjay didn't know that Bund was going to kidnap him, though?" asked Windflower.

"No, that was unexpected," said Majesky. "But I think he played his part pretty well, don't you?"

Windflower was stunned. "Yeah, I guess so," he finally said.

"Don't tell anyone," said Majesky. "But I thought you should know, okay?"

"Okay," said Windflower.

"While I have you, I wanted to check with you on Tizzard. Is he inspector material? Honest appraisal?" asked Majesky.

"Tizzard is a great cop," said Windflower. "But I'm not sure he would be the best choice in the long run. And I don't think he wants it."

"Thanks for that," said Majesky. "My assessment as well."

Majesky hung up, and Windflower was left to ponder that last conversation. He wandered outside to process it by himself. But after a few minutes of gazing at the night sky, he was still confused. Did Sanjay really play out a role with Robert Smart? It must be true because Majesky told him so. He couldn't wait to see the doctor again to talk with him about it. But first to extricate his uncle from Mary Brown and get some sleep.

Once both he and Uncle Frank were safely back in their rooms, Windflower had a chance to think a bit more about what Superintendent Majesky told him. He was shocked at the news about Robert Smart. And Sanjay was in on it. Amazing. But all that thinking didn't keep him from falling asleep; he was dead tired.

But as he was drifting off, he could almost feel himself being pulled into another world, the dreamworld. This time he was in St. John's at the waterfront. That was different, he thought. What wasn't different was that both Harvey Brenton and his old pal the seal were back.

The pair was playing some kind of game on the water. Brenton would throw a ball out into the ocean, and the seal would catch it and bring it back to the wharf. Then they switched places. The seal would throw the ball, and Harvey Brenton would grab it and bring it back. They kept doing this until Windflower interrupted them.

"Hey, I'm here," he called out.

"We know," said Brenton. "But we are engaged in the life-and-death struggle that has pitted man against beast for eternity."

"Looks to me like you're playing catch," said Windflower.

"We see what we want to see," said the seal, holding up the ball. Now, Windflower could see that it was actually glass, and inside there were people and animals, all looking like they were trying to get out.

"If we get it just right, the sunlight will find a way to sneak into the globe, and the light will melt the glass," said Brenton.

"And those inside can escape," said the seal. "As long as we don't drop it and break the glass." The seal fumbled with the ball and looked like he was going to drop it. "Oops."

"Not funny," said Windflower, whose heart had sunk as the ball nearly dropped. "You have to be more careful."

"Good advice," said the seal. "Maybe you should try it yourself."

Windflower was almost in a daze as he started to wake up. As he did, he heard another voice. He started to tell them to go away; he needed the sleep. But he felt a cold, hard jab in his back. "Get up," said a voice.

Windflower opened his eyes. He sat up in bed and tried to get his bearings. "Don't talk. Don't make a peep," said the man, who was holding a gun. "Get dressed."

Windflower pulled on his pants and his shirt and stood as still as he could. Sudden moves could get you killed in a situation like this. The man went behind and pushed him forward and out into the hallway. The bright lights temporarily blinded Windflower, but the man kept pushing him towards the end of the hallway. He opened the door to the stairwell and urged Windflower to go ahead.

Luckily, there were only three flights of stairs, and soon he was back out in the moonlight. They walked towards a car that was running at the back of the building, and the man opened the back door and propelled Windflower inside. The car took off from the hotel parking lot, and not long after they were in what looked like a quiet subdivision. The car pulled into a driveway. Two people pushed him ahead of them and into a house.

Windflower was pushed into a back bedroom and didn't hear or see much for about twenty minutes. Then Frederik Bund came into the room, followed by the man who had surprised Windflower in his hotel room.

"We meet again, Windflower," said Bund. "But I am a little less happy this time. It seems that I fulfilled my part of the bargain and you have not. We will need to remedy this situation."

"I don't know what you're talking about," said Windflower.

The man behind Bund stepped forward and hit Windflower on the side of his head with his weapon. Windflower keeled over from the impact, and when he put his hand to his pulsating skull, he felt wet. Blood, he thought. He thought that more blows might be coming, but Bund preempted that. "Mitch," he said. "No. We need him alive."

He turned to Windflower. "We need you alive because you are going to meet the bargain we struck. We can do it the easy way, or I can let my friend here do what he seems to really like to do: hurt people. Your choice."

Windflower was in too much pain to argue.

"So, here's what you're going to do," said Bund. "Call your boss and tell him I want my diamonds. Or I will kill you."

"I don't really have a boss," said Windflower. "I'm just a friend of the family."

"Come on, Sergeant, I know who you are," said Bund.

"Then you must know I'm no longer a Mountie," said Windflower. "I have little value to them."

"*Au contraire*," said Bund. "They will not want your blood on their hands. Me, I don't care either way. I'm a businessman. I have promised suppliers some product that they have paid me well to deliver. If I do not, I am expendable. And I do not ever want to be expendable. So, make the call. Or Mitch will help you make up your mind."

With that, the other man stepped closer to Windflower. "Okay, okay, but I still don't think it will make any difference."

Windflower thought about calling Majesky. But that might intimate that he knew more about the missing diamonds. Or that the ones he had handed over were fake. He called Tizzard.

33

"Eddie, it's me," said Windflower. "I have a problem. Bund wants his diamonds."

"I thought you handed them over already," said Tizzard. "What's the problem?"

"Bund is not satisfied. I need your help," said Windflower. He could almost hear Tizzard thinking. "Or else they'll kill me."

"Let me make some calls, and I'll get back to you," said Tizzard.

"Hurry," said Windflower.

"That would be wise," said Bund as he grabbed the phone. "Very wise. I will call back in two hours. I want the diamonds."

Bund and his friend left Windflower in the bedroom. He could hear a click as the door locked him in. He took a look around the room for the first time. Not much unusual. More of a spare bedroom than anything. But it had two things that interested him. The first was a window with venetian blinds pulled tight. He didn't want to open them fully because of the possible noise. He wasn't going to do anything that brought that Mitch guy back.

But he could lift an edge of one blind and peered outside. Not much to see, and the morning fog and his throbbing head made it even fuzzier. But he could see a wooded area behind him and could see over the fence into a neighbour's yard. There was a dog wandering around. Then he saw a man open his back door and call the dog, which reluctantly went in.

That might be promising, thought Windflower. If only the neighbour would come out into the back and stay there for a while, he might be able to get his attention somehow. Trying to think of how to do that hurt his aching head even more. His attention turned to the second item on his list: the bed that he was sitting on. He lay down and held his head in his hands.

Maybe it was the tiredness, or maybe it was the shock of everything that was happening. But before he knew it, he had fallen asleep.

Two people who were not sleeping right now were Eddie Tizzard in Marystown and Uncle Frank in St. John's. And they were on the phone with each other.

"So you woke up in the night and went downstairs?" said Tizzard. "What did you see?"

"I was walking down the stairs to see my buddy at the front desk. I don't really like elevators. I thought maybe I'd get a cup of tea. Then I heard a noise on the stairs above me. It sounded strange, so I ducked out into the second floor. Then I saw them go by," said Frank.

"Who?" asked Tizzard.

"Winston," said Uncle Frank. "With a guy behind him, kinda pushing him along. He had his head down and didn't look too happy."

"What did the other man look like?" asked Tizzard.

"I dunno," said Frank. "He was pretty short, but bulky. Like a fire hydrant. He had a baseball cap on, but I couldn't really see what kind it was."

"Then what happened?" asked Tizzard.

"Winston and this man went to a car in the parking lot behind the hotel and got in the back seat," said Frank.

"What kind of car was it?" asked Tizzard.

"It was a newish car, black," said Frank. "I'm not good with models and stuff. But I did see something else. I saw the license plate. CRH 737."

"Good job," said Tizzard. "Did you see the driver?"

"Only caught a glimpse," said Uncle Frank. "All I could see was that he was wearing glasses."

"Great," said Tizzard. "Stay put there. The local guys may have more questions."

Tizzard hung up with Uncle Frank. He had already talked with Majesky, who gave him carte blanche to access resources anywhere in Newfoundland, including St. John's. He had a message in to Sergeant Terry Robbins, who was running the RCMP in St. John's, and Carl Langmead at the Constabulary.

Langmead called back first. "We can track the car," he said after he got the information from Tizzard. "Sounds like we know who the other guy is, too. Mitchell Raymond. Bad dude. What's going on with the diamonds? I thought that was fixed up."

"I don't have the whole story yet," said Tizzard. "But I guess what Windflower handed over wasn't good enough."

"That puts him in a bad spot," said Langmead. "We'll pull out all the stops now to find him. We can do a faster neighbourhood scan with the license plate."

"Be careful," said Tizzard. "We don't want to do anything that spooks Bund."

"Absolutely," said Langmead. "We're not making any moves without talking to you. But let's see if we can find him first."

"Okay," said Tizzard. "I'm getting more resources from our guys in St. John's. I'll get Evanchuk to coordinate with you once I know more."

Tizzard hung up with Langmead, and almost immediately his phone rang again. It was Carrie.

"I just saw Frank. What's going on?"

"They picked up Windflower last night," said Tizzard. "Did you and him know the diamonds were fake?"

"Fake? What do you mean?" asked Carrie. "I was pretty sure they were the real deal, and I'm pretty sure Windflower did, too. Who exactly has him?"

"Bund," said Tizzard. "Him and a local thug named Mitchell Raymond. It's not good. I've talked to Langmead, and now I'm waiting for our guys to check in."

"Is Terry Robbins still the C.O. here?" asked Carrie.

"Yes, that's who I'm waiting to hear from. I'll get you to liaise between him and the RNC," said Tizzard.

"Okay," said Carrie. "Have you talked to Sheila yet?"

"No, and not looking forward to that," said Tizzard. "It's early. Maybe she's not up yet."

"She has two kids," said Carrie. "She's up."

"I'll call her now," said Tizzard. "I'm sick to my stomach already about this."

"I know," said Carrie. "But we can just do our jobs and hope it works out."

"I love you," said Tizzard.

"I love you, too," said Carrie.

He called Sheila in Grand Bank. Stella answered the phone, and he could hear Amelia Louise in the background yelling for her turn. As gently as he could, he asked to speak to their mother.

"Hello," said Sheila.

"Sheila, it's Eddie. How are you this morning?" said Tizzard.

"I know you and the RCMP too well," said Sheila. "You don't call people early in the morning to see how they're feeling. But I'm fine. What's going on?"

"There's been a situation. And Winston is involved," said Tizzard.

"What do you mean involved?" asked Sheila.

This was the hard part, thought Tizzard. "He was taken and is being held hostage."

"By whom and for what?" said Sheila. Tizzard could hear her yell at the children in the background to stay quiet. Sheila never yelled at the kids.

"By the guys who had Sanjay," said Tizzard.

"I thought that was all dealt with," said Sheila.

"So did we," said Tizzard. "But there's been some misunderstanding." The phone line was deathly quiet.

"Sheila, we'll do everything we can to get Winston out of this safely." He started to talk about all the resources they had, but Sheila cut him off.

"But you can't guarantee anything," said Sheila. "Maybe he should have just stayed in the RCMP. At least he'd have insurance. Listen, Eddie, be honest with me. How much danger is he in?"

Tizzard thought carefully about this question. "He's in danger, no doubt. But we're going to figure this out. Those guys who are holding him are looking for something. Once we give them that, they don't need Winston."

"Then give them what they want," said Sheila. "Call me when you know anything. Anything."

34

Sheila hung up, and Tizzard exhaled a long, deep breath. Then he called Superintendent Majesky.

"What the heck is going on with the diamonds?" asked Tizzard after he explained the current situation to a very quiet Majesky.

"We thought we could get through this, but I guess not," Majesky finally said and told Tizzard about Sanjay and Robert Smart.

"Do you have the diamonds?" asked Tizzard. "Or can we get diamonds?"

"To be frank, I don't know," said Majesky.

"We have another hour to find out," said Tizzard.

"I'll get back to you," said Majesky.

Tizzard sat in the silence of his house and thought about Windflower. He remembered back when he'd been shot; the first person he saw was Windflower. He could feel him hovering around the hospital room even before he woke up. He could hear his voice saying to hang on, that he could make it. He knew now that Windflower hadn't actually been there during this time; he came a little later with his dad, but he was certainly there in spirit.

Windflower had become the older brother that Tizzard needed. He had lost his own brother years ago to a roadside bombing in Afghanistan. Sean would have been around the same age as Windflower now, thought Tizzard. His second thought was that he would do anything to save his friend. His best friend. His brother.

The quiet was broken by little Hughie's cries from the bedroom. Not really crying, just telling his father that he was awake. Tizzard went into the bedroom and picked him up. The little boy giggled at his dad, and Tizzard smiled back. It was a brief moment of joy in what felt like a terrible morning. He took it as a sign of hope.

What was it his dad always said? "'Hope for the best and prepare for the worst,'" Tizzard said out loud to his son. "Let's hope for the best to start with." Hughie seemed to agree.

True to his word, Majesky was back to Tizzard right after he'd managed to get the baby changed and fed. "We'll need some more time," he said.

"How much time?" asked Tizzard.

"A couple of more hours," said Majesky. "I've located the diamonds and now have to get clearance to take them out. Not easy. I need an assistant commissioner to sign off. It doesn't help that Windflower isn't on the Force anymore."

"It's Windflower," said Tizzard with more than a touch of exasperation. "He's given more to the RCMP and our community than anybody I know. And we tricked him the first time around."

"Still need approval," said Majesky. "You'll have to stall."

Tizzard was angry when he hung up with Majesky. But a surprise visit from his dad shook him out of that.

"You look stressed out of your mind, son," said Richard Tizzard. "Is everything okay? Hughie seems fine. Is Carrie okay?"

"They're both great," said Tizzard. "It's Windflower. He's in a spot of trouble in St. John's."

"'Clouds come floating into my life, no longer to carry rain or usher storm, but to add color to my sunset sky,'" said his dad. "I got it from Doc Sanjay. Pretty good, isn't it?"

"I had a guy in a dream say that to me," said Tizzard. "What does it mean anyway?"

"It's a Tagore quote, of course," said Richard. "To me, it means that I should view challenges and problems as opportunities to grow. We will always have problems, but they should not stop us from living our lives."

"Thanks, Dad, that's helpful," said Tizzard. "I guess we also need to be grateful for what we have."

"Exactly," said Richard. "Gratitude is very important. A wise man once said, 'I try to hold fast to the truth that a full and thankful heart cannot entertain great conceits. When brimming with gratitude, one's heartbeat must surely result in outgoing love, the finest emotion that we can ever know.'"

"Who said that?" asked Tizzard. "It's beautiful. And profound."

"I think it's anonymous," said his father. "Now how about we practice gratitude together. You make breakfast, and I'll look after Hughie."

"Deal," said Eddie.

While Eddie and his dad were eating breakfast, Windflower was coming out of his fog again. He managed to sit up, but that hurt too much, so he lay back down. After another effort, he got up and crawled along the way to the window. He peeked out again through a slat, but nothing was moving in the backyard next door. Then he realized he had to go to the bathroom. This was going to be tricky.

He tapped on the door, lightly at first, and then a little harder. No sound from outside. He called out. Nothing. He gently turned the door handle, but the door was locked. He sat back down on the bed. He looked around for something to use to maybe jimmy the door, but the room was pretty bare. Then he remembered.

He put his hand into his jeans pocket and checked the small pocket in front. There it was. Beulah's hairpin from the other day. In a few seconds he had unlocked the door and opened it a crack. Still no noise from outside. He opened it a little wider and went out into the hallway. There didn't appear to be anybody in the house. First things first, he went to the bathroom. When he came out, he was about to walk out the front door when the car he had arrived in came into the driveway.

He ran back to the bedroom and quickly locked the door behind him, just in time. He heard people come into the house, and one of them went and checked his door to make sure it was still locked. Not going to get out that easily, he thought. He stayed as quiet as he could and tried to listen in on whatever might be said on the outside. He heard one of them talking, and not too happily, either. It sounded like Bund.

"Do not screw me around," said Bund. "I want my diamonds."

Windflower couldn't hear anything else for a while and assumed that it must be Tizzard or somebody else talking.

Then, Bund spoke again. "Two more hours. That is it. When I call you next, you will tell me where the diamonds are. Or else we're done. And so is your friend."

"I think they're stalling," Windflower heard the other man say.

"Shut up, you don't get paid to think," said Bund. "Check on Windflower."

35

Windflower lay on the bed and pretended to be sleeping. The lock clicked and the door opened. A blast of light hit him, and he had to move to shield his eyes. The door shut again as quickly as it had opened. "Still there," the other man said. The next thing Windflower heard was the sound of racing cars and an announcer. Somebody had turned on the TV.

That might be good news, thought Windflower as he sat up again and went back to the window, peeking outside again. This time the man was back, and it looked like he was dressed for work. He had some kind of uniform on. Not police or paramedic or firefighter. Bus driver, maybe, thought Windflower. He stuck his head inside the blinds and held them with one hand to keep them still. He waved, but the man didn't see him.

He then tried tapping on the window, but still no response. Should he risk tapping even harder? There didn't seem to be any other option. Luckily, he only had to do it once more. The man looked over. Windflower waved. The man waved back. Then, he started to walk towards Windflower. Windflower started to panic and frantically waved at him to go back. But the man kept coming.

Windflower had to think fast. How could he tell him he was in danger and not to come closer? There was a sign he'd seen recently developed by women's groups who wanted to help women in abuse situations to show they were in trouble and needed help. Windflower put his hand up and then he laid his thumb across the four fingers. Then he closed his fingers over his thumb. He had to do it three times, very slowly each time, before the man seemed to get the message. The man gave him a thumbs-up and went back inside.

Tizzard, meanwhile, had bought himself some precious time after grovelling to Bund. That would be enough time for a chopper to get from Halifax to St. John's. In fact, the helicopter was already on its way. It had to make one stop in Marystown to pick him up. Majesky wouldn't trust anybody else to do the handover. Tizzard wouldn't have wanted anybody else, either.

Half an hour later, the chopper was landing in the parking lot of the RCMP building in Marystown. As the rotors were slowing, Tizzard was already on his way to jump in. Minutes later, he and pilot Ted Reid were floating over the little communities along the southeast coast and cutting across Placentia Bay towards St. John's

In St. John's, Langmead got the 911 notification about the same time as Tizzard was lifting off from Marystown. Evanchuk was sitting alongside Langmead when the call came in. So was Uncle Frank, who refused to be left waiting at the hotel.

"Let's get an unmarked car to go take a look," said Langmead. "And can somebody call the 911 caller back and tell them to quietly get out of the neighbourhood?"

"Do you think it's Windflower?" asked Evanchuk.

"He flashed the sign that only a few of us know," said Langmead. "The Metrobus driver didn't know what it was, but he could tell that somebody was in trouble. We'll know in a few minutes if the car in the driveway matches."

A few tense minutes later, they got the confirmation. They were sitting in a makeshift war room, and Langmead had a map of Airport Heights laid out on a boardroom table. Evanchuk and the lead from the RCMP tactical squad were there, along with the sergeant from the RNC Tactics and Rescue Unit.

"There's only two ways in and out, and we've got them covered," said Langmead. "Coming out, they either have to come back this way to the airport or the other way to Portugal Cove. We're thinking that they will most likely want to have their boat ready, but we haven't received that call yet. Our marine unit is on top of that. Now, all we need to know is what your inspector intends to do," he said, looking at Evanchuk.

"I'll call him," she said.

Tizzard wasn't able to take the call because he was landing with Ted Reid at the airport in St. John's. He'd called ahead, and Terry Robbins was waiting for him on the tarmac. He waved goodbye to Reid and jumped into the car with Robbins. They drove out of the airfield and parked on a service road.

"You hear anything else?" he asked Robbins.

"No, Evanchuk has the tactical squad with her at the Constabulary," said Robbins.

Tizzard looked at his phone and saw the message from Carrie first.

"I'm in St. John's. Just landed," he said.

"We think we found him," said Carrie. She ran through what Langmead had told her. "So. We know where he is, and the RNC has the area covered. How do you want to handle things going forward?"

"Let me talk to Langmead," said Tizzard. The RNC detective came on the line.

"Have everybody stay completely out of sight," said Tizzard. "The last thing we want is to scare Bund. I have what he wants and will make the exchange. Do you have the boat covered?"

"Yes," said Langmead. "All exits and routes out of the area are controlled, and we have our marine unit watching the boat that Bund leased."

"Okay, now we wait for the phone call," said Tizzard. "I'm going to open another line so you can hear what happens. We'll call you right back." Robbins nodded and turned on his car phone. He called into Langmead's line.

Everybody in the RNC war room was quiet, even Uncle Frank. It was almost as if the whole world was holding their breath. Then they heard a cell phone ring and Tizzard answering.

"Have you got my property?" asked Bund.

"Yes," said Tizzard. "Is Windflower okay?"

"He's fine," said Bund. "Here's what I want you to do. I want you to go the airport and arrange a helicopter for me, with a pilot."

"I can't get a helicopter," said Tizzard.

"I think you can," said Bund. "How did you get here so fast?"

Tizzard said nothing.

"So, I'll need you to call off all those local cops that are circling around.

And I want to be able to access the tarmac and be able to drive right to the helicopter. You meet me there. Now."

"Okay," said Tizzard. The line went dead.

"Why does it feel like he's always one step ahead of us?" asked Tizzard to no one in particular. "Langmead, you got that?"

"Roger," said Langmead. "What do you want us to do?"

"I guess we ensure a clear route to the airport to start with," said Tizzard. "Have someone at the security checkpoint to make sure they can get through. Then stand by. Evanchuk, can you have your squad deployed around the airport perimeter? Close enough to intervene if they need to. But not visible."

He hung up the phone and turned to Robbins. "I need to brief Majesky. Can you make sure Ted Reid is ready on the tarmac? And talk to the airport to get them to clear everything else out of the way. We don't need anybody else involved in this."

He called Majesky.

"Where's he going in the helicopter?" asked Majesky.

"I have no idea," said Tizzard. "But I assume it's pretty easy to track. I'm more worried if he wants to take Windflower with him."

"You can't let him have both," said Majesky.

"Agreed," said Tizzard. "That's a deal-breaker."

The phone line went silent as both Majesky and Tizzard tried to think about the next steps. They didn't seem to have any answers. That silence was broken by the chatter on Robbins's radio. "Suspects leaving the house and heading towards Portugal Cove Road."

"Let's go back on the tarmac," said Tizzard. They drove back through the security area and were waved through by security. The airfield was eerily quiet, and the only aircraft was the RCMP helicopter. "Can you call Reid and tell him to start up the chopper? He may have to take off quickly, one way or another. Also, tell him that if I raise my hands in the air, he is to take off immediately. Okay?"

"Got it," said Robbins.

The car radio cackled again. "Car heading onto Portugal Cove Road towards airport."

36

They will be here in a few minutes, thought Tizzard as he watched the blades of the helicopter start to spin slowly and then faster. He took a deep breath and got Robbins to drive right up to the chopper. They parked and waited until they saw a car come through the security zone and up to their vehicle. Tizzard got out of the car and stood there as still as he could. But he could feel his heart racing.

Bund was shorter than Tizzard imagined, with a receding hairline and glasses. Like a pharmacist or something normal, he thought. The thug beside him was predictable, heavy-set and mean-looking. Tizzard could see Windflower in the back seat.

"So, how do you see this working?" asked Tizzard.

"Give me the diamonds, and we'll be on our way," said Bund.

"Hand him over first," said Tizzard.

"He comes with me," said Bund. "He'll be released when we are safe and on our way."

"No deal," said Tizzard. "Let him go and I'll give you the diamonds." He opened his hand to show Bund the package of diamonds."

"Okay, I'll let him go, and you come with us," said Bund with a half-smile that looked positively evil to Tizzard.

"Okay, I'll just hang on to them for now then," said Tizzard, putting his hand into his pocket.

Bund pulled a gun out of his pocket and pointed it directly at Tizzard. He nodded to Mitchell, who opened the back door of their vehicle. Windflower stumbled out of the car and half walked, half ran to Robbins's vehicle. Mitchell then opened the trunk and took two bulky packages out. He carried them with him to the helicopter. Bund indicated that Tizzard should follow Mitchell.

"Hand them over," said Bund as Tizzard and he met just below the whirling rotors. Tizzard pulled the jewels out and passed them to Bund. "I'll take your cell phone," said Bund. When Tizzard handed it over, Bund dropped it on the ground and crushed it under his heel. "And your weapon, of course." Tizzard's gun he put in his pocket.

"After you," said Bund, and first Tizzard and then Mitchell and then Bund climbed into the chopper.

"Where are we going?" asked Tizzard over the noise of the helicopter engine.

Bund pointed one finger in the air. "Up," he said. "But a little business first." He reached over and yanked at Reid's helmet, pulling the receiver out of its holder. Then he used Tizzard's gun to smash the radio console. "Let's go."

Now the airfield was swarming with police of all sorts. Langmead and Evanchuk raced to Robbins's car where Windflower was sitting, looking like he was in shock.

Evanchuk couldn't believe what just happened either. Windflower gingerly got out of the car, looking much worse for the wear. "Oh my god, they got Eddie," was the first thing he said.

Carrie was trying to act professional but looked ready to crumble. Langmead stepped into the breach. He introduced himself to Robbins, and the two men had a quick chat while Windflower and Carrie had a long hug. "I'm glad you're okay," she whispered to Windflower. He just hugged her back harder.

"Why don't you take him to the hospital? He needs to get checked out," said Langmead to Evanchuk. "Robbins and I will work things out, and he'll talk to your superintendent."

Evanchuk started to protest, but Robbins held her back. "We got this," he said. "I've got your cell phone number, and we'll call you as soon as we know anything." She knew what they wanted: to get her out of the way. Didn't want to have an emotional spouse hanging around. But she did what she was told. Their new friend Davis was assigned to drive them both to the Health Sciences.

As soon as they left, Robbins phoned Majesky with an update.

"We've got them on radar," said Majesky, "so at least we can track them. Last report was that they were over the ocean, likely heading for Nova Scotia. We've got people all over the Atlantic provinces on alert. How is Windflower?"

"I'd say battered and bruised, but okay," said Robbins. "Might have a concussion, and he's gone to get checked out. Evanchuk went with him."

"How is she?" asked Majesky.

"Probably still in a bit of shock," said Robbins. "But she's a trooper."

"She is indeed," said Majesky. "We'll pick it up from here. Unless they make a U-turn and head back your way, it seems like they are heading west right now."

"Okay, we'll update you on Windflower, sir," said Robbins. "Can you keep us in the loop? Evanchuk." He didn't need to say anything else.

"Absolutely," said Majesky.

Windflower's head hurt. A lot. But while he was in the waiting area, he got Evanchuk to call Sheila and hand him the phone.

"Yes, yes, I'm fine," said Windflower. "Just a knock in the head. Can't really hurt anything up there." He started to laugh, but that hurt too much. Evanchuk walked away to give him a little privacy.

"I'm so glad you're okay," said Sheila.

"But they took Eddie," said Windflower.

"What do you mean took?" asked Sheila. "And how is Carrie?"

"They got away in a helicopter, and Eddie was with them," said Windflower. "Carrie is not okay. Do you want to talk to her?" Sheila did, so he called Carrie back.

He watched Carrie as she listened to Sheila. She didn't say much but at the end said thank you and handed the phone back to Windflower.

"Do you want me to come to St. John's?" asked Sheila.

"No, I'll be okay," said Windflower. "I bet they'll just take a look at me and let me go."

"And where's Uncle Frank?" asked Sheila. "You didn't lose him, too, did you?"

That question stumped Windflower, and he mouthed the question to Carrie. "He's at the RNC," said Carrie. "He's fine."

"Uncle Frank is fine," Windflower said to Sheila. "Making new friends with the Constabulary. Okay, I have to go, the nurse is coming."

The admitting nurse took Windflower, who was sitting in a wheelchair now, and brought him into reception. Carrie waited outside with Davis. Her cell phone rang. It was Terry Robbins.

"Any news?" asked Carrie, expectantly.

"Not much," said Robbins. "But Majesky says that they are able to track the chopper on radar. They were over the ocean, likely heading to the mainland."

"That's not much," said Carrie.

"Sorry, that's all I got so far. As soon as I hear anything else, I'll call," said Robbins.

Windflower was wheeled out of reception and moved into an observation room shortly afterwards. He looked at Evanchuk to check how she was doing. Not well by the looks of it. "Anything?"

"They've got them on radar and think they're on the way to Nova Scotia or somewhere off the island," said Carrie. "Could be anywhere."

"I have a feeling he's going to be okay," said Windflower. His optimism didn't seem to sway Carrie. He tried another approach. "Eddie is tougher than he looks. I was there after he was shot. Three times. Lots of people didn't think he'd pull through. But I knew he would." That brightened Carrie's eyes a little.

"I know it's really hard. It was tough back then," said Windflower. "I know we're not supposed to pray that people get better. That's kind of Creator's job. But we can pray that the person be given the strength to go through whatever they're facing. That's what I'm going to do."

"Me, too," said Carrie. "Me, too." Silently she whispered to herself, "Because he has to."

37

Eddie may have been the one who was least confident about the outcome of the current situation. That was until he saw Mitchell open one of the packages and then the other. He'd forgotten about those. He had been more intent on trying to figure out where Bund was taking them and what he planned to do once they arrived at whatever destination was in his warped mind.

Bund had been barking out instructions to Ted Reid all the way along. The only thing Tizzard knew for sure was that they were over water. Lots of water. The Atlantic Ocean. And that they were heading west. When they hit the coastline, Bund gave Reid coordinates in longitude and latitude. A specific location. Tizzard couldn't tell where they were because low-level clouds kept visibility at a minimum. Plus, they were far too high up to really pick out anything other than dots on the ground.

After about twenty minutes flying over land, Bund told Reid to start coming down. Now Tizzard could see more of what lay below them: some towns and a highway snaking its way across the land like a ribbon. Must be the Trans-Canada, he thought and couldn't tell but it seemed like they were moving north as well. They kept going down, and by the time they got to 5,000 clicks on the altimeter, Mitchell had given Bund his package and both had opened them and put them on.

Parachutes, of course, thought Tizzard.

"Don't hang around here. We have people on the ground who will take you down," said Bund. Those were his last words before first Mitchell, and then Bund jumped out of the helicopter. Tizzard watched as the two men floated and then saw the chutes open in a flash of white below them.

Reid looked at him. "Let's get out of here," said Tizzard.

"I think we're near Amherst," said Reid. "There's a detachment there."

"Let's go," said Tizzard.

Ten minutes later, they were on the ground at the Amherst Nova Scotia RCMP and Tizzard was on the phone with Majesky.

"Glad that you're safe," was the first thing Majesky said. The second thing was more surprising. "We know where they are."

"What?" asked Tizzard. "We just dropped them off, and we have no idea where they are."

"We're tracking them," said Majesky. "There's a microchip GPS in the bag of diamonds."

"What?" said Tizzard again. "How is that possible? What if Bund finds it? What if he saw it when we were doing the exchange?"

"That's a risk we had to take," said Majesky. "But the chip is only three-eighths of an inch, and it blended into the bag of diamonds. He'll find it eventually, but we're hoping to get him before that."

Tizzard was quiet, and outside he looked calm. But inside he was fuming. When Majesky talked about taking a risk, it was Tizzard and Windflower who were really at risk. Both had ended up being taken hostage by a madman. Both could have ended up dead. There was a lot he wanted to say, and he would say somewhere along the way, but this was not the time or place for that.

"Where are they now?" was all he said.

"They appear to be travelling by car or some sort of vehicle," said Majesky. "They're moving too fast to be on foot. We think they may have had somebody waiting to pick them up. Right now, they are in New Brunswick. We've got people stationed all along the main highway, closing the road behind them as they pass. We are planning an interception."

"Thanks," said Tizzard. "I have to call my partner."

"Sure, sure, go ahead," said Majesky.

Tizzard hung up and called Carrie. To say that she was relieved would be a major understatement. She tried not to cry and almost made it. "I'm just glad you're okay," she said when she could finally speak.

"I'm fine," said Tizzard. "Not very happy, but I'm fine."

"What happened?"

"I can't talk about it right now," said Tizzard. "I'll tell you when I get back home."

"Where are you now?"

"Amherst, Nova Scotia," said Tizzard. "But I'm going to see if I can't get a ride back with Ted Reid."

Reid overhead the last of this conversation. "I don't see why not," he said. "You certainly outrank me, Acting Inspector."

"You got any assignments at the moment?" asked Tizzard.

"I'm all yours."

"Excellent," said Tizzard. "Let's go to St. John's. And if nothing else happens, maybe you can give us a ride back to Marystown as well." He called Majesky to tell him his plans, but his line was busy, so he called Carrie instead. "Reid is just refuelling the chopper," he said. "We'll see you in a couple of hours."

Carrie went to find Windflower to tell him the good news, but he was being examined. It turned out that he might have a concussion. The doctor gave him some painkillers and said that he should stay overnight. He tried to protest, but he had to admit that lying down appealed to him more than just about anything right then. He had a chance to talk with Carrie and found out the good news about Eddie and got her to phone back to Sheila to let her know he would be staying overnight at the hospital. He promised to call her, and that was the last thing he remembered until he woke up. Or almost woke up, in a dream.

This time there was nothing but water as far as he could see. He thought it was the ocean, but then he saw that it was a large lake. A very large lake, with an enormous moose wading through shallow water and coming directly towards him. Maybe he should have been afraid, but he didn't feel it one bit.

The moose came splishing and splashing its way towards Windflower. When it got close, it shook itself vigorously. And all over Windflower. He thought he heard the moose laugh. Then the moose spoke. It had a female voice that he quickly recognized.

"Auntie Marie, is that you?" he asked.

"Yes, my boy. Isn't this a great outfit? I always wanted to be a moose," said the animal. "Even though we don't have clans in our nation, we are certainly people of the deer family. And the moose is the largest and a symbol of our endurance and survival through the long, cold winters."

Windflower nodded at the moose, still surprised that his beloved Auntie Marie was with him and in the shape of this majestic animal.

"Do you want me to tell you a story?" asked Auntie Marie.

"Yes, please," said Windflower.

"This was a story told to me when I was a little girl. It's about how our people came to hunt the moose," said Auntie Marie.

"There once was a family of moose who were standing around a fire when they smelled the sweetest smoke. A pipe came floating through the air and all, but the smallest and youngest moose let it pass. He took a puff. When he did, his elders scolded him, for this was the pipe of the humans. They said that this would help the humans find them and kill them.

The young moose said he wasn't afraid. He could run faster than any human. The next morning the humans came looking for the moose. The young moose tried to outrun the hunters, but they were wearing snowshoes and quickly caught up to him in the deep snow. They killed the moose and thanked him for smoking their pipe and giving up himself so they could survive. They also treated his body with care and acknowledged his spirit.

That night the young moose woke up among his people. He had a gift that had been given to him by the humans. He said that he had been treated with respect and that it was okay to allow the humans to catch them. And so that is true to this day. The lesson for humans is that if we respect the animals we hunt, we will be successful."

"That is a great story," said Windflower. "Thank you, Auntie." Then he added something else, because he knew there was more. "And what is the lesson?"

"Be strong but be gentle and always show respect to others," said Auntie Marie as the moose slowly walked back into the lake. Windflower watched as the moose disappeared into a mist that hovered over the water. He was sad and missed his auntie but felt filled up by her visit. He was still thinking about that when he woke up in the unfamiliar surroundings of his room in the St. John's hospital.

38

Eddie Tizzard was there, and so was Carrie Evanchuk. And Uncle Frank.
"Wow, this is a greeting party," said Windflower as he struggled to wake from the haze of the painkiller. "And Eddie, you're here."

"In the flesh," said Tizzard.

"Me, too," said Uncle Frank. "Although nobody seems to know I'm even around."

"Ah, we all love you, Frank," said Tizzard.

"So, what happened to you?" asked Windflower, waking up a little more. "Obviously, you're okay."

"Good as new," said Tizzard and told the story of Bund and Mitchell bailing out over Nova Scotia. "God knows where they are. He's a slippery one, that's for sure. How are you feeling?"

"The painkillers help a lot," said Windflower. "But they really make me sleepy."

"We'll let you get some rest," said Tizzard.

"Okay," said Windflower. "But Uncle Frank, can you stay for a minute?"

"Sure," said his uncle. "I'll see you outside," he said to Tizzard and Carrie as they left the room.

"I had a dream," said Windflower. "Auntie Marie was in it."

"Sometimes she comes to me in dreams," said Uncle Frank. "It's nice when she comes, but when she leaves it feels even harder."

"I know what you mean," said Windflower. "She came as a moose."

"Did she tell you the moose story?" asked Uncle Frank.

"She did," said Windflower. "Why did she come as a moose, and why did she tell me that story?"

"She seems to like that appearance," said Uncle Frank, chuckling. "I think she finds it funny to imagine the looks on our faces. As for the story, you must have needed to hear that message again."

"About being strong and showing respect to others?" asked Windflower.

"And also being gentle," said his uncle. "It's easy to be a strong man. It's harder to be a gentle man."

"Like being polite?" asked Windflower.

"That, and about being strong and gentle at the same time. Like grass," said Uncle Frank. "You've heard this before. Grass is strong because it is not afraid to be stepped on. It waits for the pressure to be released, and then it springs back up, good as new."

"Got it," said Windflower. "Thank you, Uncle."

"No worries," said Uncle Frank. "Now I gotta go and catch Tizzard before they takes off on me."

Windflower laughed and waved goodbye to his uncle. He called Sheila to let her know that he was okay and that he'd definitely be home tomorrow. Sheila and the girls, both of whom insisted on talking to him, were happy to hear that news and that their great-uncle would be coming too.

"Does he have any presents for us?" asked Stella.

"Pwesents," he heard Amelia Louise yelling in the background, with Sheila trying to calm them both down.

"I'll call in the morning," said Windflower as he hung up. He had a brief thought of food, but sleep soon overpowered him and he was out cold. When he woke up, it was morning.

Eddie and Carrie woke up early, too. They'd already been down for breakfast and were hoping to get out of town soon. Ted Reid had his RCMP helicopter at their disposal and they were meeting him at the hospital. There was a large landing pad there and they could say goodbye to Windflower before they left.

They were checking out of the hotel when Uncle Frank came into the lobby from outside. "It's a grand day out there," said Uncle Frank. "Are you leaving?"

"We're going to see Windflower and then head out," said Tizzard. "Ted Reid is giving us a lift to Marystown in his chopper."

"Wow, that would be something," said Uncle Frank. "I've never been in a helicopter before. Lots of small planes. Bush planes, float planes. But never had a chopper ride."

"Would you like to come to Marystown with us?" asked Tizzard, getting the hint and a nudge from Carrie. "I'm guessing Windflower will be coming back later today, and he can pick you up."

"That would be wonderful," said Uncle Frank. "Let me get my stuff."

Carrie and Eddie settled into their comfy chairs to wait for Uncle Frank.

Windflower had finished his breakfast, too. Not that a spoonful of eggs, a soggy piece of toast and a prepackaged fruit cup was anything to write home about. No coffee, either, just a cup of lukewarm tea. The good news was that the nurse told him he could likely go home this morning. He had to wait for the doctor to do their rounds.

He was about to call Sheila when the door to his room opened. It was a doctor, just not the one he was expecting.

"Good morning, Winston," said Doctor Sanjay. "It looks like you're on the mend."

"You look great," said Windflower. "Have you been discharged?"

"Yes, yes," said Sanjay. "A few bumps and bruises are no reason to be in hospital. I wanted to check on you, though. I do feel somewhat responsible for your circumstances."

"Not you," said Windflower. "Although I am more than a little perturbed with Superintendent Majesky."

"I think we all got caught up in his, what's the word for it? Shenanigans, I think," said Doctor Sanjay. "But I regret very much that you were put in such danger. And I have a major apology to give when I get home."

"Me, too," said Windflower. "How are you getting back, by the way?"

"I was going to call my son to come get me," said Sanjay.

"Don't have him bother," said Windflower. "Assuming I can get out of here, why don't you come with me? I'll have to arrange transport for me and Uncle Frank anyway."

"That would be wonderful," said Doctor Sanjay as they heard a knock on the door and a young doctor came in with the nurse. "I'll see you in a little while," said Sanjay as he left the room.

Doctor Martha Henderson examined Windflower briefly and reviewed his chart. "You are good to go," she said. "But no driving for the next twenty-four hours. And if you have bad headaches, come back or see your doctor right away."

Before he could call Sheila with the good news, Tizzard, Carrie and Uncle Frank came in as soon as the doctor left.

"How are you?" asked Tizzard.

"I'm ready to go home," said Windflower.

"I'm getting a ride on a chopper," said Uncle Frank.

"You're going on a motorcycle to Grand Bank?" asked Windflower.

"No, I'm going on the helicopter with Eddie and Carrie," said his uncle.

"That's great," said Windflower. "But how am I getting home? I just got the green light to get out of here. But the doc said I can't drive for the next day."

"All fixed up," said Tizzard. "Terry Robbins will send over a driver with Carrie's cruiser to take you back. As soon as you are ready."

"Make the call. I'm ready to go anytime," said Windflower. "Oh, and see if you can find Doctor Sanjay. He's still around here somewhere. He needs a ride, too."

39

Carrie went off to find Sanjay, and Eddie went to make his call to Terry Robbins.

Uncle Frank sat with Windflower to keep him company.

"The girls are pretty excited to see you," said Windflower.

"I can't wait to give them a big hug," said Uncle Frank.

"Let's call them while we're waiting," said Windflower. He dialled Sheila, and she picked up almost right away.

"How are you feeling, and when are you coming back?" she asked.

Windflower laughed. "I guess you need a break. I'm great and ready to come back as soon as I can get a car lined up. I still have a headache, but that will pass. Uncle Frank is here with me. Are the girls around?"

It didn't take long for the girls to get on the phone with Uncle Frank. It was hard to tell who was more excited. Windflower watched the joy on his uncle's face as he listened to his daughters. Despite his headache, he felt pretty good about his life right at this moment. He said a quiet prayer of gratitude while he waited his turn to say hello.

"Okay, we'll see you all later today," said Windflower. "Let me talk to your mommy again."

"So, we'll see you and Frank in a few hours," said Sheila.

"He's going on an adventure first, though," said Windflower. "He's hitching a ride with Eddie and Carrie on the helicopter. It helps knowing the inspector, I guess. I'll pick him up in Marystown."

Carrie came back soon after with Doc Sanjay and Eddie with the good news that someone had been dispatched from the RCMP in White Hills to pick up Windflower and Sanjay to drive them home.

"Okay, let me get organized and checked out of this place," said Windflower as he shooed the others out of his room. He met Doctor Sanjay a

little while later as the nurse brought him to the reception area. He had
stubbornly resisted the offer of a wheelchair, but now he was a little shaky
and grateful that they had a ride home.

Sanjay was talking to the young RCMP constable who'd been assigned
to them.

"Winston Windflower, meet our chauffeur, Henry Blackmore," said
Sanjay.

"Morning, Constable," said Windflower. "Thanks for doing this."

"It's an honour, sir," said Blackmore. "I'm very pleased to meet the
great Sergeant Windflower."

"I'm not an RCMP officer anymore," said Windflower. "And you certainly don't have to call me sir."

"You will always be Sergeant Windflower to me and most of the men I
know," said Blackmore.

"Me, too," said Sanjay. "Shall we depart?"

"Absolutely," said Windflower. "I'll be glad to be out of this place."

"'The past is always with us, for nothing that once was time can ever
depart,'" said Sanjay as they walked to Carrie's cruiser.

"''Tis in my memory lock'd, And you yourself shall keep the key of
it,'" replied Windflower. "You and I have a lot to talk about. I look forward
to hearing your story."

Sanjay laughed and got into the back seat while Windflower jumped
into the front to keep Blackmore company. As they departed, they could
hear the sound of a helicopter taking off from the heliport at the back of
the building.

They looked up as they moved out of the parking lot to see the familiar
RCMP helicopter flying in the same direction they were going.

Onboard, Uncle Frank could barely contain his excitement. He kept
pointing out things he recognized on the ground. "There's Mount Pearl,"
he said. "And I think that's Paddy's Pond." But as the helicopter started to
rise to its cruising altitude, it was harder and harder to identify anything
more than large bodies of water below them.

Carrie smiled at Tizzard and squeezed his hand. She mouthed, "I love you," and he squeezed back.

"How long will it take?" Tizzard yelled to Ted Reid over the noise of the chopper.

"Less than an hour," said the pilot. "Depends on the wind."

About forty minutes later, they started their descent, and once again Uncle Frank started calling out familiar landmarks. It wasn't hard to tell the massive body of water that was Mortier Bay, and all four on the helicopter marvelled at this beautiful sight. Another fifteen minutes later, they were landing on the large X behind the RCMP building in Marystown. Carrie went off with Uncle Frank to get coffee, and Tizzard and Ted Reid went inside the building.

"Superintendent Majesky is here," said Terri Pilgrim when Tizzard reached his office. "He's looking for you, too," she added to Ted.

"Probably wants a ride back," said Reid. "That's good with me."

"And Murphy wants to talk to you. I think we're all set for the ceremony, but he's freaking out because all the bigwigs are coming," said Pilgrim.

"Who all is coming?" asked Tizzard.

"Well, we've got the mayor and council, MP, the provincial member and the minister of justice, along with reps from every RCMP division in the country and just about all police services in Atlantic Canada. We've had to move the ceremony to the arena because so many people wanted to come," said Pilgrim.

"Is there a program?" asked Tizzard.

"Getting it printed right now," said Pilgrim. "Here's Murphy to tell you all about it."

A red-faced and flustered Murphy came into Tizzard's office. "Good work," said Tizzard. "Both of you. I knew I could count on you. Murphy, why don't you run through the event? It will make me more comfortable." Tizzard sat back and watched Murphy fumble through his papers until Pilgrim handed him the cheat sheet she had prepared.

"Thanks," he mumbled. "So, there will be a procession. A parade, really. Starts here and goes right through the middle of town. We got the Salvation Army band to lead, followed by a riderless horse and honorary pallbearers who accompany the hearse. There's no body, of course. It's all symbolic."

"Go on," said Tizzard.

"All of the official mourners have been invited to march in the procession," said Murphy. "Those who wish will join Kirk Forsythe at the head of the march. After that, representatives of all the RCMP divisions and police forces will have their delegations. All RCMP officers from this province in attendance will line the route and salute as the hearse passes." Murphy stopped for a breath. "Inside the arena will be the speeches. First by Kirk Forsythe, followed by the politicians, and then Superintendent Majesky. Did you wish to speak, sir?"

"No, thank you, Sergeant," said Tizzard. "The superintendent can speak for us."

"Are you using my name in vain, Inspector?" asked Majesky, who had slipped into the room.

"No, sir, just saying that I have confidence in your ability to represent us," said Tizzard.

"I like that," said Majesky. "I already have some notes prepared. I see you've brought our helicopter with you. Can you take me back when we're done here today?" he asked Reid.

"Yes, sir," said Reid. "I'm going to go get fuelled up and check everything out on the chopper."

"Thanks, Ted," said Tizzard.

"Is there a reception afterward today?" asked Majesky.

"Yes, sir," said Pilgrim. "At the Legion."

"Great, thank you both for your work," said Majesky. "I need a few minutes with the inspector."

Terri Pilgrim and Murphy left, and Majesky closed the door to Tizzard's office.

40

"We should do a debrief," said Majesky.

"That would be good," said Tizzard.

"But first, an update," said Majesky. "We found the car and Mitchell. Near the airport in Montreal. Mitchell was dead. Shot in the head."

"That seems to be a pattern now," said Tizzard. "Do we know where Bund's gone?"

"The GPS tracker appears to have been turned off. Bund probably found it and is likely on a plane somewhere," said Majesky. "But he can't easily go to Europe. He's high on the Interpol wanted list. Maybe somewhere south, but then he would have to clear customs. We assume he's got a disguise and maybe some false papers, but even the developing world has better detection systems now."

"So, after all this, you might still lose Bund and the diamonds," said Tizzard. "I know there's a rank system, but you gotta know how pissed I am about this. You let me, Windflower and Sanjay get exposed to this madman who has probably killed at least two people and maybe more."

Majesky started to speak, but Tizzard cut him off. "I don't want to hear about the case or the best interests or any of that…" He wanted to say some really bad and crude things but somehow resisted. "Your job, our job, is to protect each other. You didn't do that."

Now Majesky was deliberately silent.

"I'll finish out the week, and then I'm done as inspector," said Tizzard.

"Okay," was all Majesky said as he stood and left Tizzard's office.

Windflower and Sanjay were sitting in the restaurant at Goobies. Blackmore joined them after filling up the cruiser. They'd decided to stop for a late breakfast. After a hearty meal of eggs and bacon and toast and home fries, they sat and enjoyed their coffee.

"Well, that was something we just went through," said Windflower. "I'm still pretty upset about Majesky putting all of us in danger."

"Do you want me to leave?" asked Blackmore.

"No, stay," said Windflower. "Neither the doctor nor me are RCMP officers. We can say what we want."

"And we don't care who hears it, either," said Doctor Sanjay with a laugh. "My biggest regret is the worry that I caused for my poor Repa."

"I'm just glad that I came out relatively unscathed," said Windflower. "Otherwise, Sheila would have killed me."

"I thought it would be a simple operation, pardon the pun," said Sanjay. "I was not expecting to be abducted in that fashion."

"Did you know the diamonds were fake?" asked Windflower as Blackmore looked at them with his mouth wide open. "You can leave if it makes you uncomfortable."

"If it's all the same, I'd like to stay, sir," said Blackmore. "Might be good for my professional development. We did hear a rumour about the diamonds that everybody was chasing not being the real deal."

"That caused some complications for me," said Windflower. "Especially when the bad guys found out."

"I did know that the diamonds were not genuine, but I couldn't say anything. That was difficult. But we are none the worse for wear. And I have a wonderful tale to relate to my grandchildren. A real adventure. Who would have thought that possible at my age?" said Sanjay.

"I'm not sure I want any more of those adventures," said Windflower. "I guarantee you that Sheila doesn't."

"'Let me not pray to be sheltered from dangers, but to be fearless in facing them,'" said Sanjay.

"I don't know, Doc," said Windflower. "I trust the Bard on this. 'Be wary then; best safety lies in fear.' You ready, Constable?"

"I am," said Blackmore. "On to Marystown."

Tizzard met up with Carrie and Uncle Frank at the coffee shop. As they sat in the window, they could see the different police force reps arriving and being directed by Murphy to their places in the procession. The dignitaries were already there and were being greeted by the mayor and council at the hotel.

"This is quite a proceeding," said Uncle Frank. "Kind of reminds me of what we do back home."

"What do you do in Pink Lake?" asked Carrie.

"If it's an elder, we have a parade just like they are having here, and then we have a community feast where we share our memories of the person who has gone over to the other side," said Uncle Frank. "It's a celebration because we don't believe they are leaving us forever, just until they get comfortable over there. Then they can come to visit."

"That's very civilized," said Tizzard. "Anyway, I've got to go put on my dress uniform. You can stay here with Carrie if you want and then come over to the arena afterward. You'll get to see everything from here."

"That would be grand," said Uncle Frank as Carrie went to get them both another coffee.

Tizzard stopped for a second to talk with Carrie while she waited in line. "I told Majesky I'm quitting."

"Good," said Carrie. "When?"

"End of the week. He didn't bother arguing with me."

"I'm glad," said Carrie. "We don't need that aggravation in our lives. I miss Hughie too much already and can't imagine doing this over and over."

"Me too," said Tizzard. "Maybe we'll take a few days off next week and take Hughie to Golden Sands."

"That would be great," said Carrie. "All we got to do is get through this week."

"Get through today first," said Tizzard. "I'll see you later."

Tizzard got one last briefing from Terri Pilgrim and put on his dress uniform. She had already sewn on his inspector's insignia, a crown that was placed on the shoulder epaulettes on the scarlet/blue tunic and blue jacket. She had even arranged to have his brown boots polished, and they gleamed in the sunlight as he walked outside.

He joined Murphy, and they made their way through the ranks of local and regional and national police officers who had come to pay their respects. There was a lot of gentle laughter and camaraderie, but that soon grew quiet when the riderless horse draped in the RCMP colours was led to the front of the group.

Even the Salvation Army band that was tuning up went silent as a sign of respect and to acknowledge the moment. Tizzard helped Murphy line up the dignitaries, including Superintendent Majesky and Kirk Forsythe at the front of the procession. Then he nodded to Murphy, who gave the signal to the band major to begin. The band started slowly walking to a single drumbeat to set the pace. About fifty yards in, the major raised his staff and they began to play "Amazing Grace."

There was hardly a dry eye among the police officers present at this sad lament, and many of the hundreds of bystanders who lined the route also dabbed away a few tears. Some of it was surely for Diane Forsythe, thought Tizzard as he joined the march. But maybe it also reminded everyone of someone else, someone close to them that they had lost.

The band continued playing until they reached the parking lot at the arena and then reverted to its single drummer to keep the beat for the wave of marchers who came behind them.

As the last of the procession moved into the arena, everyone stopped and waited for the honour guard to come and greet them and the horse without a rider and the hearse with the Canadian flag and RCMP insignia on top.

41

That was just when the trio from St. John's made it into Marystown and Blackmore became the last RCMP car in the procession. He parked and along with Windflower and Doctor Sanjay went to join the parade of police officers who were passing by the honour guard into the arena.

Inside, the place was packed, and since it was clear that not everyone could be seated in the arena for the ceremony, large speakers had been erected outside. Windflower and his crew found a seat on the last row of the section set aside for police officers. Even though neither he nor Sanjay were in that class, the other officers nodded and moved over to accommodate them.

Windflower hadn't planned on being here for this ceremony, but as anxious as he was to get home, he was very pleased to be present and to be part of it. It hadn't been that long since he was wearing the same uniform as so many around him, and even though he'd left, he still felt the pull of belonging to this community. That sense was never greater than when there was a crisis, an emergency, or in this case, something that had happened to one of their RCMP family.

A local singer began the ceremony with a chilling version of "Ave Maria," which the crowd soon learned from Kirk Forsythe was one of his late sister's favourite hymns. Kirk didn't speak long, but he gave everyone a bit more insight into the kind and courageous person that his family and this community had lost. The other special guests offered their public condolences to the Forsythe family and to the police officers gathered there. The final speaker was Superintendent Majesky.

Windflower had heard Majesky speak in public before and wasn't surprised by his ease and eloquence in delivering his remarks. But he did sense that there was something more in the superintendent's voice than sympathy as he spoke of the late inspector. That was interesting, he thought. And something to check with Tizzard about later.

He didn't have much more time to think, however, as the singer was back on stage to close out the program. This time she sang "Hallelujah" by Leonard Cohen. And for anybody who hadn't been moved to tears already, this was the moment. Windflower let the beautiful music wash over him and said his own silent prayer for the spirit of Diane Forsythe. That her journey to the other side be smooth and that she find peace and comfort at the end.

Windflower, Sanjay and Blackmore stood with the crowd as the exiting procession began, and after the dignitaries had departed, Windflower left Sanjay to go back to the car with Blackmore and sought out Tizzard. He found Tizzard with Carrie and Uncle Frank near the entranceway to the arena.

"Boy, that was something," said Uncle Frank.

"It was indeed," said Windflower. "How was your helicopter ride?"

"That was absolutely wonderful," said his uncle. "You could see everything as you were flying along. It was almost like you were an eagle."

"Great," said Windflower. "Are you coming back to Grand Bank with me?"

"Yes, b'y," said Uncle Frank. "I just have to get my bag, and then I'm ready to go."

"Why don't you help Frank get his stuff?" said Tizzard to Carrie.

"Sure," she said. "Come on, Frank. You can meet us over at the RCMP building."

She and Uncle Frank went back over to pick up his luggage. Windflower stayed with Tizzard, who was busily shaking hands with the other police officers who were now leaving the arena. When there was a break in that action, Windflower pulled him aside.

"Anything new on Bund and his buddy?"

"Mitchell is dead, and Bund is on the lam again. They found the body and the car in Montreal," said Tizzard. "Majesky thinks he may be flying somewhere down south."

"You talk to Majesky about all this?" asked Windflower.

"Yeah. Told him I was quitting as inspector," said Tizzard. "He just basically used all of us."

"It's always the same, Eddie," said Windflower. "Majesky looked a bit upset, emotional when he was giving his speech. Did you notice that?"

"I did," said Tizzard. "I think there was more than a collegial relationship between them."

"Interesting," said Windflower. "I think you are making the right decision, by the way. You're either all-in and in their way all-in, or you'll just get eaten up by them and the system."

Tizzard nodded. "You staying around for the reception?"

"Nah, we better get home," said Windflower.

"I don't have that luxury," said Tizzard.

"Have fun," said Windflower as another group of departing officers came to say hello to Tizzard. Outside the arena, Uncle Frank was chatting with Sanjay, and Evanchuk was making plans with Blackmore to get her cruiser back after he dropped his passengers off in Grand Bank.

"Is there anywhere to stay in Grand Bank?" asked Blackmore.

Windflower caught that last question and replied for Carrie. "There's a great little B&B," he said. "Right down by the water."

"He and his wife own and operate it," said Carrie. "It's very nice."

"And the food is superior," said Sanjay. "I can attest to that."

Windflower smiled at the support offered by his friends. The old B&B that he and Sheila had lovingly restored was a busy and bustling concern now. Levi and Beulah Stokes kept the place going and he and Sheila were happy to sit back and see their investment thriving.

"Great," said Blackmore. "I'll be back in the morning with your vehicle, and I'll talk to your boss about getting a ride to St. John's."

Windflower jumped in front with Blackmore; Uncle Frank and Doctor Sanjay were already chatting away in the back seat. Carrie left them and went to find Tizzard. She found Eddie near the front door to the reception, still glad-handing the guests. He looked exhausted but had his official smile pasted on. She got a chance to pull him aside.

"I'm going to get Hughie and go home," said Carrie.

"I'll be there as soon as I can," said Eddie. They couldn't kiss in public,

too unprofessional, so they settled for that lover's smile that meant everyone who had a pulse could see how much they loved each other.

He hoped he could get out relatively quickly, but as the senior officer
he was the host, and the host can't leave until at least the important guests
have left. By the looks of it, that might take some time. So he got himself a
few of the fancy sandwiches and a glass of club soda and did his best imi-
tation of a mix and mingle. Slowly, the VIPs started to make their exit. As
the crowd thinned, Tizzard noticed that Kirk Forsythe and Superintendent
Majesky were heavily engaged in a conversation in the corner.

Shortly after that, Kirk came up to him.

"Thank you for your assistance with all of this," said Forsythe.

"I didn't do much," said Tizzard. "Sergeant Murphy and Terri Pilgrim
did all the work."

"Please pass along my thanks to them as well," said Forsythe. "It has
been a hard week, but my family will always be grateful that Diane was
acknowledged in this way. And now I have some closure as well."

Tizzard was going to ask him about that, but the mayor was motioning
him to come over to talk to the MP who was standing beside him. Tizzard
shook hands with Forsythe and wished him a safe journey home. The may-
or engaged Tizzard and the MP in a long debate about how the municipal-
ity couldn't afford the pay increase that had been negotiated by the federal
government and the new RCMP union. Both the MP and Tizzard's eyes
glazed over as he droned on and on about a situation that neither of them
had any capacity to assist with.

As Tizzard extricated himself as gently as he could from that conversation, Majesky was waiting to talk with him. "Let's go back to the office,"
said Majesky. "Those who want to hang around now can do so on their
own." Tizzard did not disagree and followed Majesky as he led the way
back to the RCMP building and up to Tizzard's office. Once again, Majesky closed the door behind them.

42

"You're wasting your time if you're trying to convince me to stay," said Tizzard.

"You can do what you want," said Majesky. "But I want to give you some information that as the commanding officer of this area you should have. I just spoke to Kirk Forsythe. You are aware he was making enquiries about the paternity of the unborn child that Diane Forsythe was carrying. I told him that I was the sperm donor."

Tizzard tried to keep his jaw from dropping to the floor.

"I did this to spare the Force any further embarrassment, since Forsythe did tell me that his family would spare no effort or money to find answers to their questions," continued Majesky. "Diane and I were friends but not lovers. She asked me, and I agreed. That was a mistake. A serious error in judgement on my part."

Tizzard was still a little unsure how to respond before Majesky hit him with another stunner.

"I intend to resign my position, and if the Force agrees I will retire," said Majesky. "Not the way I wanted to end my career. But... In any case, I thought you should know."

"I'm sorry you have to leave," said Tizzard. "But I understand."

"I'm sorry, too," said Majesky.

Suddenly it felt to Tizzard like the whole world had shifted. He was in a superior position, at least morally, to the superintendent. And he wasn't sure if Majesky wanted anything from him.

"You're a good man, Tizzard," said Majesky. "Stay on that path. Be true to yourself."

Majesky stood and left his office. Tizzard thought for a few minutes about what he'd just heard and the final message Majesky had left with him. Then he closed his computer and walked back outside. That was just in time to first hear and then see Ted Reid pilot the RCMP helicopter high into the sky above him. Tizzard got in his car and drove home.

Windflower was already home and well into his second round of games with the girls.

"Be careful with Daddy. He's got a sore head," said Sheila. But that didn't seem to slow down his daughters' enthusiasm, and they continued to pile more pillows on top of him in advance of jumping all over him. When he finally came up for air, he begged off and went to see Sheila, who was putting the final touches on an apple pie.

"Dessert?" he asked hopefully as she put it in the oven.

"Sorry," she said. "It's for the United Church bazaar and bake sale on the weekend. "Come with me and we'll buy someone else's pie to take home."

"I'll be starving by then," said Windflower.

"Me, too," said Uncle Frank, who had come downstairs from his nap. The girls swarmed him, and he was quite content to let them hug and squeeze him as much as they wanted.

"I've missed you so much," said Uncle Frank. "Run upstairs in my room. There's two bags on the bed. One for each of you."

The girls did not have to be asked twice and raced upstairs. By the squeals that the adults heard from below, the girls were pretty pleased with what they found. They came down, each clutching a doll. "I think they're twins," said Stella.

"They are the kind of dolls that children had when we were young," said Uncle Frank. "You see they each have a deer-tail dress. The tattoos on their faces are like the ones the old people used."

"I love mine," said Amelia Louise.

"Me, too," said Stella. Both girls went to their great-uncle to give him a hug.

As the girls started playing with their dolls, Uncle Frank talked a little more about the dolls. "You'll notice that they are faceless."

"Why is that?" asked Sheila.

"There's an old story, not from my people, about a beautiful doll that was created and passed from community to community, where the doll was told how pretty she was. The doll became big-headed, and the Great Spirit punished her by making her faceless," said Uncle Frank. "In recent years, so many Indigenous women and girls were murdered or went missing that many people felt they were not just nameless but faceless as well. So a campaign started to make and share faceless dolls in their honour."

"That is so sad," said Sheila.

"It is," said Uncle Frank. "But now we have more awareness, and hopefully they will no longer be nameless and faceless, like these dolls."

"Where did you get them?" asked Windflower, thinking he might have got them from a doll-maker in his community.

"Where you get everything now," said Uncle Frank. "From the other great power, Amazon. What time is supper? I'd like to go see Jarge if I have time."

"What are we having?" asked Windflower.

All eyes turned to Sheila. "Well, Herb Stoodley dropped off half a dozen rainbow trout."

"Perfect," said Windflower. "I can grill them on the barbeque if you make a salad and some potatoes."

"Great," said Sheila. "Supper will be in an hour."

"See you then," said Uncle Frank. He left for his friend's house while Windflower went to inspect the trout in the fridge.

As Windflower was contemplating his fresh trout, Eddie Tizzard was walking around Marystown with his lovely bride by his side. Hughie was dozing in the stroller, and the day was glorious and sunny and warm.

"So, Majesky told me that he is the father of Diane Forsythe's baby," said Eddie. "Or he was going to be before the accident. Not an affair. He donated the sperm."

"What?" exclaimed Carrie. "That's a shock, but not a super surprise."

"I guess so," said Tizzard. "He was a logical choice, but I was still surprised."

"Why did he tell you that?" asked Carrie.

"I thought he was setting me up to stay. But instead, he's the one that's leaving," said Eddie.

"Now I'm surprised," said Carrie. "Leaving as super or from the RCMP?"

"Retiring," said Eddie. "If there's no discipline. And I don't think there will be. The Force will try to bury this one."

"That's quite a fall from grace for Majesky," said Carrie. "I have to admit I always thought he was one of the good guys."

"'Some rise by sin, and some by virtue fall,'" said Eddie.

"And all's well that ends well," said Carrie. "Let's get Chinese take-out for supper. I don't feel like cooking."

"Me either," said Tizzard. "Let's get him home, and I'll go pick it up."

Windflower was pretty happy with the trout Herb had delivered. Even better, they were cleaned and deboned. He'd even taken the heads off, which made Amelia Louise happy. She couldn't stand to look at dead fish. She said their eyes were always staring at her.

He'd seen a marinade for trout that he wanted to try out before putting them on the grill. It called for maple syrup, soy, vinegar, and a little olive oil with seasoning. He put together the mixture, adding some cayenne pepper and a little of the spicy paprika that had become his favourite spice. Then he put the marinade in a flat baking dish and laid the trout in the mixture and put them back in the fridge.

He had to find and clean the fish cage to put the trout in. He could put them directly on the grill, but then he might lose some of that precious fish. Better to be careful, he thought as he scrubbed the fish cage in the back sink while Sheila got the potatoes peeled and started in on the salad. The girls were watching TV, and for once the household was calm and relatively quiet.

43

He took the opportunity to go to Sheila and give her a quick hug and a shoulder rub while she was working at the kitchen counter.

"That will get you everywhere," said Sheila.

"Then, I'll remember to keep it up," said Windflower as he nuzzled into her neck.

"Are you kissing Mommy like a horse does?" asked Stella, who had drifted into the kitchen unannounced. "I saw horses on a TV show, and that's how they were kissing. Can I have a horse?"

"Mila wants a horse, too. A pony," said Amelia Louise.

"I don't think we're allowed to have horses in Grand Bank, are we, Mommy?" asked Windflower.

"Nice deflection," said Sheila. "No, girls, we're not allowed horses in town. It's a by-law."

"What's a by-law?" asked Amelia Louise.

"It's when the government lets some strangers decide what you are allowed to do on your own property," said Windflower.

"It's still the law," said Sheila. "I tried to change it when I was mayor. But the council was afraid of upsetting some people. No livestock, including horses, inside town property."

"That's stupid," said Windflower.

"Stoopid," said Amelia Louise.

"Now see what you've started," said Sheila, chasing him out of the kitchen with a dishcloth. His two girls were happy to grab their own and join in that fun. He managed to escape with Lady out to the deck. When he looked around, Molly had snuck out, too. She found a quiet and sunny place at the far end of the deck and lay down so that she could observe all proceedings.

Windflower started the barbeque and looked over at the cat. "I'll save some for you," he whispered as he went back in to get the trout and the fish cage. It seemed to him like Molly smiled back.

She was still watching him closely when he came back out with the trout in his fish basket and the remainder of the marinade in a bowl. Lady, on the other hand, had found something incredibly interesting under one of Sheila's rose bushes and was expending all her efforts on that front. Windflower smiled at the differences between the two pets, one calmly waiting for what she believed she deserved and the other frantically trying to get something that she probably shouldn't have.

He placed the basket on the grill on a medium heat, poured some of the juice over the trout and allowed the fish to brown on the bottom. He went back inside and popped open a beer to enjoy while he waited, an Iceberg Lager from his favourite brewery in St. John's, Quidi Vidi Brewery. It claimed to be made with pure iceberg water that was over twenty thousand years old. He didn't know about that, but he had to admit that it was "sum good b'y'."

After he had finished about half of his beer, he turned the basket over and poured the remainder of the marinade over the nicely browned skin of the trout. The aroma coming from the barbeque was amazing, and it was all he could do not to fork out a piece to try out the fish. He somehow resisted and drank the last of his beer. By that time, the trout looked perfect. He put the fish on a serving plate and called the pets to come in with him.

Lady trooped in quickly, and Molly dawdled along behind the Collie, never really taking her eyes off Windflower as he held the door open. "Don't worry," he said to the cat. "Yours is coming."

"Who are you talking to?" asked Sheila when he finally got inside. He ignored that question, since he couldn't really say he was talking with the cat.

"Aren't these gorgeous?" he said to Sheila.

"They are indeed," said Sheila. "Why don't you put some on our plates, and I'll get the potatoes and veggies?"

Windflower put one of the smaller trout on each of the girls' plates and a larger one for him and Sheila. As he was putting the remainder on the counter, he took a large forkful and put it in Molly's bowl. When Lady looked at him expectantly, he added a piece to her bowl as well. Just as he was about to sit down, Uncle Frank walked in.

"Right on time," said Uncle Frank as he sat at the table.

"You are indeed," said Windflower as Sheila passed him another plate and he put the largest trout in the pack on his uncle's plate.

"Why don't you say grace tonight?" Sheila said to Uncle Frank, who had a forkful of trout almost to his lips. He paused and finally laid down his utensil.

"Okay," said Uncle Frank. He closed his eyes for a moment. Then he spoke first in what sounded to the girls like a strange language. "You didn't understand what I said, did you?" he asked the girls, who were staring at him wide-eyed.

They both shook their heads.

"That was Cree. That's what your father heard when he was growing up," said Uncle Frank. "Although he has probably forgotten most of it by now. My prayer was in Cree. I said that I was grateful to be given another day. That I am healthy. That I am with all of you and that you are healthy. That I no longer put poison in my body and that I can now hear the singing birds and see the beauty in the world."

All the others around the table were now completely quiet, waiting to see if Uncle Frank had any other important words to tell them. He did. "Let's eat."

Eddie and Carrie were enjoying their Chinese food. He'd gotten the usual: chicken fried rice, beef chow mein, sweet-and-sour chicken balls and a double order of egg rolls. He also asked for extra red sauce, and while he skipped the chopsticks, he'd made sure they got their fortune cookies. Wouldn't want to miss that, he thought as he opened the bag and started laying the dishes out on the table.

Carrie put Hughie in his highchair and gave him a bowl with some rice and a very small piece of chicken ball, mostly just the outside pastry that he could chew on while they had their supper.

"I love this red sauce," said Eddie. "I don't know what's in it, but it is amazing."

"Me, too," said Carrie. "Everybody does. I looked it up one time. It said that it was a mixture of sugar, vinegar, and spices with the addition of pineapple juice and ketchup. That gives it the red colour."

"And some magic food colouring to make it glow in the dark," said Eddie.

Carrie laughed, and little Hughie laughed along, too. When they were finished, Eddie cleaned up the table and Carrie looked after the baby. He made them some tea that they sipped on in the living room while Hughie crawled around on the floor beneath them. "Dessert?" asked Carrie.

"What have you got?"

Carrie smiled and went to the kitchen. She came back with a box of May West cakes. "Since we were going bad, I thought we'd go all out," she said.

"I haven't had one of these in forever," said Eddie, tearing open the box and taking out an individually wrapped treat for each of them. They were large, round cakes with chocolate on the outside and a vanilla crème inside. He bit into his and exclaimed his delight. "This is so good. I can't believe my luck." Then he remembered something and got up and ran to the kitchen.

He came back with their fortune cookies.

Eddie opened his first. "'To thine own self be true,'" he read. "That's what Majesky said to me, too."

"Pretty clear message from the universe," said Carrie. She tore open her plastic package.

"What does it say?" asked Eddie.

"'Don't worry about money. The best things in life are free,'" she read.

"Isn't that the truth," said Eddie. As he spoke, Hughie started to fuss on the floor. That was Carrie's cue to put on his pajamas and get him his last bottle of the night. She came back fifteen minutes later, and they watched TV until they both realized how tired they were. Eddie turned out the lights and checked in one more time on the baby before going into the bedroom with Carrie.

44

As Eddie and Carrie were settling in for the night, Windflower was just coming back from the last walk with Lady. He filled the pets' bowls with water and their usual dried food. Molly came over to check if any more of that tasty trout was available. When it wasn't, she slunk back to her bed in the corner, giving Windflower what he perceived was a snarl along the way.

"That's not very nice," he said. "I gave you your share already."

Molly seemed to ignore that remark and closed her eyes, pretending to sleep.

"Oh well," said Windflower. He smiled his best fake smile just in case the cat could actually read his mind. But what came into that mind was a quote from science fiction master Robert Heinlein. He said it out loud to an attentive Lady, who was hoping for a treat. "'Women and cats will do as they please, and men and dogs should relax and get used to the idea.'" Seeing that a treat was not going to be on offer, Lady went to her corner and closed her eyes as well.

"Goodnight," said Windflower, and he turned out the lights and went to see Sheila upstairs.

"Who were you talking to?" asked Sheila.

This time Windflower did not try to evade the truth. "I was saying good-night to the pets."

Sheila laughed. "You are one crazy man."

"People think I'm crazy because I talk to my pets," said Windflower. "What am I supposed to do when they ask me a question?"

"Go to sleep, Winston," said Sheila.

Though miles apart, Windflower and Eddie Tizzard were both soon having the same experience: sleeping solidly in the arms of their loved one.

And the good news was that it lasted through the night for both of them.

Eddie was up first. He heard Hughie on the monitor and rose as quietly as he could without waking Carrie. He changed the happy little baby and warmed up his bottle. While Hughie had his milk, Tizzard checked his phone for messages. One was from Terri Pilgrim about trying to set up a meeting with the mayor. He deleted that one. It could wait until next week.

There was another from Murphy about an "incident," and he did put in quotes that it happened in the bar after the reception. Not a big deal, and he sorted it out but wanted to let Tizzard know in case there were any complaints. How bad was it? thought Tizzard. Then he deleted that one, too. His last message was from a strange number. Ontario, maybe Ottawa area code. He scrolled to the bottom to see who it was from. All it said was Ron. Ron who? He thought.

The first sentence gave it away. Hi Eddie, it's Quigley. It was Ron Quigley, a former inspector who Eddie had worked for in Marystown. He'd been transferred to Ottawa, where he was working on the national drug squad. What did Quigley want? Tizzard wondered. That would have to wait. The message talked a little about what he was doing and then said to call Quigley as soon as he got up.

Eddie took the empty bottle from Hughie and took him to the kitchen with him while he made coffee. He was just pouring the first cup when Carrie came out of the bedroom. He handed it to her and poured his own.

"I have to make a quick call," he said as he handed over Hughie. He called Quigley's number.

"Hey Eddie, how's it going? I hear congratulations are in order on your appointment," said Quigley.

"Thanks, Ron," said Eddie. "But the congrats may be premature. I'm quitting as inspector."

"Let's talk," said Quigley. "I might have to make you an offer you can't refuse. I'm at the airport heading to Halifax. I'm taking over as superintendent, at least temporarily. I need you to stay."

Tizzard started to say that his mind was made up, but Quigley cut him off.

"I need you, Eddie," said Quigley. "Will you at least think about it?" When Tizzard didn't immediately respond, Quigley jumped in again. "I'll call you again in a couple of hours. Just think about it. It'll be like old times."

"I'll think about it," said Tizzard. He started to say more, but Quigley cut him off again.

"Thanks, Eddie. I'll call you."

"Who was that?" asked Carrie

"A blast from the past," said Eddie. "Ron Quigley."

"What did Ron want?" asked Carrie. She had also worked with him in Marystown a few years back.

"He's coming back," said Eddie. "Not here. Halifax. To take over from Majesky."

"That was fast," said Carrie.

"I guess there's too much going on for them to leave that job vacant. Ron is coming by temporarily for now. He asked me to stay," said Eddie.

"What did you tell him?"

"I tried to say no, but he asked me to think about it," said Eddie. "He's going to call back later today when he gets to Halifax."

"Well, either way it sounds like you still have a job, and you've got me and Hughie." Hughie was grabbing for his daddy in Carrie's arms.

Tizzard took the baby and swung him over his head to great peals of laughter from Hughie. "I do indeed. Are you going to Grand Bank today?"

"I'm off," said Carrie. "My leave form is in your basket. Sergeant Windflower will have to look after Grand Bank by himself today."

Windflower was up early, too. The girls had decided to sleep in a little, and Sheila was happily joining them. He'd woken with the birds, and although he was tired, he felt the pull to get up. He went downstairs and put the coffee on. Molly barely stirred. She was clearly in the "what have you done for me lately?" camp. Lady, on the other hand, was overjoyed, and Windflower let her out to calm her down.

It was foggy this morning. Not unusual, even in summertime. But it was still nice and mild, and often the fog would burn off as the sun got warmer. Or it would be blown back out into the Atlantic Ocean. He hoped that would happen, because soon the warm sunny days would give way to the cooling breezes and much cooler days of autumn in these parts. He thought about getting his smudge kit. But today he reached up into the closet for his ceremonial pipe.

The pipe had belonged to his Auntie Marie, one of his touchstones in this world, in addition to helping him understand the dream world. She'd left it to him to care for and use as he needed. Today, after all he'd been through, he felt like that time was now. He went outside and unbundled the pipe from the blanket he had stored it in. He admired its long, hand-carved wooden handle and catlinite bowl. It was almost as if he could feel his aunt's presence as he touched her pipe. Now his pipe, he thought.

He put a pinch of sacred tobacco in the bowl and lit it with a wooden match. He took one puff to get it going and then watched as the smoke rose and cut through the fog above him. He tried to clear his mind of thoughts and let the smoke from the pipe envelope him. The combination of smoke and fog transformed his backyard into a hazy mist, but as he looked closer, he thought he could see a light emanating from the middle of the yard.

He could not see much, only shadows. But as he walked nearer, he could start making out shapes as well. There was a moose and a rabbit and a beaver and a large deer. They were all sitting or standing around a fire. Perched on a rock overlooking the fire was an eagle. It was the eagle that spoke.

45

"We have been watching you," said the eagle. "You like to live dangerously."

"I'm not doing it deliberately," said Windflower. It seemed to him that the other animals around the fire guffawed at that.

"Exactly," said the eagle. "Listen, we've all had to work our butts off to keep you safe."

"What do you mean?" asked Windflower.

"We sent several dreams to help you out. I followed you when you were with that crazy guy and told them where to find you," said the eagle.

"That was the GPS thingy," said Windflower.

"Oh, yeah, then how did they know you got taken in St. John's?"

"That was Uncle Frank, I think," said Windflower.

"After I knocked on his window ten times," said the eagle. "When are you going to understand that we are all connected and that every action has a reaction? In here and out there?"

Windflower had no answer for that. "Thank you for looking after me," he said after a moment's pause. "I know you are my allies and my friends."

As he spoke, he could feel the light growing dim, and the creatures and fire in front of him faded into the early morning fog. Lady was looking up at him and wondering what the heck was going on.

"It's okay, girl," he said. "Let's go inside."

Windflower put away the pipe and got himself a cup of coffee. He was surprised by the first person who came downstairs this morning.

"Good morning, Winston," said Uncle Frank. "You made coffee, great." He poured himself a cup and sat across from Windflower at the kitchen table.

"You're up early," said Windflower.

"It's funny," said Uncle Frank. "At my age you either can't stay awake or can't stay in bed. I was just lying there when I smelled the coffee. I thought you might be up."

"I'm glad you're here, Uncle," said Windflower. "We've missed you, and the girls are so happy when you are around."

"They bring me great joy," said his uncle. "I see you have been using the pipe."

"Sometimes," said Windflower. "I usually smudge, but this morning felt like a pipe morning."

"I know that feeling," said Uncle Frank. "I can hear my pipe calling me sometimes, too. Anything interesting today?"

"Just another great reminder to be grateful and that I am never really alone," said Windflower. "You got plans for today?"

"I thought I'd wander down to the wharf to catch up on the latest gossip," said Uncle Frank.

"Why don't you come with me this morning?" asked Windflower. "The doctor said I should be careful driving, and I have to go to Fortune to see the mayor. You can be my chauffeur."

"That would be grand," said his uncle. "But I hope there's breakfast first. I can't work on an empty stomach."

Windflower laughed. "Absolutely, Uncle. Bacon or bologna?"

"It's Newfoundland," said Uncle Frank. "I'll have bologna, Newfoundland steak."

Windflower laughed and took out the frying pan.

Carrie was already cooking breakfast while Eddie was playing with Hughie: pancakes with bacon. She piled a stack on Eddie's plate and laid a row of bacon rashers beside the pancakes. Eddie put a squirming Hughie in his highchair and tore off a piece of pancake for him. That settled him down.

Eddie took the maple syrup and poured a more than generous amount over his pancakes. He took a couple of bites and proclaimed their goodness to the chef.

Carrie smiled. "I love to see a man eat."

"In that case, I'm definitely your man," said Eddie.

"So, what are you going to tell Quigley?"

"Well, if it's okay with you, I'd like to tell him that I'll continue in the role while they find somebody." Carrie nodded, so he continued. "I'm pretty sure I don't want that job in the long term. Too much politics for me. But if I don't do it, we'll only end up with Murphy."

"Or worse," said Carrie. "I think it makes sense for now. If it gets too difficult, you can always back away."

"Thanks, Carrie, I really value your opinion," said Eddie. "I'm also going to call Windflower. He knows me better than I know myself sometimes."

"That's a good idea, too," said Carrie. "He does seem to have a good handle on the bigger picture."

"Exactly," said Eddie. "Can you pass me the maple syrup? I could use a little touch more."

Carrie laughed and handed it over. Eddie added his syrup and then gave Hughie another piece of pancake.

"He likes the syrup," said Eddie as the baby giggled and smeared syrup all over his face.

"Just like his father."

"Not a bad thing," said Eddie. "Could be worse."

"Could be indeed," said Carrie.

Meanwhile, over at Windflower's place the girls were showing Uncle Frank their latest library books in the living room while Windflower was setting the table for breakfast when Sheila came down.

"Good morning, beautiful," said Windflower. "Grab a coffee. Breakfast is almost ready."

"Wow, this is great service," said Sheila, pouring a cup of coffee for herself. "Thanks for getting up early. I really needed a few extra winks this morning. And breakfast, too. I'm impressed."

"Well, Uncle Frank helped by looking after the girls," said Windflower. "Come and get it."

Stella and Amelia Louise raced Uncle Frank to the table. They won, but not by much.

Windflower served everybody eggs, fried bologna and home fries while Sheila made sure both girls had a good helping of fruit to go along with all the carbs their daddy was providing.

"Pass me a slice of that toast, please," said Uncle Frank. "Is that the special molasses raisin bread from Goobies?"

"It is indeed," said Windflower. "I had to wrestle two little old ladies for the last loaf when we were coming through yesterday."

"Is that true, Daddy?" asked Stella.

"Your dad was just joking," said Sheila. "Right?"

"Yes, I was joking," said Windflower. "But I would have done so, if I had to."

"Winston," admonished Sheila. He was saved by the ringing of his cell phone. "Excuse me," he said and walked out to the living room to take the call.

46

"Winston, how are ya b'y?" asked Ron Quigley.

"I'm the best kind," said Windflower. "Nice to hear from you, Ron."

"I hear you got a new gig. How's that working out for you?"

"I only started this week, and in case you haven't heard, I have been doing RCMP proxy work all week," said Windflower.

"Haven't had my briefing yet," said Quigley. "I'm on my way to Halifax. Taking over as super for a few months."

"What happened to Majesky?" asked Windflower. "He was leading the charge the last time I checked."

"Don't have all the details on that yet either," said Quigley. "All I know is that he's out. Retired. And I'm moving in on a temporary basis."

"Well, if you get down here, we'll all be happy to see you," said Windflower.

"I have a favour to ask," said Quigley.

"Shoot," said Windflower. "Although I have to remind you that as I am no longer a member of the Royal Canadian Mounted Police, I reserve the right to say no. And Sheila holds a veto on all decisions."

Quigley laughed. "I may have something more formal for you to discuss with your new commander-in-chief, but for now I'd like you to talk to Eddie Tizzard."

"What do you want me to talk to Tizzard about, exactly?" asked Windflower.

"I want him to stay on as inspector," said Quigley. "I'm coming in blind, and I need someone down there to stabilize that region. Just for the short term."

"I think you should ask him that yourself," said Windflower.

"I have," said Quigley. "He's agreed to at least think about it. I told him I'd call him later today for his answer. I'm looking for back-up."

"I'll call him if you really want me to," said Windflower. "But I support whatever Eddie thinks is right for him and his family. I'm not going to pressure him."

"Fair enough," said Quigley. "I really appreciate your help. It will help me and the Force through a difficult period."

"Okay," said Windflower. "But 'I am not bound to please thee with my answer.' Or his, for that matter."

"Be brave, my friend," said Quigley. "Remember that 'our doubts are traitors and make us lose the good we oft might win by fearing to attempt.'"

Windflower tried to think of another Shakespeare quote to toss back at Quigley, one of their old-time passions, but before he could, the line went dead.

"Who was on the phone?" asked Sheila when he came back in.

"Ron Quigley," said Windflower. "He's moving back East. Taking over as Superintendent."

"What happened to Majesky?" asked Sheila.

"Ron didn't know, but I bet Tizzard will. Do you mind cleaning up? I'm going to give him a call," said Windflower.

"And I'm ready to go to work when you are," said Uncle Frank. "How much is the pay, by the way?"

"I think it will almost cover your room and board," said Windflower. This time he went outside to make his call, and of course, Lady snuck out with him. She went to do some further exploration under the rose bushes while he called Tizzard.

"Good morning, Sarge," said Tizzard. "You're on the go early. I thought you'd be in bed resting up."

"No rest for the wicked," said Windflower. "Ron Quigley called me."

"I had the same experience," said Tizzard. "Did he ask you to pressure me to stay?"

"He did, but I told him you could make up your own mind," said Windflower. "Have you?"

"I'm leaning towards staying on for a bit 'til they get someone else," said Tizzard. "What do you think?"

"That sounds reasonable, plus you could negotiate an arrangement with Quigley that works for you," said Windflower.

"That's good. I didn't think of that," said Tizzard. "I just don't want to be away too much, and I'd like to stay out of the politics."

"Well, tell him that," said Windflower. "By the way, what happened to Majesky? That's a bit of a shock."

Tizzard told him about Diane Forsythe and their arrangement. "I don't think he had much choice."

"That's something, isn't it?" said Windflower. "I guess we never really know people, do we? Is my sidekick coming over today?"

"She says there's a leave form in my in-basket," said Tizzard with a laugh. "So not today."

"Why don't you come over tomorrow, all three of you?" asked Windflower. "We'll go have por' cakes and pea soup at the Mug-Up."

"That sounds really nice," said Tizzard. "Unless something crazy happens, we'll be over."

Windflower and Lady went back inside, where Sheila was just finishing up the breakfast clean-up. Stella was standing on a chair putting plates in the cupboard while Amelia Louise was drying a cup and singing a song to herself.

"Great, you have helpers," said Windflower.

"We're trying," said Sheila. "But she's been drying that same cup for a while now," she added, pointing to Amelia Louise.

Windflower smiled and gave all three of his girls a kiss. He gathered up Uncle Frank, who was watching TV in the living room. "Ready to go?" asked Windflower. "Oh, and I invited Eddie to come over for por' cakes tomorrow," he said to Sheila.

"Is he okay?" asked Sheila. "There seems to be a lot of turmoil going on in Marystown."

"I think so," said Windflower. "He and Carrie and the baby will be over tomorrow, so you can find out for yourself."

"Let's go," said Uncle Frank. "I hope there's snacks along the way.

What time is break time anyway?"

"Wish me luck," shouted Windflower to Sheila as he and Uncle Frank went out to the car. The day was turning out to be better than Windflower had expected. The fog had almost completely disappeared back into the ocean from whence it had sprung, and the sun had warmed up the air considerably. Windflower lowered the window on the passenger side to let the fresh air stream in.

"It's a grand day to be alive," said Uncle Frank.

"It is indeed," said Windflower as they drove along the water's edge on the brief ride to Fortune. Once there, Windflower went to the town office, but the mayor wasn't in yet. He was expected in an hour or so. Windflower went outside, where his uncle was standing next to his car.

"How about we go for a bit of a drive?" said Windflower.

"Great," said Uncle Frank. "Which way?"

"Let's go down towards St. Lawrence," said Windflower.

They drove out of Fortune and into the wild barrens that made up most of this part of the world. As they drove, they drifted in and out of the fog that hugged the shore along the way. They passed through a series of small communities before taking a side road down to a little place called Point au Gaul. It wasn't a very big spot on the map, and its population couldn't have been more than a hundred, but Windflower knew some of the history of the place.

47

"There was once great sorrow in this place," said Uncle Frank. "You can feel it in the air."

"Yes," said Windflower as he and his uncle walked down towards the water, passing a giant foghorn along the way, feeling the cooling breeze of the fog on his face. "Back in 1929 a tidal wave hit the area around here. The water started rising around seven thirty in the morning. Giant waves swept in and swept out everything in their path. Twenty-eight people were killed on the Burin Peninsula. Right here, at Point au Gaul, they say that as many as a hundred buildings were taken away. Never to be seen again."

"The power of the ocean," said Uncle Frank. "Let's say a prayer for the spirits of those who once lived here. Some of them are still around."

Windflower stood silently with his uncle as they acknowledged the damage and loss that had taken place here so many years ago. Their reverie was broken by a very loud rumble that started low and grew into an unbearable noise. "Let's go," yelled Windflower as he and Uncle Frank scrambled back up the rocks and into their car just as the foghorn was ending.

"Let's go back to Fortune," said Windflower.

This time the mayor was in, and Uncle Frank did a walkabout on the wharf while Windflower spent a few minutes chatting with the mayor and the town manager about their policing needs.

"We don't have too many problems," said Mayor Jeremy Rose. "This time of year is the hardest, actually, because the kids are bored. They've run out of things to do."

"That's when we get most of the vandalism," said Peter Reddy. "And the summer programming is just about over."

Windflower listened carefully to the town officials and then spoke.

"Sounds like they need something to do."

"Like what?" asked the mayor.

"I don't know," said Windflower. "Maybe a small soccer tournament with some prizes for everybody. Not too competitive. Just for fun. All you need are a few balls and some pinnies. I can probably get Constable Evanchuk to help me set up registration, and if your staff can supervise, we can probably get going next week."

"That's a great idea," said Mayor Rose. "Why didn't we think of that?" he said to Peter Reddy.

"Maybe because we were focused on trying to stop the vandalism and really spending our time cleaning it up," said Reddy. "We've still got two students on staff who can help organize this, too."

"Okay, you set things up on your end. Put up a poster and pick a day early next week for registration. Let me know," said Windflower. He shook hands with both men and went to look for Uncle Frank. He found him sitting on the wharf next to a fishing stage, talking to one of the local fishermen. He and his new friend had a Styrofoam cup that looked like coffee, and the fisherman had laid an open tin on the bench between them.

"Winston, this is my new friend, Walter Hogan," said Uncle Frank. "He's a fisherman."

"Nice to meet you," said Windflower. "Winston Windflower."

"You used to be the police feller," said Hogan.

"Used to be," said Windflower. "Now I'm just helping out the town."

"Well b'y, they could sure use it," said Hogan. "Care for a biscuit? Me wife made them fresh this morning."

"Thank you," said Windflower. He took one of the tea biscuits out of the tin and took a nibble. "They are incredible. My compliments to your wife."

Hogan smiled, and the three men sat there in silence, enjoying the sunshine and their snack until Windflower finally stood up. "I guess we better be getting back," he said.

Uncle Frank left his friend with a promise to return and an offer of some fresh fish when he came back. "I'll be here, for sure. See ya."

"You make friends wherever you go," said Windflower as they were driving back to Grand Bank."

"It's easy," said his uncle. "You show them your hands are empty and you ask them questions."

"That's very wise," said Windflower.

"It's very simple," said Uncle Frank. "I just assume that everyone is 'nitotem,' my friend. They can decide otherwise, but I choose them as my friends."

Windflower laughed as they drove down to the wharf. When the old guys congregated there saw Uncle Frank get out of the car, they all came to greet him.

Windflower slid over to the driver's side.

"You okay to drive?" asked his uncle.

"I think I'm good now," said Windflower. "Thanks for your help. See you later."

Uncle Frank was now enveloped by his old buddies, and Windflower smiled as he left the wharf and drove home.

Eddie Tizzard had been hard at work all morning pushing paper and dealing with his subordinates, all of whom seemed to have a special request today. He finally got a break and walked outside the building. His cell phone rang, and he thought about not answering it. It was Ron Quigley.

"So, Corporal, you got an answer for me? A positive one, I hope," said Quigley.

"That depends on what you call positive," said Tizzard. "I'm prepared to stay on until you find someone, but I have some conditions."

Quigley readily agreed to Tizzard's conditions. "If I have to ask you to do more, I'll give you time to check with the boss at home."

"Okay, then I guess we have a deal," said Tizzard. "But I might kill a whole lot of my subordinates before I leave."

Quigley laughed. "I've got some information on Bund. He's back in Newfoundland."

"What?" said Tizzard. "I thought he flew the coop down to South America somewhere."

"Apparently not," said Quigley. "A guy was spotted trying to use a credit card with a link to Bund, stolen, of course. At the rent-a-car counter at St. John's airport. The card was refused, but by the time our guys got there, he had taken off in a taxi."

"Are the RNC guys on it now?" asked Tizzard.

"Terry Robbins is talking to Langmead. Is he the guy?" asked Quigley.

"Yeah, Carl Langmead. He's been working with me and Windflower on this all along," said Tizzard. "Have you talked with him?"

"No, I was hoping you could do that," said Quigley. "If you agreed to stay on, which you have."

"I'll call him right now and get back to you."

"Good morning, Inspector," said Langmead. "How can the Royal Newfoundland Constabulary help you today?"

"Now, that's the attitude I'd like my crew to have," said Tizzard. "You looking for a new job?"

Langmead laughed. "No, b'y," he said. "I got my hands full here. I assume you're calling about our world traveller, the elusive Mister Bund. I already talked to Robbins."

"Yeah, now I'm calling for the upper levels," said Tizzard.

"Majesky?" asked Langmead.

"He's out," said Tizzard. "Ron Quigley is the new superintendent."

"In any case, we've tracked down the cab driver who took Bund from the airport. He dropped him off at a house downtown. A place that is well known to us. A biker hangout. But he's not there."

"Where is he?" asked Tizzard.

"We're looking," said Langmead. "I got a call from the chief to say we had unlimited resources, so we've got twenty guys on the street looking for him. There are few places to hide and even fewer ways to get out of St. John's."

"That's interesting," said Tizzard. "Only a few ways out... Didn't Bund have a boat lined up? What's going on with that?"

"Good question," said Langmead. "We kind of left that lead alone once he took off in the helicopter. But let me get on it and get back to you."

Tizzard thought about Bund and how much chaos he had caused along the way. Probably killed two people already and might still do more damage unless they could find him. But he didn't have any more time to think.

Terri Pilgrim was standing in his office doorway as he tried to leave. "The mayor is here," she said.

Before she could stop him and before Tizzard could escape, Mayor Keith Hynes barged into his office. "Somebody's got to do something about this," said Mayor Hynes.

"Come in and sit down," said Tizzard. "Would you like a coffee?"

48

Windflower was back at the house and had already been assigned to childcare duty. Sheila had a meeting with some of her suppliers and needed some peace and quiet. That wasn't possible with two little kids running around, so Windflower was given directions to take them out, as quickly as possible.

"Let's go for a hike," he suggested.

Both girls looked at him with so much disappointment that he added an extra. "Maybe we'll get ice cream on the way back."

Their spirits lifted considerably, Stella and Amelia Louise grabbed their knapsacks while Windflower got a couple of bananas and juice packs to put in his bag. They drove to the hospital with Lady in tow and headed for the trail that led up Farmer's Hill.

"Did they really have farms here one time?" asked Stella.

"With horses?" asked Amelia Louise.

"Yes, years ago all the area on the way to where the trail starts was farms," said Windflower. "This is where they grew all their vegetables, and I do believe they did have horses. Although they were working horses, not riding ones."

"I would still ride one," said Amelia Louise.

"Me too," said Stella.

Lady broke up this conversation by starting to run around to show how happy she was. She was so excited that she didn't see a rabbit, actually a snowshoe hare, pretending that neither the dog nor the humans existed. It stood perfectly still; not even a whisker twitched while it hoped that these larger creatures would pass by.

Windflower saw the rabbit and pointed it out to the girls, who thought they could try and touch it, like a pet rabbit they had seen one time at a neighbour's. But as soon as they got close, the animal jumped, hopped and was gone in a flash. Only then did Lady realize she had missed something and went frantically running into the brush. But the hare was long gone, much to her dismay and that of the girls.

That excitement over, the hike continued up to the top of the hill. Windflower took the bananas and drinks out of his bag and shared them. He took a moment to look out over Grand Bank from this perch near the peak of the trail. It looked so calm, so serene, nestled in and around the harbour where people and boats had worked and lived for hundreds of years. He said a quiet prayer of gratitude for the opportunity to live in such a paradise with his beautiful wife and two healthy children.

His period of reflection was broken by a very noisy Lady, who was busily engaged in rooting something out under the boards of the lookout.

"Hey, Lady, what's going on?" he called out.

Lady had found a white plastic bag. Windflower managed to get it away from the Collie with some difficulty, and when he did, it broke open. Lying on the ground were three sealed baggies with what looked like diamonds inside. Maybe ten times as many as what they had found before in Sanjay's secret hideaway at the clinic.

"Are they jewels?" asked Stella, who had come to take a closer look.

Her little sister was, as always, not far behind. "Are they jools, Daddy?"

"I don't know, but we'll take them back and check them out," said Windflower. "Now, let's go down the hill and get our ice cream."

Going down was much faster, especially with the prize of ice cream waiting for them. Minutes later, they were in the line-up at the dairy bar. Both girls wanted identical caramel sundaes with a little whipped cream and a cherry on top.

Windflower was waiting in line to order his Moose Tracks cone and the sundaes when he heard a familiar voice. It was Doc Sanjay and Repa along with their son, Anil.

"Winston, how's she going b'y?" said Sanjay. "You remember Anil."

"Nice to see you again," said Windflower. "And very nice to see you, too, Repa."

"Thank you again, Sergeant," said Repa. "We are so happy to have him home and safe."

"I'm glad he's safe, too," said Windflower.

"Let me buy your treats," said Sanjay. "It's the least we can do."

Windflower tried resisting, but that was futile. Both Repa and Doctor Sanjay insisted.

The girls and Repa and her son got their order first and started walking away from the dairy bar. "We're just going up to the park," said Repa. "Come and join us."

"We'll be there in a minute," said Windflower as he and the doctor got their cones and went across the road to sit on the steps of an abandoned garage. "I need to talk to you about something," said Windflower. When they were well away from the ice cream place and prying eyes, he took one of the sealed baggies out of his knapsack.

"Oh, my goodness," said Sanjay. "More diamonds."

"I know," said Windflower. "The dog found a bag with three pouches like this inside. I guess my big question after all we've been through is are they real?"

"That's important," said the doctor. "There's several ways to tell." Windflower looked at him strangely. "I looked it up," said Sanjay. "Although I never expected to have to use that knowledge."

"Me either."

"I'm guessing you don't have a magnifying glass," said the doctor.

"Not on me."

"Let's try this then," said the doctor. He went back across the road to the dairy bar and came back with a glass of water. "Give me one of the diamonds."

Windflower opened the baggie and carefully took out one of the larger gems. He passed it to Doctor Sanjay, who dropped it into the water. The stone started to fall and then floated to the top of the glass.

"It fails the first test," said the doctor. "Real diamonds are much heavier than water and would sink to the bottom. But that test is not foolproof. Let's try one more. Can I have another stone?"

This time the doctor took the diamond and put it between his fingertips. "This is called the fog test." He put his fingers with the gem directly in front of his mouth and blew on it. Windflower watched carefully as the stone started to fog up. It stayed fogged up for what seemed like a long time and then cleared.

"Fake," pronounced Doctor Sanjay. "Real diamonds can conduct heat and thus disperse that fog right away. Of course, you will have to check with a professional."

"Thank you, Doc," said Windflower. "That is indeed my intention."

The men finished their ice cream and walked to the park, where the girls were playing on the swings under Repa's watchful eye. Windflower thanked Repa and went back to get their car and drove home. Sheila was finishing up her calls and offered to take the girls to Riff's, the local discount store. The girls were thrilled and Windflower relieved that he could continue to investigate the diamonds, or whatever they were, that Lady had uncovered.

He called Eddie Tizzard in Marystown, but of course he was in a meeting. He left a message with Terri Pilgrim and went to see Betsy Molloy.

49

"**H**i, Betsy," said Windflower when he arrived. "Did we keep any fingerprint kits?"

"For sure," said Betsy. "You never know when you might need one of those. I kept one of just about everything and five fingerprint kits. I know how useful they can be. Let me get one for you."

Betsy went to the back and came back with the fingerprint kit.

"Thank you, Betsy," said Windflower. He tore open the package under Betsy's watchful eye. Then he took out the baggies from his knapsack.

"Are they diamonds?" asked Betsy.

"We think they're fake," said Windflower. "But I'm hoping that we can get prints off the bags so that we can trace the owner."

He sprinkled some powder on one of the bags and used the brush to spread it over the surface. Then he blew away the excess powder and could see a few prints were visible. He used the tape to lift the fingerprints and placed them on a card.

"Here you go, Betsy," he said. "Can you scan them and send them to Terri Pilgrim in Marystown? Ask her to run them through the system and give the results to Inspector Tizzard."

"I'll tell Terri to let me know if they find anything," said Betsy.

"You're the best," said Windflower. "I'm going to leave these bags with you for safekeeping."

Betsy beamed and went off with the prints and the baggies.

Eddie Tizzard had almost gotten out of his office after the meeting with the mayor when one of his sergeants came in and wanted to talk about the leave schedule for the fall. Tizzard would rather get his eyes poked out than deal with this, but he stayed and listened as the sergeant droned on. Finally, Terri came in to rescue him.

"You are going to want to hear this," she said.

Tizzard apologized to his sergeant and shooed him out. "I support whatever decision you make," he said as the other officer was leaving.

"What's up?" he asked Pilgrim.

"I talked to Betsy Molloy," said his assistant. "Sergeant Windflower found three bags of jewels in Grand Bank. He thinks that they may not be real. But he got some prints off the bags, and I ran them through. The prints match somebody named Robert Smart. A lot of red lights went off when I punched it in. And there are several calls from HQ and an email from Interpol." She handed him several yellow message slips.

Tizzard called Ron Quigley.

"Hey, Eddie, what's up?" asked Quigley. "I'm just on my way to my office. I have to find it first. It's somewhere in an industrial park in Dartmouth."

"Good luck with that," said Tizzard. "We've had some more diamond developments."

"What is it with you guys and diamonds?" asked Quigley. "So, what's going on?"

Tizzard ran through what he knew and suggested Quigley talk to Windflower for more detail. "But you'll have to deal with HQ and whatever is going on with that Robert Smart guy. I thought he was working with us."

"All new to me," said Quigley. "But you can send the HQ guys to me. Did you say Interpol was involved, too?"

"That's what my admin said," said Tizzard. "Said everybody was interested in Robert Smart."

"Okay," said Quigley. "Anything from the RNC on Bund?"

"Langmead is on it," said Tizzard. "He's clearly in the St. John's area, but nobody knows where. Or his next move."

"Stay on Langmead," said Quigley. "I'll check in later."

Tizzard gave the message slips back to Terri Pilgrim and once again tried to leave his office when his cell phone rang again. He took a quick peek. It was Carrie.

"You hungry?" she asked.

"Famished."

"Want some macaroni and cheese?" asked Carrie.

"I'll be right there," said Tizzard. He waved goodbye to Pilgrim, scooted out of the building before anyone else could stop him and raced home.

Windflower was full from his banana and ice cream but still didn't need much encouragement to join the girls in a tea party with real cookies that Sheila had taken out of the freezer. He was having quite a relaxing time when Ron Quigley called.

"Mister Superintendent," said Windflower as he recognized the number.

"Can I still call you Sergeant?" asked Quigley.

"Everybody else does," said Windflower. "I'm tired of trying to stop them."

"'If we are true to ourselves, we can not be false to anyone,'" said Quigley.

"Ah," said Windflower. "'To thine own self be true.'"

"Indeed," said Quigley. "I'm calling you about diamonds. Tizzard says you have some."

"Well, we have three bags of something," said Windflower. "Doc Sanjay did the water test on them, and they failed. But I don't know for sure."

"Can you get them to Marystown?" asked Quigley. "Then they can be couriered to HQ."

"Would tomorrow be okay?" asked Windflower. "Eddie and Carrie are coming over in the morning."

"Oh, yeah, Saturday in Grand Bank," said Quigley. "Pea soup and por' cakes. I miss that. The jewels are secure?"

"Absolutely," said Windflower. "In the safest hands in Grand Bank."

"That has to be Betsy Molloy," said Quigley. "Okay, then. Thanks for talking to Tizzard, by the way. You know he's agreed to stay on."

"I didn't do anything and would have supported any decision he made," said Windflower. "He'd already had his mind made up when I talked to him."

"Anyway, it's a big relief. 'I can make no other answer but thanks, and thanks,'" said Quigley.

"'But where there is true friendship, there needs none,'" replied Windflower, but once again Quigley had hung up with the last word.

Windflower went back to the tea party, which was just wrapping up. The girls were now focused on discussing what movie they were going to watch. Friday night was movie night at the Windflower-Hillier household. The girls got to pick a kids' movie for early viewing, and Windflower and Sheila would find one for themselves after the children had gone to bed.

The girls were having their debate, and it seemed to be narrowing down to *Tom and Jerry* as proposed by Stella and *Clifford the Big Red Dog* argued by Amelia Louise. They tried to get their father to choose sides, but he wisely went to the kitchen to help Sheila clean up their tea party dishes.

"Supper?" he asked.

"I thought we'd just have hot dogs," said Sheila. "I got some fresh corn, too. Something fast and simple. It's been a long week."

"That sounds great," said Windflower. "I think we all need a break."

50

Someone else who needed a break but couldn't quite get there was Eddie Tizzard. He had spent the last couple of hours with Terri Pilgrim going over leave charts and finances. He was bug-eyed from the numbers and happy when Carl Langmead phoned to give him a break from that mind-numbing activity. He told Terri to pack up and go home and picked up his phone.

"Carl, what's the good news?" he asked. "Have you got our bad guy yet?"

"Not yet, but we're on his trail," said Langmead. "We got a tip that he's hanging around with the bikers, and we've got a watch on the Outlaws clubhouse in Mount Pearl. No sign of him yet, but if he shows, we're ready."

"Great," said Tizzard. "Anything on the boat?"

"That's an interesting situation," said Langmead. "Apparently the owner has left town but has conveniently stocked the boat with a full locker, including food, liquor and a loaded shotgun with lots of ammunition."

"That is interesting," said Tizzard. "Keeping an eye on that, too?"

"Absolutely," said Langmead. "Our marine crew is on the water, and Terry Robbins has sent a team to monitor the shore side. I think we've got it covered."

Tizzard hung up with Langmead, turned out his lights and closed his door. He was ready to go home and relax. But he couldn't help thinking that they'd had Bund cornered and covered several times before, and he managed to somehow get away. A more pleasant thought was that it wasn't his problem tonight. An even better thought was seeing Carrie and Hughie and having some good, quality family time.

He drove the short distance home with a gigantic smile on his face. That only grew wider when he opened his front door.

Windflower handed out the hot dogs and corn while Sheila poured drinks. The movie debate had ended peacefully. *Tom and Jerry* tonight, *Clifford* the next possible movie opportunity. Stella had thrown in an old doll that Amelia Louise had coveted to seal the deal.

"Good negotiation skills," said Windflower to Sheila as he picked up drinks to bring around to the girls.

"They're starting to work things out on their own," said Sheila. "And that's a very good thing."

The girls were busy chatting and playing with their food, and that gave the adults a chance to talk.

"So, what's new with you?" Windflower asked. He had learned to ask the first question. Other people, especially your person, would love that, and he could eat his supper and listen.

"Things are good," said Sheila. "The business is really taking off. We have twenty-five suppliers producing all kinds of knitted and home-made items, and we are getting lots of online orders since we got our social media accounts running."

"Facebook?" asked Windflower, finishing off his second hot dog.

"That's good, but more for interaction than sales," said Sheila. "Our customers, who are primarily women, love Instagram. I think because it's all pictures. How are you feeling after your big adventure?"

"I'm good," said Windflower. "Headache is just about gone, and I feel much better. Not sure how many more adventures I have in me."

"None would be good as far as I am concerned," said Sheila. "Don't let Ron Quigley talk you into anything."

"He hasn't asked for anything except to try to get Tizzard on board," said Windflower.

"Yet," said Sheila. "What is Eddie going to do?"

"He's going to stay on until they can find a permanent replacement," said Windflower. "I think he was more afraid of who they would appoint if he didn't take it."

"Are you talking about Unca Eddie?" asked Stella.

"Is he coming to visit?" asked Amelia Louise.

Without waiting for an answer to their questions, the girls started marching around the kitchen, chanting, "Unca, Unca, Unca."

"I'll clean up while you put the movie on," said Sheila.

Windflower picked up both girls and carried them to the living room.

Uncle Eddie Tizzard was having a great time with Carrie and little Hughie. They'd had a simple supper too, fish sticks and French fries, and the baby had more ketchup on his face than Eddie thought was in the bottle. He cleaned him up while Carrie warmed a bottle. She gave him half now and saved the other half for when he'd had his bath and was ready for bed.

The bath was Eddie's job. He ran it warm and filled it with bubbles, just the way Hughie liked it. The way he liked it, too. After bath time, he put the baby into pajamas and delivered him to his mommy for the rest of his bottle. Fifteen minutes later, Hughie was sleeping peacefully in his mother's arms. Eddie gently extracted him and brought him into his crib. He kissed him goodnight and went back to see Carrie.

She was flipping through the guide on the TV. She found *The Amazing Race*, the Canadian version. Both she and Eddie loved this show. It had finally come back online after being postponed during the pandemic. In this episode, contestants were in downtown Vancouver and had to find a package in the dangerous Hastings and Main area and deliver it to the airport before the other teams. It was always frantic and always fun.

After the show, Carrie made another pot of tea, and Eddie just lounged around playing on his phone. They found a *Bourne* movie on TV and enjoyed as much of that as they could before they admitted that they had done all they could for the day, turned out the lights and went to bed. Even though it was early, Eddie fell asleep quickly and did not move a muscle until he heard Hughie in the morning.

Windflower's night was pretty peaceful, too. After the girls' movie and putting them to bed, he and Sheila watched some TV, and he took Lady for a quick walk around the block. Sheila was already in bed, reading, when he got back. He joined her and tried to read too, but that didn't last long. He vaguely remembered Sheila turning off the lights and not much more.

Until he woke up in a dream. This time he was flying. Well, he wasn't really flying. He was on the back of a giant eagle, and they were flying over what he soon recognized was St. John's. He could see the harbour and Signal Hill, and as the eagle swooped lower, he could see the Basilica and the RNC headquarters building. The eagle went down even farther, and Windflower could see people on the ground and almost make out their faces.

The eagle rose up again and headed what Windflower felt to be west, and he was right. Soon, they were over the Waterford Valley and past Bowring Park, where they'd just missed getting Frederick Bund. On the eagle flew, and as they were descending again Windflower recognized Mount Pearl, and on its outskirts, an industrial park. Donovan's Industrial Park. As they came even closer to the ground, Windflower could see motorcycles outside one of the units on a dead-end street.

The eagle landed, and Windflower carefully dismounted. The doors to the building looked reinforced, and there were closed shades on all the windows. He stepped back when the doors opened, and a couple of men staggered out into the light. But they didn't appear to notice him. Of course. He was in a dream. The men got on two of the motorcycles and started them up. As they drove away, Windflower noticed the patches on their vests.

Outlaws was written across the top. In the middle was their well-known skull trademark and *Canada* in large letters across the bottom. The eagle swooped down, and Windflower could see even more detail, like the men's faces. Even with sunglasses and a motorcycle helmet, he recognized one of them as Bund. The eagle trailed behind the motorcycles as they left the industrial park, and Windflower was able to catch a glimpse of the second man on a motorcycle behind Bund. He knew him but couldn't quite place him.

Then it came to him. That was Robert Smart, the dead man at the B&B. Or the one he had thought was dead. But he was gone to Europe or somewhere, wasn't he? The motorcycles got on the highway and headed down towards St. John's. Before they got there, they turned off on the Southern Shore Highway. As they took this exit, the eagle continued on the highway towards downtown. Windflower tried to get the eagle to turn around, but the bird not only wouldn't turn back, it started flying higher. When it reached the clouds, it lifted its wings and Windflower fell off, tumbling over and over.

He started to fall, but it was more like floating, and instead of coming directly down, he kind of drifted and drifted until he finally woke up back in his bed with Sheila.

It was light but still quiet around the house. He crept downstairs and let Lady out in the backyard. He got his phone and joined her moments later. It was early, but he took a chance that Eddie Tizzard might be up. He was correct.

51

Eddie had been up for an hour already with Hughie and was happily watching his little boy crawl all over the carpet in the living room. He had to be vigilant, since the kid could really scoot along now. Hughie was pulling himself up on tables and anything else that would hold his weight. Eddie was surprised when his cell phone rang. He took a quick peek at the number.

"Morning, Sarge, what gets you up early?"

"I had a dream," said Windflower. Then he paused, realizing that once again he was about to talk about something that he wasn't one hundred percent sure was true. But his instincts propelled him forward as Eddie waited on the other end of the line.

"What happened in the dream?" asked Tizzard. He tried to sound as normal as possible in what seemed like an abnormal situation.

Windflower decided to just spill the beans. "I saw Bund in the dream. And I think I saw Robert Smart as well. Isn't that weird?"

Tizzard didn't really want to answer that question. "That's interesting. That would mean Robert Smart may not be the friend we thought he was and in fact is a person of interest for multiple police forces across the globe. Where did you see Bund and Smart?"

"It was in Donovan's Industrial Park," said Windflower. "Looked like an Outlaws clubhouse."

"Langmead said that they thought Bund might be hooked up with the bikers," said Tizzard. "Were they coming or going?"

"Going," said Windflower. "It seemed like they were heading up the Southern Shore Highway." He omitted the parts where he was flying with the eagle. That might be too much, even for a friend like Eddie.

"Even more interesting," said Tizzard. "That boat Bund had leased is up that way. Petty Harbour, I think."

"Okay," said Windflower. "What are you going to do with what I just told you?"

"I'm going to phone Langmead," said Tizzard. "Is that okay?"

"Are you going to tell him about my dream?" asked Windflower.

"You think I'm crazy?" said Tizzard with a laugh. "I'm going to say our intelligence says that Bund and maybe even Smart are with the Outlaws. And that they might be heading for that boat."

Windflower laughed nervously. "Do you think I'm crazy?"

"Yes, but I've known that for a long time," said Tizzard, this time laughing harder than the first time. "We'll see you later today for por' cakes."

Windflower hung up and went inside with Lady. Two little girls in pajamas were waiting for him.

"There's a bear in Uncle Frank's room," said Stella.

"A big bear," said Amelia Louise.

"Okay, let's take a look. But we have to be very quiet," said Windflower. He led them upstairs as the trio tip-toed towards the spare bedroom where Uncle Frank slept.

He had to admit two things. First, it was very loud. Secondly, it did sound what he thought a bear might sound like, if it was snoring. The girls wanted him to open the door and look inside, but he resisted. "It's just your Uncle Frank snoring."

"Are you sure?" asked Stella.

"I think it's a big bear," said Amelia Louise.

Windflower couldn't convince them otherwise but did manage to get them downstairs again without waking Sheila. "Let's have some fruit, and you can watch TV. Then I'll make waffles." All worries about wild animals seemed to vanish with that offer, so Windflower made them each a fruit bowl and put on a large pot of coffee for himself and Sheila. When they were all organized in front of the TV, he and Lady went back outside. This time he brought his smudging kit.

His first thought as he went back outside was that he had a lot to be grateful for. As he filled his bowl with his sacred medicines, he thought about how Eddie Tizzard had listened and not judged him about his dreams. That was true friendship. He also peeked back in through the patio doors at the two happy and healthy little girls who were smiling and eating their fruit together. That was joy. Then as he lit the mixture, he saw Lady staring back up at him. That was loyalty and pure love. He truly did have a lot to be grateful for.

After smudging and a few more prayers of gratitude, he went back inside and got his waffle mix ready.

Eddie Tizzard waited until Carrie got up before making his call to St. John's. Carl Langmead wasn't around yet, so he left a message. He called Ron Quigley next. Quigley was up. He was always up, thought Tizzard.

"Inspector, how are you this fine morning?" said Quigley.

"I'm well," said Tizzard. "Just wanted to give you a quick update. We have some reports of Bund being in St. John's and with the bikers. No surprise there. But we've also heard that Robert Smart is there as well."

"With Bund?" asked Quigley.

"Appears so," said Tizzard. "I've got a call into Langmead to follow up. They might be heading for a boat that Bund had rented some time ago."

"Where's the boat?" asked Quigley.

"Petty Harbour, I think," said Tizzard.

"Okay, I'll start lining up our resources from this end," said Quigley. "We'll send Ted Reid back with the chopper for reconnaissance, and I'll talk to the Coast Guard. How competent are the RNC?"

"Langmead is great," said Tizzard. "But they've let Bund slip away a couple of times now."

"Well, we haven't exactly been stellar on that count," said Quigley. "I'll talk to Terry Robbins as well. If I need you, can you go to St. John's?"

"Not today," said Tizzard. "I need a day off. But if you need me, I can go tomorrow."

"Thanks, Eddie," said Quigley. "I appreciate it. Enjoy your por' cakes."

"Everything okay?" asked Carrie when Eddie finished his call. "You're not going to work, are you?"

"No, my dear," said Tizzard. "We're going to Grand Bank for por' cakes. Aren't we, buddy?" With that he took Hughie and swung him over his head. The little boy squealed with laughter, so he did it several more two happy and healthy little girls who were smiling and

"Breakfast?" asked Carrie.

"I thought you'd never ask," said Eddie.

52

The Windflower clan was just finishing up their breakfast when Uncle Frank came downstairs. "Did I miss it?" he asked.

"No," said Windflower. "I've got a little batter left that I can make you a waffle with if you'd like."

"That would be grand," said Uncle Frank. "What's the big plans for today?" he asked Stella and Amelia Louise.

"We're going for por' cakes," said Stella."

"And a brassar," said Amelia Louise.

"It's a bazaar at the church," said Sheila as she poured Uncle Frank a cup of coffee.

"That's what I said," said Amelia Louise.

"Why don't you girls go clean up your toys and put them in the toy box?" said Sheila.

"That usually means they want to talk grown-up stuff," said Stella under her breath to Amelia Louise as they went to the living room.

"How are you feeling these days?" asked Sheila. "It must be hard without Auntie Marie."

"It is," said Windflower's uncle, growing quieter. Windflower placed his waffle on his plate and Sheila passed over the berries and maple syrup.

"It's like a piece of you isn't there anymore," said Uncle Frank. "I know that she is in a good place, but I do miss her." He took a bite of waffle and pronounced it wonderful.

After a few more bites, he started speaking again. "It's also a vivid reminder that we are just passing through this place. It was always temporary, but we pretend that this is all there is."

"But you'll be around for a while longer," said Windflower, speaking more quietly so as not to alert the girls in the living room.

"I am on my final miles," said Uncle Frank. "I wasn't going to tell you this." He paused for another moment. "I have a growth. A tumour."

"Oh, Frank," said Sheila.

"Don't be sad or feel sorry for me," said Uncle Frank. "My moccasins are nearly worn out from my journeys. But I wanted to come back here for one more visit. To see you and the girls and my friends."

Sheila and Windflower sat in stunned silence.

"Is there anything they can do?" asked Sheila.

"Only what we all can do," said Uncle Frank. "Pray. Not that I be given a miraculous cure, but that I have the strength to go through what I have to go through."

"We will do that," said Windflower. "Auntie Marie will help you."

"I know," said Uncle Frank. "The good news is that I still have my appetite." He finished off his waffle while Sheila and Windflower cleaned up.

"You want to come for por' cakes?" asked Windflower.

"I have to go see Jarge," said his uncle. "But I may catch up with you at the Mug-Up later."

"That would be good," said Sheila. "Eddie and Carrie and the baby are coming, too."

"I'll make sure I get there, then," said Uncle Frank. "See you around noon."

Windflower and Sheila watched as Uncle Frank ambled down their driveway to visit his friend.

"You okay?" asked Sheila, knowing that Uncle Frank was Windflower's last living close relative.

"I'm okay," said Windflower. "And I know he said not to, but I still feel sad."

"It's okay to be sad," said Sheila. "It's just a feeling. There's a great quote by the Indian poet Osho. It really helped me after my mom died. Let me get it." She ran upstairs and came back with a notebook. She found the page she was looking for and read from it.

"'Sadness gives depth. Happiness gives height. Sadness gives roots. Happiness gives branches. Happiness is like a tree going into the sky, and sadness is like the roots going down into the womb of the earth. Both are needed, and the higher a tree goes, the deeper it goes, simultaneously. The

bigger the tree, the bigger will be its roots. In fact, it is always in propor-
tion. That's its balance.'"

"Wow," said Windflower. "But I'm still sad."

"That's okay," said Sheila. "But I think we should also try to make the
best of the time we do have with Uncle Frank."

"Good reminder," said Windflower.

"I'll clean up while you go have your shower," said Sheila.

He went to Sheila, and they held each other for a long time. Long
enough to attract Lady from her bed and their daughters from the living
room. After the group hug that ensued, Windflower finally got his shower
and the opportunity to reflect on what his uncle had told him.

As he towelled off, he thought about the many acts of kindness Uncle
Frank had shown him over the years. Besides his grandfather, Uncle Frank
was one of the few consistent male role models in his life. Yes, his uncle
had had his struggles with the bottle, and that had caused more than a few
embarrassing incidents. But his recovery from addiction and the desire to
live a positive life was still inspiring to Windflower. He would miss him.

His next thought was that he wasn't dead yet. Not even close. So, instead of focusing on the loss that was to come, why wouldn't he celebrate
and enjoy this time with such a special relative? Windflower came out of
the bathroom feeling happy at that thought.

He was still smiling when he came back downstairs.

Sheila noticed. "Your mood has certainly changed."

"'Death, a necessary end, will come when it will come,'" he said. "I
have peace about that."

"And we try to live our lives anyway," said Sheila.

"Exactly," said Windflower. "How about a walk before we try and eat
again?"

"That sounds like a plan," said Sheila. She rounded up the girls, threw
a bottle of water and two boxes of raisins in a bag and was ready to go. So
was Lady, who was waiting with Windflower on their front steps.

"Let's go down to the beach," said Windflower.

53

While Windflower and Sheila and their gang were heading out for their walk, Eddie and Carrie were packing up their car to come over to Grand Bank.

Eddie strapped Hughie in his car seat and helped Carrie load the stroller and the two baby bags into the trunk.

"Why do we need so much stuff?" he asked

"I know," said Carrie. "It's like you have to take your whole house with you when you go out."

"At least he's happy," said Eddie, looking back in the mirror at the baby as they started to drive off.

"That's what's important," said Carrie. "Our lives as Mommy and Daddy."

"My dad says 'a baby is an inestimable blessing and a bother at the same time,'" said Eddie.

"That's Mark Twain again," said Carrie. "But here's another one that probably applies to you: 'My mother had a lot of trouble with me, but I think she enjoyed it.'"

Eddie laughed and drove out of Marystown and onto the highway. He gave a quick glance in the mirror at Hughie. He was already fast asleep. That didn't last long when Tizzard's phone rang. He passed it to Carrie, who put it on speaker and held it while he talked.

"Good morning, Carl," he said.

"You're an early bird," said Langmead. "What time did you leave that message?"

"We've got a little boy. Just over a year old," said Tizzard.

"Gotcha," said Langmead. "Mine are older. But I still have to get up in the middle of the night all winter to take them to hockey. Anyway, your info was correct. We've managed to track Bund, and yes, he has another guy with him. They're on the boat in Petty Harbour."

"Have you been in contact with Terry Robbins?" asked Tizzard.

"Not yet," said Langmead. "Next call. But we've got the marine unit waiting just outside the harbour and a full crew onshore watching."

"Do they know you're there?" asked Tizzard.

"I don't think so," said Langmead. "They don't seem too concerned. Bund is out this morning doing grocery shopping in the Goulds."

"Are they getting ready to leave?" asked Tizzard.

"They might be, but they're not likely going anywhere today," said Langmead. "It's blowing a gale and expected to get worse overnight."

Tizzard had noticed some strong winds this morning, but that wasn't unusual around here. Plus, the weather could be completely different around St. John's. "Okay," he said. "Sounds like they're stuck there at least for another day. Don't intervene unless you have to."

"It is our jurisdiction," said Langmead.

"I think we have a shared interest in this," said Tizzard. "Let's not have a cornflakes contest over this. We have lots of resources we can bring, and you have expertise on the ground. Take it as a suggestion."

"Got it," said Langmead. "Plus, we don't know what kind of weaponry Bund has, but we can safely assume he has some."

"Okay," said Tizzard. "Talk to Robbins. He will have carte blanche on the resource side. My new super will look after that."

"Is it Ron Quigley?" asked Langmead. "We heard it might be."

"It is indeed," said Tizzard. "You know him?"

"We grew up in the same neighbourhood. He was on Mayor Avenue, and I lived on Freshwater Road," said Langmead.

"Near Leo's?" asked Tizzard.

"You got it," said Langmead. "I'll treat you next time you're in town."

"Thanks," said Tizzard. "Keep me in the loop. I want to know if anything happens."

"Will do," said Langmead.

"Just like you to start talking about food," said Carrie after Langmead had gone.

"And I got a free meal coming," said Eddie. "How good is that? Fish and chips and dressing and gravy. I'm hungry already."

"You're always hungry," said Carrie. "Is there anything you don't like?"

Tizzard thought for a moment. "Cauliflower," he said finally. "I'm not big on all vegetables, but cauliflower tastes like chalk to me. My dad says 'cauliflower is nothing but cabbage with a college education.'"

Carrie laughed. "I'm sure that's Mark Twain."

"If it was, he's a pretty smart man," said Tizzard.

Carrie groaned as they drove along the highway and came closer to Grand Bank.

Windflower and the girls were coming back from their walk with Sheila and Lady. The girls had insisted they couldn't walk and were now sitting and laughing in the wagon that Windflower was pulling along.

They arrived back at their house as Eddie and Carrie were pulling into their driveway. Sheila helped Carrie by taking Hughie out of his car seat and bringing him into the house, while Windflower grabbed the baby supplies and followed behind. Eddie Tizzard would have come, too, but he was being chased around the lawn by two little girls and one very happy dog.

Of course, they had the "Unca, Unca, Unca" chant going strong, and finally Eddie relented and fell on the lawn, where Stella and Amelia Louise and Lady happily covered him with kisses and hugs and dog licks. Windflower came out to rescue him.

"Let Uncle Eddie come in and visit for a few minutes. Then we're going to the Mug-Up," said Windflower. The girls released their grip, and everybody went inside to see the baby. Hughie was pleased with all the attention and stared wide-eyed at the girls, who watched his mommy change him and then give him a bottle that Sheila had warmed up for them.

Once Hughie had been looked after, the whole gang started off on the way to the Mug-Up. When they got close, Windflower saw Uncle Frank on his familiar perch with his friends near the wharf. He went and got him to join their group who had set up at a large picnic table on the outside of the café. This was a relatively new and welcome addition to the Mug-Up, and on a fine day you could sit in the sun and feel the sea air blow through your hair.

Today, the wind was a bit more than that gentle breeze. But it was still warm and sunny, and they made themselves comfortable while Windflower and Eddie went in to order. Minutes later, they were back with juice for the girls and coffee for everybody else, and not long after that they were called to the wicket to pick up their pea soup and por' cakes.

Eddie was finished first and took the baby to let Carrie enjoy her lunch.

"I was thinking that I should have gotten him an order of por' cakes, too," said Eddie.

"You would have had two orders then," said Uncle Frank. "That was smart."

"It won't be smart when you have a tummy ache later," said Carrie.

"I'm not worried," said Eddie. "My dad says that 'part of the secret of a success in life is to eat what you like and let the food fight it out inside.'"

"Mark Twain," said Carrie with a sigh. Everybody but Eddie nodded in agreement.

54

After lunch and putting all the paper plates in the garbage, Windflower suggested going down to the wharf to take a look around. Eddie put Hughie into a snuggly, and while the girls hung on to both sides of Sheila, who chatted with Carrie, the men walked right down to the end past the bait shed.

"You should know, too," said Uncle Frank to Eddie. "I'm telling everybody. I saw your dad this morning. I have a tumour, and there's not much they can do."

"I'm so sorry," said Eddie.

"Don't be," said Uncle Frank. "It's a natural part of life. A doctor friend of mine says that we will all get cancer at some point of our life. Unless we die first. I like the quote by Sanjay's Tagore: 'Death is not extinguishing the light; it is only putting out the lamp because the dawn has come.'"

All three men were silent now as the wind started blowing harder and the waves lapped up against the wharf.

"We'll still miss you," said Eddie as Carrie and Sheila and the girls came closer.

"I'll miss you too," said Uncle Frank. "But I may come back to visit."

Eddie smiled and went and gave Uncle Frank a hug. Soon, he had two sets of arms around his legs hugging him, too.

"We have to go visit my dad," said Eddie. "And then we'll head back."

"You're welcome to stay for supper," said Sheila. "We're going to the bazaar at the church, so there'll be lots of dessert."

"Tempting," said Eddie. "But I think we'll head back." He looked at Carrie, and she smiled her agreement.

Eddie and Carrie went off to see Richard Tizzard while Windflower and his gang walked home. This time Windflower got a few minutes alone with his uncle as Sheila took the girls into the library on the way home.

They sat on the bench outside and watched as a busy stream of Saturday went by.

"People are always coming and going somewhere," said Uncle Frank. "They can't seem to be content to stay in one place and just be."

"It's the way our world works now," said Windflower. "Even if you are going somewhere, you have to check your phone to make sure you don't miss anything along the way." Both men laughed as two teenagers walked by with their hoodies up and their faces glued to their individual phones.

"When will you go back?" asked Windflower.

"I was thinking right after Labour Day," said Uncle Frank. "I have an appointment with my oncologist in Edmonton in late September. Mostly for measurements and to see how I'm doing."

"You seem fine right now," said Windflower.

"I'm better earlier in the day," said his uncle. "But I need to nap a lot more. In fact, I think I'll pass on the church event and head home."

"Okay, Uncle, we'll see you later," said Windflower. He sat on the bench and watched his uncle walk slowly away in the direction of their house. He could feel sadness well up inside him. It almost leaked out, but he was saved by two happy faces who wanted to show them the books they'd gotten from the library.

"Where's Frank?" asked Sheila.

"Gone home for a nap," said Windflower. "Just a bit tired, I think," he added when he saw the look on Sheila's face.

Sheila put the girls' books in her bag, and they continued to walk up the road to the United Church, where there was already a large crowd of people gathered around tables that had been set up in the parking lot. There were all kinds of crafts and homemade goods, and to Windflower's delight, every second table had a selection of pies and cookies.

Sheila spent a few moments wandering around to all the tables, since many of the craftspeople were part of her co-op. Windflower and the girls focused on the food. He selected a beautiful lemon meringue pie and a package of date squares. The girls settled on a package of chocolate chip cookies with Smarties on the front to look like faces. They also insisted on opening them up to try them out.

"We have to see if they're any good," said Stella, a sentiment her younger sister heartily agreed with. Both of them had chocolate-smeared faces when Sheila came back with a small, hooked bath mat.

She took a Kleenex and cleaned them up while giving Windflower that "how dumb are you?" look. He shrugged. "They said they had to try them out."

Sheila laughed and led their happy troop back home.

Eddie was pretty happy, too. Hughie was having a nap, with Carrie joining him. Eddie and his dad were playing a game of crib. His dad won the first one, but Eddie had just squeaked out the second. Now they were on the "who shall" game. Like who shall be the victor. But Eddie's cell phone interrupted the action on that front.

"Sorry, Dad," he said as he went outside to take the call.

He didn't even bother to look and see who it was this time. He was pretty sure it wasn't good news.

"Tizzard," he said.

It was Terry Robbins. "Quigley said I should call you. I'm with Langmead out near Petty Harbour. It's not good. Bund has figured out we're here. And he has a hostage, a young RNC officer. You may have seen him at the hospital. Davis."

"He seems to be good at that. Taking hostages," said Tizzard. "Why are you calling me?"

"Quigley wants you to lead the negotiations," said Robbins.

"Have we heard anything from Bund?" asked Tizzard.

"No, and we haven't tried to yet," said Quigley. "Langmead's guys chased him back to the boat, but nobody has seen sight of him or our guy. Right now, it looks like he couldn't get out anyway with the wind that's blowing. But that is supposed to change by noon tomorrow."

"So that's our window," said Tizzard, almost to himself. "I can come in tonight," he added. "In the meantime, keep the area well lit and clear out the harbour. It wouldn't surprise me if he has explosives. Get a megaphone and call out to him. Tell him he is surrounded and we want to end this peacefully. We want him to release Davis. Then we can talk. Give him my number if he wants to talk."

"Got it," said Robbins. "Anything else?"

"Tell Quigley I want Windflower to come with me. I need him. And he has to call and convince him to come."

Tizzard hung up and went back inside. Despite the seriousness of the situation, he finished off the game with his dad. He lost, which pleased his father greatly. Eddie was almost as pleased that he'd forced himself to put his family first for a change. He smiled as he went to wake up Carrie with the bad news that he was going to St. John's.

"You've got to be kidding me," was Windflower's response when Ron Quigley called him. "I got beat up the side of the head, pistol-whipped, got a concussion, taken prisoner and put in the trunk of a car and you want me to help you? Forget it."

"Tizzard needs you," said Quigley. "He asked me to call you. He needs your advice and support. You can't let him down."

"I can and I will," said Windflower. "I just got back. Even if I was to agree, there's no way Sheila would sign off on this."

"I'll talk to Sheila," said Quigley. "If she agrees, will you go?"

Windflower thought about that, and pretty sure what Sheila's answer would be, replied, "Sure, go for it. Let me get her."

55

Sheila was in the kitchen, putting away their treats. Windflower handed her the phone and walked away. "Ron Quigley," he said as he went out to the living room to see what the girls were up to.

He could hear Sheila's voice rising as she talked to Quigley. He asked for it, thought Windflower. Then there was quiet, and Sheila came back into the room smiling. She handed him back the phone. "You can go. But if you die, I'll kill Ron Quigley."

Windflower walked outside to talk to Quigley more privately.

"What did you say to her?" asked Windflower. "How did you convince her?"

"Charm, my dear boy," said Quigley. "'The way to a woman's heart is through your wallet.'"

"You bribed her?" asked Windflower incredulously.

"I wouldn't call it a bribe," said Quigley. "More of an enticement. I made her an offer she couldn't refuse."

"What did you offer her?" asked Windflower.

"A trip to Montreal, airline tickets, hotel, and $200 spending money," said Quigley.

"Can you do that?" asked Windflower. "You're supposed to be the RCMP, not *Wheel of Fortune*."

"It's your bonus, if you accept the job to accompany Tizzard to St. John's," said Quigley.

"Now that's an offer I can't refuse," said Windflower. "You are shrewd, Ron Quigley."

"'Some are born great, some achieve greatness, and some have greatness thrust upon them,'" said Quigley. "Will you call Tizzard?"

"I'll call him," said Windflower. "But I want to remind you that 'a fool thinks himself to be wise, but a wise man knows himself to be a fool.'"

Quigley laughed. "I'll let you have the last word today. Thank you for doing this."

Windflower hung up and went back to find Sheila.

"You sold me out for a shopping trip?" said Windflower.

Sheila laughed. "You were going anyway. I decided to get something for myself." And she laughed again.

"Well, I guess we'll get a nice trip to Montreal," said Windflower.

"We?" said Sheila. "I don't think so. I want a weekend away. I was thinking Moira might like to come with me. We both need a break."

For the first time in a long time, Windflower was speechless. He walked away. He thought he could hear Sheila laughing again but didn't turn around to give her any more satisfaction. The truth was that he really didn't mind. The girls were not a lot of trouble once he bribed them with movies and ice cream. And they were in bed by eight thirty. It might be fun, he thought as he called Eddie Tizzard.

"How did you get Sheila to buy in?" asked Tizzard. "I was sure she'd say no."

"Quigley bought her off," said Windflower and told Tizzard about Sheila's plan.

"Don't let her tell Carrie," said Tizzard. "I'll be doomed."

"When do you want to go?" asked Windflower.

"I thought we'd have an early supper with my dad and head back to Marystown," said Tizzard. "You might as well come with us. I'll be over around six. After we get Carrie and Hughie straightened away, we can head out."

"Sounds like a plan," said Windflower.

"When do you have to go?" asked Sheila as she came to give him a hug. "Don't let anything happen to you, okay?"

Windflower hugged her closer. "Tizzard is going to pick me up around six."

"You better get moving on supper, then," said Sheila. "What are you making us?"

"Any of those nice salmon steaks left in the freezer?" he asked. "Maybe I'll barbeque."

"Absolutely," said Sheila. "Let me go get them for you." She went downstairs and came back with a large plastic bag with four salmon steaks in it.

"Perfect," he said. "There's a new recipe I saw I wanted to try out with the salmon. It has a garlic lime butter sauce. I guess I need a couple of limes and some fresh garlic."

He drove to the supermarket and picked up his supplies, plus a loaf of garlic bread. Couldn't go wrong with that. Sheila had the salmon steaks lined up on a platter and was cutting up vegetables.

"That's good," she said when she saw the garlic bread. "I'll pop that in when you start on the salmon."

He briefly thawed the salmon in the microwave while he got his sauce ready. First, he had to smash the garlic. That meant he broke off a couple of cloves and individually hit them with the flat of the blade. Then he peeled back the cloves to reveal a gooey mess of garlic. Then he squeezed the juice from two of the limes; the other was for garnish. He added the juice to the bowl where he had placed the smashed garlic. The recipe called for fresh dill, but he didn't have any, so he added a teaspoon of pickle juice from a jar in the fridge and a little basil because he liked that flavouring. A dash of salt and his usual heavy hand of black pepper and a quick stir gave him the base for his sauce.

He melted some butter in a saucepan and poured in his bowlful of garlic and juice and spices. He let it simmer for about a minute and then spooned some of the sauce over the salmon. It already smelled wonderful. He went outside to light the barbeque.

The girls were playing with Lady out in the backyard while Molly was giving them a sneaky peek through her almost closed eyes. When she saw Windflower, she opened her eyes and stared right at him. She knows I'm going to cook fish and she's putting in her order, he thought. Then he tried to stop thinking because he wasn't really sure if the cat could read his mind. Just in case she was really paying attention, he mouthed "I'll save you some" as he went back in get the fish.

He laid the salmon skin-side down on the medium-hot grill and poured some of the sauce over it. Within a minute, the aroma of the salmon and garlic and lime filled the whole area around the barbeque. When the skin was brown and crackling, he turned the salmon over and poured almost all of the rest of the sauce over the fish, turned down the heat, and closed the cover.

A few minutes later, he turned it one more time and spread the remaining sauce overtop of the salmon. He opened the door, called out to Sheila that he was ready and ushered the girls and Lady back inside. Molly lingered and would not move until Windflower and his plate of salmon were safely back inside. She slunk past him and went to her corner. She lay in her bed but eagle-eyed Windflower and licked her lips.

"This smells glorious," said Sheila as she took a bite of the salmon. "Oh my God, it tastes even better."

"What is that smell?" asked Uncle Frank, who had wandered into the kitchen.

"Just in time as usual," said Windflower. He put most of the remaining salmon on Uncle Frank's plate.

"Perfect," said Uncle Frank, and soon he was quiet and enjoying his supper.

Windflower cut off a piece of salmon and savoured the flavours as the scent of garlic and lime and fish enveloped him. "Hmmm," was all he said. The fish was divine. The skin was blackened and crispy, and the salmon flaked on his fork. "Ahhh," he added. "Not bad, if I do say so myself."

56

"You know, your mom was a good cook," said Uncle Frank as he finished off the last bite of salmon and reached for another piece of garlic bread.

"I can remember Auntie Marie being the cook of the family," said Windflower.

"Marie was a great cook. That's who taught your mom," said Uncle Frank. "She made the best Saskatoon berry pie I ever ate."

"I remember that pie," said Windflower.

"Well, tonight we have lemon meringue pie," said Sheila. She cut everybody a piece of the lemon meringue pie from the bazaar and made some coffee. They didn't normally have coffee in the evening, but Windflower thought he needed it for the road. Sheila made a Thermos for him to take with him.

"I am sufficiently sufficed," said Windflower, making quick work of the pie. "I'll clean up," he offered while Uncle Frank and the girls went out to the living room. They wanted to show him how to play Jenga.

"No, you go and get ready," said Sheila. "Eddie will be here soon."

Windflower gave her a hug and started to go upstairs. Then he remembered. It was hard to forget with two beady little eyes watching your every move. He took the last piece of salmon, a nice chunk, and placed it in Molly's bowl. She ate it as fast as Windflower had devoured his pie. Then she licked her lips and looked to Windflower to see if there was any more. Seeing no more on offer, she closed her eyes and pretended to sleep. Windflower murmured a silent "you're welcome" and went to pack his bag.

He could hear the girls squealing and Uncle Frank laughing as he came down the stairs. That was something he would surely miss. But enjoy the moment, he reminded himself. He walked past the kitchen and peeked in at Molly. She looked like she was fast asleep, but almost like magic she opened her eyes when he looked in. She started to get up, then realized that Windflower didn't have anything else for her and slumped back down.

"Sorry, bud," he whispered. But Molly was gone off into cat land. Lady, on the other hand, was almost overjoyed to see him. In return, she got a Milk Bone, and she happily and loudly crunched it as he went out to the living room.

"You play, Daddy," said Amelia Louise. "Mommy was my pardner, but she jus' knocks it over."

Sheila feigned outrage but was happy to give up her seat on the floor. It was Windflower and Amelia Louise against Stella and Uncle Frank. And the competition was fierce. Uncle Frank was very good at the game, probably because he had a lot of patience. But Windflower prided himself on being lightning swift. At least that's what he told himself.

But patience beats speed every time, Windflower learned as his and Amelia Louise's stack came tumbling down, to the cheers of Stella and Uncle Frank. Amelia Louise demanded a rematch, but Windflower spotted Eddie Tizzard's car in the driveway. Rather than alert the girls to his presence and risk another round of their favourite chant, he kissed them both and went to give Sheila a hug. They held each other so closely that Windflower's ribs hurt, but he wouldn't release until she did. When she did, she wiped the tears from her eyes and looked him intently. "Don't do anything stupid," she said. Windflower smiled and hugged her again. As he was leaving, Uncle Frank came out and gave him a hug, too.

"Be careful, Winston," said his uncle as they embraced. "Doc Sanjay gave me this quote from Tagore that I pass along to you today: 'Let me not pray to be sheltered from dangers, but to be fearless in facing them.'"

"Thank you, Uncle," said Windflower, once again not letting go until his uncle did. Then, before another round of hugging could begin, he grabbed his bag and Thermos and rushed out to the car and jumped in the back seat with Hughie. As they left the driveway, he could see the girls rushing out and the "Unca, Unca, Unca" chant starting up. "Get away fast, driver," he joked. "Before it's too late."

Tizzard laughed and pulled away. A few minutes later, they were on the highway to Marystown. Little Hughie was fast asleep as soon as they hit the blacktop. Windflower wasn't far behind, and he only opened his eyes when he felt the car slow to a stop at Tizzard and Carrie's house.

"You stay there and rest," said Tizzard as Carrie took Hughie inside and he helped with the baby bags. Windflower did as he was told until he heard the car door open again. He woke with a start and moved out into the front seat with Tizzard.

Tizzard had brought a bag of cookies, and Windflower poured half of his coffee into Eddie's coffee cup. That kept them going along the winding roads out of Marystown into the barrens that made up most of the journey to Swift Current and then on to St. John's. The sun was beginning to set, and they got to watch it make its glorious descent over the naked landscape and out towards Fortune Bay. As it finally dipped beyond the horizon and darkness overtook them, Tizzard's phone rang. He passed it to Windflower, who put it on speaker.

"Well, we meet again," said Bund.

"Is our guy safe?" asked Tizzard. "Because there's no point talking if he's not okay."

"He's fine," said Bund. "I haven't really hurt any of your people yet. Even when I had the chance. Remember?"

"What do you want?" asked Tizzard.

"I'm a businessman," said Bund. "I have an offer to make you that you cannot refuse."

"What's that?" asked Tizzard.

"Call off the dogs and I'll let your young chap go," said Bund. "Free passage to the Atlantic Ocean, and that will be the last you'll see of me."

"That might be difficult," said Tizzard.

"I have great confidence in you, Eddie. Is that what your friends call you?" asked Bund mockingly. Tizzard ignored that remark, so Bund continued. "Mark this down, Eddie. I will not be taken into custody under any circumstances."

"You can't threaten us," said Tizzard.

"It's not a threat," said Bund. "I have three propane tanks and a stick of dynamite. It will be more than me and your buddy that explodes if there happens to be an accident."

Tizzard looked at Windflower, but again did not reply.

"You have until noon tomorrow or when the wind dies down, whichever comes first," said Bund. "Call me when you have everything arranged."

The phone blinked off. "Call Quigley," said Tizzard. "He's in my favourites now."

Quigley was upset but remarkably calm. He'd been through many difficult situations before with the National Drug Squad in Ottawa. "Let's try and keep him talking," he said. "I'll phone Robbins, and you get on the blower to Langmead. If they haven't already, get them to evacuate anybody close to the harbour."

Tizzard called Langmead and left a message. They were passing through Swift Current when Tizzard's phone rang again.

"Carl, how are you?" said Tizzard. "I've got Windflower with me, too."

"I'm good," said Langmead. "The old tag team reunited. What's up?"

"You need to get the area around Bund's boat cleared. He says he has explosives," said Tizzard.

"He wouldn't need much," said Langmead. "There's at least two large propane tanks that you can see."

"Maybe more in storage," said Tizzard. "Me and Windflower are on our way in. We're almost at Goobies. Bund says we have until the weather clears to arrange safe passage for him and the boat. Has anybody sighted your guy?"

"Nope," said Langmead. "Not a peep from Davis. We know he's got him, since he sent a text to our HQ. With a picture of Davis tied up."

"I'm going to try to get a status report on Davis when I call him back from Goobies," said Tizzard. "Maybe try to talk to him. Any sense of what weaponry he might have?"

"Not really," said Langmead. "We took the shotgun and didn't see any more when we took a look around. But we weren't really looking for guns. Or dynamite. He could have arms hidden anywhere on that boat."

Tizzard looked at Windflower. Windflower frowned. Both of them knew that wasn't good. They were heading into a fight blindfolded.

"I guess we have to assume that he has some high-powered gear," said Tizzard. "Make sure your guys are well back. Whatever he has, he likely knows how to use it."

"We're not going to just let him go, are we?" asked Langmead.

"Not until we get Davis out, that's for sure," said Tizzard.

57

Windflower and Tizzard were quiet on the short ride to Goobies from Swift Current. They were both processing what they'd heard and pondering what to do next. "Might as well get a snack," said Tizzard. "'An empty stomach is not a good political adviser.'"

"Your dad or Mark Twain?" asked Windflower, thinking he was covering all his bases.

"Albert Einstein," said Tizzard, laughing despite the seriousness of the situation.

They had blueberry pie and coffee in the restaurant, and Tizzard called Bund.

"We need a sign that Davis is okay," said Tizzard.

"I sent a picture," said Bund.

"Not good enough," said Tizzard. "They tell me that they need to see him, and I need to talk to him."

"I'm not going up on deck until we have a deal," said Bund. "You guys are not very good, but I'm sure you have at least one sharpshooter with a long-range rifle."

"Let me talk to him, then," said Tizzard.

Bund hesitated, and the line went silent. A few moments later Tizzard heard another voice.

"Davis, is that you?" asked Tizzard. "Are you okay?"

"I'm okay," said Davis, although from his shaky voice it was clear that he was not.

"That's it," said Bund. "When the wind dies down, I want to see a clear path for me and my little boat to cruise out through the harbour."

"We want Davis released first," said Tizzard.

Bund laughed. "That's not how this is going to work. I agree to not harm him, and you let my boat go. That's the deal. Make it happen." The phone went dead.

Tizzard turned to Windflower. "Suggestions?"

"Not yet," said Windflower. "We need to think about his weaknesses, although he doesn't have many."

Tizzard nodded, and the two men left the restaurant. Tizzard made his check-in calls along the way, and there were several reports back and forth between the RCMP and Constabulary, but nothing really changed on the ground. Tizzard drove into St. John's and went all the way down to the RCMP building in the White Hills. They thought about heading over to Petty Harbour, but they both needed a break.

Tizzard had rooms booked for them at the apartment building behind the RCMP building. That would do for the night. He ran and got their keys from the duty officer, and he and Windflower walked into the apartment building. As they were waiting for the elevator, Windflower spoke up.

"I've been racking my brain trying to think up an angle, how can we approach this. But with Bund it really is hard to think of something he hasn't already planned for. He's been one step ahead of us all the way along," said Windflower.

"I agree," said Tizzard. "I've been doing the same thing. But nothing."

"So, what's different about this situation?" asked Windflower. "Anything?"

"Looks the same," said Tizzard. "He's got a hostage to hold us back and a means of escape, if we get out of his way. And he's got a partner."

"He's got a partner, Robert Smart," said Windflower. "Who he hasn't killed yet."

"Hey, maybe that's something," said Tizzard. "Does Smart know that Bund has killed all his other partners in crime?"

"Can we get to Smart somehow?" said Windflower. "He was working for us for a while."

"If he turned once, maybe he'll turn again," said Tizzard. "Come to my room. Let's call Quigley."

"It's an option," said Quigley when he answered the call. "Worth a shot. I'll see if I can find his contact info."

"Maybe somebody can text him," said Windflower. "Tell him that Bund has killed his last two partners and offer him a deal."

"We'll try," said Quigley.

Neither man could sleep now. But luckily, they had teabags and a kettle, so they could make tea. They sipped on that, and each man called back home to let their folks know they had arrived safely in St. John's.

Carrie had gotten Hughie asleep and was heading to bed soon herself. Sheila was still dealing with two wound-up little girls, but they too would eventually wear themselves out. Both wished their partners to be extra cautious and said goodnight.

"I guess we should put Plan B into effect," said Tizzard.

"What's Plan B?" asked Windflower.

"We arrange for safe passage for Bund's boat," said Tizzard. "If we can't make a connection with Bund, I don't see any choice."

"We still need to protect Davis," said Windflower.

"But how?" asked Tizzard.

"Maybe get our dinghy or inflatable boat to accompany Bund's boat out through the harbour," said Windflower. "One man to operate it, unarmed, to show Bund there's no danger. When he clears the harbour, he hands Davis over. Then off he goes."

"Not bad," said Tizzard. "Who would we get to go on the boat?"

Windflower didn't want to say it, but now he knew why he was here. "I can do it," he said.

"You sure?" asked Tizzard. "You need permission or anything?"

"I'd never get permission," said Windflower. "She'd kill me first."

Tizzard laughed. "Okay, let's see what everybody thinks of the idea."

He got on the phone to Quigley, who quickly signed off. Then Langmead and Robbins, who also agreed and would start to put things together tonight once Tizzard talked to Bund.

He called the number.

"Good news, I hope," said Bund. "I feel that the wind is already starting to subside."

"Absolutely," said Tizzard. "We will start removing our people and equipment from the area once we have an agreement."

"Agreement on what?" asked Bund.

"We clear out and let you leave. One small RCMP inflatable boat will follow you. One unarmed person in the boat. You let Davis go when you get out of the harbour," said Tizzard.

"Interesting," said Bund. "Let me think about it. You surprise me, Eddie. I didn't think you were bright enough to think of something like this."

Tizzard looked at Windflower as the line went dead. "I think you're smart, Eddie," said Windflower. "Despite what other people think."

Both men laughed, and Tizzard made them another cup of tea. They were starting to doze off when Tizzard's phone rang.

"You'll never guess what happened," said Ron Quigley. "As I was trying to find a way to contact Robert Smart, his handler called me from HQ. He was still working with us."

"Who are you talking about?" asked Tizzard as he put the phone on speaker.

"Robert Smart," said Quigley. "He'd come back as part of a plan to get Bund. The fake diamonds that Windflower found were put there by Smart. His original plan was to lure Bund back here with those and tell him he had a lot more where they came from. But when they got found, everything changed."

"You mean Smart is on our side?" asked Windflower. "Has he reached out to your guys in HQ?"

"Not for a few days," said Quigley. "That probably means Bund is watching him or is suspicious of him."

"Why is he doing this?" asked Tizzard.

"No idea," said Quigley. "I assume there's a big payoff somewhere down the line. And maybe he just doesn't like Bund."

"I get that one," said Tizzard. "So, where do we stand?"

"I've sent the message, and we hope it gets through, but I think we have to proceed as if he's not going to help," said Quigley.

"Okay, thanks," said Tizzard. He called Langmead to tell him the latest and alerted Terry Robbins to get the RCMP inflatable boat ready.

"Already docked in the harbour," was Robbins's response. "We're parked in the supermarket in the Goulds. That's where our command centre is set up."

"I guess we should go over there," said Tizzard after he made his calls. Windflower agreed. "It'll be daylight in a few hours, and we'll want to get set up."

Tizzard nodded, and the men left to drive to Petty Harbour. "Let's make a pit stop," said Tizzard as they came up past the hotel and turned onto Military Road. "I think the Tim Hortons beside the RNC HQ is open twenty-four hours."

"Of course it is," said Windflower.

They pulled into the coffee shop parking lot. There were two Constabulary cruisers in the lot, and inside there were two more officers having coffee. They both acknowledged Tizzard and Windflower as they made their order. Tizzard had the Farmer's Wrap with bacon, egg and cheese and a hash brown, and Windflower ordered an egg and bacon breakfast sandwich on an English muffin. Both got coffee and sat to wait for their number to be called.

Tizzard went up and grabbed their food, and for a few moments they ignored the suspense and danger that was awaiting them and were just two friends enjoying a late snack or early breakfast together. They took the remainder of their coffee, waved goodbye to the RNC officers who were still there and headed out towards Petty Harbour.

Tizzard drove downtown and then up onto the arterial road that would take them over the south side of St. John's and onward through Kilbride and the Goulds. They stopped at the supermarket, which was now full of RNC and RCMP vehicles and personnel. They spotted Carl Langmead and Terry Robbins and walked towards them.

"Where can we talk?" asked Tizzard.

Langmead led the way to the RNC RV that was serving as their command centre. Usually, it was their public relations vehicle that showed up at community fairs and garden parties. Today it had a much grimmer task. Langmead shooed the two officers who were in there outside.

There was a large map of Petty Harbour on the table. Langmead and Robbins took turns walking through where their assets were deployed. Most were out of sight, including three RCMP snipers who were inside or on the roofs of various buildings along the waterfront.

Tizzard ran through what they had been talking about with Quigley. "But there's no guarantee that anything can happen on that front. So, we're moving ahead with our plan to try to get Davis out before Bund leaves.

Although we haven't heard back from Bund either. But let's get ready."

"There's where Bund's boat is located." Robbins pointed to a spot on the map. "Our boat is here, about a hundred and fifty yards away."

"Okay, let's go," said Windflower. "I need someone to show me how this boat works."

"The RCMP pilot is waiting for us," said Langmead. "Do you want to come with me?"

Windflower looked at Tizzard. "You go ahead," said Tizzard. "I'll be over in a few minutes."

Tizzard stayed behind. He wanted to talk to Robbins.

"If the snipers get a shot, I want them to take it," said Tizzard. "I have no idea what Bund is up to, and he's certainly capable of killing people. He's done it at least twice."

"Got it," said Robbins. "I will give them the word." Robbins went to pass along that information. Tizzard's phone rang again. It was Bund.

"Okay, we do it your way," said Bund. "As soon as it is light, I am going to leave. If your boat is outside the harbour, I will drop off my passenger. But I warn you. If I get a whiff of anything else going on, he's not going to make it."

Before Tizzard could respond, the phone went dead. Okay, he thought, that's the end of talking. Now we move to action. And even though he was not very religious, he said a silent prayer that everyone would come out of this okay, especially Davis. He put his phone away and accompanied Robbins on the short ride to Petty Harbour.

Windflower said his own prayers on the silent drive with Langmead to the site where Bund was holed up in his boat. His prayers were similar to Tizzard's, but he added that he hoped Creator would give them all the strength and courage to carry out their responsibilities in this difficult time. He closed with thank you, as he had been taught. He knew from experience that help was already on the way.

Petty Harbour was eerily quiet. No vehicles parked along the apron, except for two motorcycles. The other boats, mostly fishing vessels, had been moved to the other side and were half-hidden in the darkness. Langmead drove Windflower to the RCMP inflatable boat that was located about a hundred metres away on this side. It was the only other vessel that was near Bund's.

A gentle hum came from the RCMP boat. Windflower and Langmead went to greet the person guiding the boat, a young RCMP constable who could barely qualify to be a skipper. He was visibly nervous. He called Windflower "sir," and Windflower didn't bother correcting him. Windflower got on board while Langmead waited alongside in his car.

The constable showed Windflower how to start and stop the engine and how to navigate using the steering wheel. "It's pretty simple, really," said the young man.

"That's good," said Windflower. "Simple is definitely good. Life jackets?"

"Under the seat, right here, sir. Flares and an emergency kit are up above. The radio is set to our internal RCMP channel. It should be secure. There's the buttons right there," he said, pointing to the knobs and dials. "And here's the headset. You'll want to wear this. It gets pretty noisy when you're on the water going full speed."

"Thank you, Constable," said Windflower. "What's your name, by the way?"

"It's Stevens," said the constable. "Brian Stevens."

"Well, thank you, Brian. I think I'm all set," said Windflower. "Detective Langmead will give you a ride back to the command centre. I'll try to not wreck your boat."

Stevens gave a wry smile. "Sir, I want you to know that I am very proud of you. I don't know exactly what you're going to do. But I know it needs courage."

Windflower nodded as Stevens got off the boat and into the car with Langmead. Windflower poked his head out of the overhang and waved to them both. The RNC car slowly drove off, and Windflower was left alone on the boat in the darkness, except for the light coming from Bund's boat down the wharf. He wondered what that guy was up to.

59

Windflower couldn't see much, but soon the night sky started to lighten. Not a lot, just a tinge of light coming from the east. He strained his eyes to see around the harbour and thought he could make out shadows on a few of the closer buildings. That would be snipers, he thought. He didn't have much more time for thinking because his radio lit up, and he grabbed the headphones. It was Tizzard.

"You set up?" asked Tizzard.

"I'm good," said Windflower. "Any news from Quigley?"

"Nothing yet," said Tizzard. "It's almost sunrise. I expect Bund will be leaving soon."

"Okay," said Windflower. "As soon as his boat starts to move, I'll be right behind him. I'll leave the radio open."

"Be careful," said Tizzard.

Windflower did not reply. The sky over the ocean was beginning to glow around the edges. Little by little, the light crept in over Petty Harbour. First pink and then bright red, the sun came up over the water. Windflower heard Bund's boat first and thought he saw Bund's shadow run out of the boat and untie it from the dock. Then he saw him in the cabin, but before he could react, the boat started to move.

He jumped out, untied the RCMP boat and was right on Bund's tail. As it grew lighter, he could see right into the cabin of Bund's boat. Suddenly, he saw another man beside Bund, and then a third man. Bund was waving his arms, and Windflower heard a loud sound. He'd heard that before. Gunshot. Then another. Then silence.

"What's going on?" screamed Tizzard over the radio. "Our guys say that there's some commotion on board Bund's boat."

"I can't tell yet," said Windflower. "I think I heard gunshots. Wait, the boat is turning around. It's heading for shore. Get bodies here fast."

Windflower sped behind Bund's boat and pulled up on the wharf beside it. He waited to see what would happen next. He could hear the sirens blaring as the reinforcements started coming into the wharf area, along with two of the snipers who had assumed positions nearby. He motioned to them to stay back for now. A few seconds later, Davis, the RNC constable, appeared on deck. When he saw the snipers and Windflower's boat, he raised his hands in the air.

"Don't shoot. Don't shoot. RNC," shouted Davis.

Windflower tied the RCMP boat and ran to Davis. "What's going on?"

"Bund is shot. I think he's dead. Smart got shot, too," said Davis. "One of them starting shooting and the other responded. I don't know what happened."

"It's okay," said Windflower. "Go and sit in the RCMP boat."

Davis did as he was told, and more police started arriving. Tizzard and Langmead ran to Windflower. "I think both of them are shot," said Windflower. "Davis is okay."

Tizzard waved the RCMP snipers over and called Robbins, who got their SWAT crew. Together they went into the cabin. They found Smart lying on the floor, bleeding profusely. Bund was below. He was dead. One of the SWAT team reported back to call the paramedics. Minutes later, they brought out Smart and put him in the ambulance that was swiftly dispatched to St. John's. Bund's body, covered in a sheet, came next.

Windflower was suddenly exhausted. All his energy had gone into managing the last couple of hours, and now that it felt like it was over, he could finally relax. He refused an offer of coffee and sat in Tizzard's car while the RCMP and the RNC processed the scene. Tizzard finally pulled himself away and got in the car with Windflower.

"Good job," said Tizzard.

"Pure luck on my part," said Windflower.

"'Fortune brings in some boats that are not steered,'" said Tizzard.

"Good one," said Windflower. "And appropriate, don't you think? But I haven't got the head to reply. Any chance of breakfast?"

"Now, that's always appropriate," said Tizzard. "I know a place…"

"Of course you do," said Windflower.

They drove to Duckworth Street in St. John's, where there was indeed a place that served breakfast and was open every day at seven in the morning. Over fish cakes and baked beans, they talked about everything except what had happened earlier this morning.

"Do you want to stick around and have a rest or go home?" asked Tizzard as they finished their meal.

"If you're okay to drive, let's go home," said Windflower. "I'd much rather spend tonight at home in my own bed."

"Me, too," said Tizzard. They drove back to the apartment and checked out and were soon on their way out of St. John's. They both called to check in and were greeted with similar reactions when they said they were coming home. Windflower didn't bother telling Sheila about his adventures. What she didn't know couldn't hurt him, he thought. Tizzard made arrangements to have someone on standby to drive Windflower back to Grand Bank when they got to Marystown, and they were well on their way to Goobies when Ron Quigley called.

"Congratulations to you both," said Quigley.

"I think I speak for both of us when I say you're welcome," said Tizzard.

"Probably the best outcome we could have hoped for," said Windflower. "How is Smart?"

"Last I heard, he's fine," said Quigley. "He's a tough nut. He's been dead before."

Windflower and Tizzard laughed.

"They also found bags and bags of those fake diamonds," said Windflower. "Bund's plan was to flood the market with them and then get out before he got caught. He had a place lined up in the Cayman Islands where he planned to live off his riches."

"What happens to Smart now?" asked Tizzard.

"Once he's on the mend, we ship him back to Europe," said Quigley. "We don't need him anymore, so I suspect Interpol will try to use him. He seems very good at that, too."

"Okay, we're heading home," said Tizzard. "Do not call me tomorrow. Even if the building is on fire, I'm off."

"No worries," said Quigley. "You sound suspicious of me."

"'Suspicion always haunts the guilty mind,'" said Tizzard.

"'One may smile and smile and be a villain,'" added Windflower.

"Ouch," said Quigley. "I have little to add to that except to say that 'ingratitude is monstrous.'"

Quigley was gone before either man could quip back, and that was completely fine. They were driving home to their families, and all was good. A quick stop at Goobies for gas and a coffee and they were headed down Route 210 towards Swift Current. Neither man spoke much as they slid past the rolling curves of Swift Current and over the bare landscape on the way home. They listened to *The Sunday Magazine* on CBC, and both in their own way gave thanks that the events had unfolded so safely and without harm to those who least deserved it.

60

When they arrived in Marystown, Tizzard drove to his house. Carrie and Hughie were sitting on the porch. The little boy was very excited to see his dad, and Eddie grabbed him and swung him in the air.

"Do you want some lunch?" asked Carrie. "I've got some cold cuts. I can make a few sandwiches."

"Stay and have a bite," said Eddie. "I'll get the guy to come in half an hour to drive you home."

"Sure," said Windflower. "That would be nice."

Windflower spent a pleasant half an hour with Carrie and Eddie and the baby. They had lunch and talked about their plans for the rest of the summer.

"Oh, that reminds me," said Windflower to Carrie. "I signed you up to help organize a soccer tournament for Fortune."

"I love soccer," said Carrie.

"She played in high school," said Eddie proudly.

"What did you play in high school?" asked Windflower.

"Mostly the fool," said Eddie.

"Not surprised," said Windflower. "Anyway, it's supposed to be a fun tournament. To keep the kids out of trouble. Hope you'll help."

"That means you have to do all the work," joked Eddie.

"I'm in," said Carrie. "It'll be fun. Something we don't seem to have much of these days."

"Better step up your game, Eddie," said Windflower.

"Here's your ride," said Eddie, looking out the window. "Just in time to stop you from creating more disturbance in our marital bliss."

"'If men could be contented to be what they are, there were no fear in marriage,'" said Windflower.

"Touché," said Eddie. "Listen, I know I am lucky to have found one of the best women in the world to be by my side. We have a love that's strong and true. 'And when love speaks, the voice of all the gods make heaven drowsy with the harmony.'"

"Please," said Windflower. "Thanks for the sandwiches, Carrie. See you next week."

Eddie walked out to the car with Windflower. Without saying a word, the two men embraced and held each other.

"Well, we survived another one," said Eddie.

"Indeed," said Windflower. "Feels like we're like cats. With nine lives. Although it seems like we've used up quite a few."

"Nah, b'y, we're good," said Eddie. "As my dad would say…"

Windflower laughed. He went to get in the front seat with the driver, another young constable named Collins. But he asked if it was okay if he sat in the back. He felt a little drowsy and thought he might have a cat nap.

That's exactly what happened. As soon as the car rolled down the driveway, he fell asleep. But soon after that, he woke up in a dream with Molly the cat sitting a foot away from his face, staring at him.

"You don't get nine lives, you know. Only cats," said Molly.

"Okay," said Windflower, trying to wake up and bring himself more into this dream. "Only cats. Okay."

"We're special," said Molly.

"Oh, I knew that," said Windflower.

"Sarcasm doesn't become you," said Molly. She started to get up and walk away.

"Wait," said Windflower. "Hello, Molly. Do you have something for me?"

"Oh, you've discovered politeness," said the cat. "Just for the record, the reason cats have nine lives is because we have earned them in servitude to humans for thousands of years."

"Okay," said Windflower, thinking how bad a life is that?

"I heard that thought," said Molly. "There is always calm after the storm. Stay watchful and alert."

"Like a cat?" asked Windflower.

"Very good," said Molly. "But you will never reach this level of excellence. And keep it up with the fish, by the way."

Windflower had many more questions, but he woke with a start as the RCMP cruiser slowed down and took the first entrance into Grand Bank.

Windflower thought about the dream he had just had. What did that mean? No more time to think about that before he saw a flash of colours and hair rushing towards him. He managed to thank Collins before Stella and Amelia Louise and Lady tackled him and brought him to the ground on the grass in front of his house.

Is this the calm I was expecting? he thought as he tumbled over and managed to briefly escape his captors' clutches. Sheila was standing in the doorway, laughing.

"I think you can handle this one, Mister RCMP Hero," said Sheila. When Windflower put on his fake puzzled look, she smiled. "I talked to Carrie. Were you going to tell me?"

"I was," said Windflower, lying. "I just didn't want to worry you."

"Kind intentions, but no deal," said Sheila. "I'm not mad, just glad you're safe. I'm glad you're home."

"I'm glad, too," said Windflower. "It's good to be home."

The End

ACKNOWLEDGEMENTS

I would like to thank a number of people for their help in getting this book out of my head and onto these pages. That includes beta readers and advisers: Mike MacDonald, Barb Stewart, Robert Way, Denise Zendel and Lynne Tyler. Allister Thompson for his excellent copy editing and Alex Zych for final proofreading.

ABOUT THE AUTHOR

Mike Martin was born in St. John's, NL on the east coast of Canada and now lives and works in Ottawa, Ontario. He is a long-time freelance writer and his articles and essays have appeared in newspapers, magazines and online across Canada as well as in the United States and New Zealand.

He is the award-winning and best-selling author of the award-winning Sgt. Windflower Mystery series set in beautiful Grand Bank. There are now 13 books in this light mystery series with the publication of *All That Glitters.*

A Tangled Web was shortlisted in 2017 for the best light mystery of the year, and *Darkest Before the Dawn* won the 2019 Bony Blithe Light Mystery Award.

Some Sgt. Windflower Mysteries are now available as audiobooks and the latest, *A Tangled Web,* was released as an audiobook in 2023. All audiobooks are available from Audible in Canada and around the world.

Mike is Past Chair of the Board of Crime Writers of Canada, a national organization promoting Canadian crime and mystery writers and a member of the Newfoundland Writers' Guild and Capital Crime Writers.

You can follow the Sgt. Windflower Mysteries on Facebook at https://www.facebook.com/TheWalkerOnTheCapeReviewsAndMore/